About the Author

Franco Rainey began his writing career covering the life of organised crime in the US, focusing on New York City's most powerful mafia families. Having worked as a proofreader and editor for almost ten years, he then dedicated his time to writing fictional crime stories. His first novel *When the Saint Burns in Their Hands* was published in 2022.

Dedication

To my father, William John Pilkington.

This one's for you, Dad.

Franco Rainey

WHEN THE SAINT BURNS IN THEIR HANDS

AUSTIN MACAULEY PUBLISHERS™

LONDON ∗ CAMBRIDGE ∗ NEW YORK ∗ SHARJAH

A CIP catalogue record for this title is available from the British Library.

ISBN 9781398444997 (Paperback)
ISBN 9781398445000 (ePub e-book)

www.austinmacauley.com

First Published 2022
Austin Macauley Publishers Ltd®
1 Canada Square
Canary Wharf
London
E14 5AA

Acknowledgements

I would like to thank the following people for their help and support:

Many thanks to former caporegime, Michael Franzese, whom I was fortunate enough to meet, and develop a true insight into the life of Cosa Nostra and organised crime. His information relating to the Mob proved to be invaluable in my research, and to which I am truly grateful.

To the team at Austin Macauley Publishers, for their meticulous work throughout the publishing process.

Finally, to my family and friends, for their belief, encouragement and support.

Part I
The Family (La Famiglia)

Chapter One

Catania, Sicily

One shot. One opportunity.

That's all he would be afforded.

Twelve months that had seemed like a hundred-year wait, and the moment that he had yearned for, had finally arrived. To take revenge on the man who had murdered his wife and their unborn child. The days without her had left a hole in his life.

And the nights were equally unforgiving. Forced to relive each moment that had led up to her death, their eyes would meet before she would fall helplessly to the ground. The moment when he would wake up and call out her name.

Michele La Barbara was sitting parked up outside the church grounds, observing the euphoria unfold as he maintained a steady eye on his target, waiting patiently for the moment when he would strike. The scene outside the church was picturesque as cameras flashed in earnest to capture the newlywed couple.

In the background, the Ionian Sea glistened as the midday sun hung aloft in an uninterrupted blue sky; further north, Mount Etna stood in all its majesty, a true image of enchantment and unforgettable beauty. It was such splendour that had drawn the happy couple to the island to be wed; an image of grandeur that could only be described as one of paradise.

Amadeo Calabrese had met his young Sicilian bride while touring the island the previous year, and having fallen in love with one another, he had decided that they would get married in Sicily as opposed to taking their vows on American soil. Amadeo had not only fallen in love with the woman of his dreams, he had fallen in love with the island, its customs and its people.

And on this special day, he was accompanied by his proud father, Alberto Calabrese, head of New York City's most powerful Mafia family, who had made the long journey to witness his son being married. Alberto had given both Amadeo and Caterina his blessing, and no expense was spared to give his son the wedding that he had wished for. The venue was the most grandiose location on the island, and with a guest list of friends and family, and a host of welcome onlookers, it was a truly spectacular setting.

'Complimenti!' came the plaudits from the crowd.

All eyes had been focused on the couple, who had just taken their wedding vows and had been blessed as husband and wife. The sighting of the black Range Rover had gone unobserved, even from those who would later claim to have noticed it, its reason for being there at that time, was unimportant.

Three men sat patiently in the vehicle, its dark tinted windows obscuring their identity. The man in the passenger seat watched intently as the celebrations continued to unfold, before finally calling to his brother, Giovanni, who sat behind him, to pass him the rifle. Murder was an act that each of these men was accustomed to, yet as the Sicilian crime lord placed the telescopic lens into position, he was more anxious now than he had been on the day of his first kill.

Michele lowered the window down to the cries of jubilation, as he sought to comfort himself for that one shot that would require timely precision. With the rifle in position, he looked through the telescopic lens and focused on his intended target.

Oblivious to the predatory eyes that lay in wait, the bride and groom graced their audience with a series of waves and smiles as they stood hand in hand at the foot of the church steps. Occasionally, the bride would turn to face her husband, who held a calm demeanour; his presence generating an air of jubilation from his gracious audience. This suave and sophisticated character was respected on every level, while for one man, he was guilty of a crime that had turned his world upside down.

Michele withdrew the rifle from the window, causing his brothers to make eye contact through the rear-view mirror. He sat upright for a moment, looking ahead with unflinching eyes into a world of emptiness, before regaining his position and his sights on his intended target.

Initially, no one had even noticed what had occurred, not even the bride, who was still smiling even as her husband's hand began to slip away from hers. Then everything went still; the sound of celebration was replaced by a moment of surreal silence. Disbelieving at first, Caterina watched in horror as her husband's body fell helplessly to the ground in front of her. The once beautiful bride, whose face was now showered in blood, fell to her knees next to her husband, and then erupted into a state of panic.

Her screams and contorted facial expression, harrowing for all to witness. The young Sicilian woman, who only moments ago had held a smile larger than life, now kneeling in despair and disbelieving that her husband was dead. The once charismatic young caporegime, who had insisted on being married in the *garden of Sicily*, murdered in cold blood.

Content that he had achieved his objective, the marksman withdrew his sights from the telescopic lens. And as the passenger side window was raised, the vehicle pulled away slowly and as surreptitiously as it had arrived. For Michele La Barbara, the months of anguish that he had had to endure would prove to be no sweeter in the coming months or even years that would follow. For life without the one woman who had brought so much joy and harmony into his world, would never be the same again.

As for the bride who had been left to despair over her husband's body, it was that Michele had considered the choice of death to be less painful than the anguish and solitude that would remain with her for the remainder of her days.

Alberto Calabrese had ordered an immediate search to find his son's killer. The island, notorious for its brutality as well as its beauty, would offer no leads as to who had murdered his son, leaving the ageing boss with no alternative but to return home empty handed.

'I want my son's killer found and brought to me alive. Do you understand?' he had told his eldest son and underboss, Benito.

As every man available took part in the search for Amadeo's killer, Alberto Calabrese knelt down at the foot of the church steps and held his son in his ageing arms. For an instant, he saw his son as a child, an infant, and for a fleeting moment, his boy looked back at him and smiled. It had been many years since the New York crime boss had shed a single tear; even when his dear wife and mother to their children had died more than seven years ago, he had merely dealt with her loss on a sombre note, but with one of acceptance. Now, with his son in his arms, he wept and screamed out hysterically to the killer that he would avenge his son's death before his dying days.

The New York boss of the Calabrese family had remained silent for the remainder of the flight home, with only constant images of that fateful shooting and the bride's screams from hell to keep him company.

The assassin who had gunned down his son was never discovered.

13

Until now…

Michele sat up in bed.

'Mary!' he called out.

He was perspiring heavily; his right hand holding on to the silver locket that hung loosely around his neck.

It had been almost two years since the death of his beloved wife, and still, the dreams came. He would be given a brief respite—two or three successive days at the most—but visions of that fateful day would continue to haunt him. It was Groundhog Day. With only seconds to act, Michele ran through the marketplace, pushing past the crowds of people who got in his way, intruding on his attempts to rescue his wife from the bullet that was already loaded and aimed at its point of contact.

He called out her name in desperation, waving his arms, imploring her to acknowledge him so she would be able to run for cover. He could see her, but she could neither see him nor hear him calling out to her. She was away from the crowds that flocked the marketplace, vulnerable and open to attack.

And then everything went still and silent. Her expression of happiness turned to one of disbelief as the bullet entered her body. Michele could do no more than watch her, unable to rescue her at her time of need, he cried out her name—his screams of anguish could be heard in the world of dreams and reality—and her name he would call out for many more nights to come.

Mary held her hand over her stomach, her expression now one of sorrow as she suddenly came to terms with her infliction. Still holding her hand over the wound, she looked up toward Michele, her face asking the question *why?* Why had her husband not been there to save her? The man who held an entire island in the palm of his hands had been unable to save the one he loved. As her lifeless body collapsed to the ground, Michele fell to his knees and wept.

For now, the voices and the images in his head had ceased despite knowing that it would only be a matter of time before they would return, ready to impose further punishment on his troubled soul. But it was the call that made his cell phone tremble violently on the bedside table that brought him back to the present. A call at such an early hour of the morning would be far from a welcome one, that much he was certain of. And as he observed the name on the screen before answering the call, his sixth sense told him that the conversation that would follow meant trouble.

It was his brother, Giovanni.

'Giovanni?' Michele said cautiously.

At first, there was no response, not even a sound to suggest that the caller was on the other end of the phone.

And then the screams came.

Michele could hear Giovanni frantically calling out for *them* not to hurt his wife. His pleas for mercy, eventually drowned out by her cries of suffering.

Helpless to act, he was compelled only to listen.

The sound of gunfire echoed around the walls of Michele's home. After a moment of silence, Giovanni could be heard, calling out to his wife. 'Aliana? Aliana!'

Seconds later, the sound of gunfire was heard once again. And then everything went quiet.

Michele held his silence.

Waiting patiently for the caller to make an introduction. As for his brother Giovanni and his wife who had been on their honeymoon in New York City, they were dead.

'I know you're still there, Michele La Barbara,' the caller said.

'I'm here,' Michele said.

'Your brother and his wife are dead'—*That much Michele understood*—'Don't worry, though. We'll be sure to forward their body parts to you, so you can give them a decent burial.'

Michele could hear the sounds of laughter follow.

'We?' Michele said.

'All in good time,' the caller said. 'By the way, be sure to check in with your other brother Luigi. I hear he's not feeling so hot today. Kind of lost his tongue, if you get my meaning.'

More laughter followed.

The message from foreign shores had been clear—murder could be committed on either side of the shore and at any time of their choosing.

Michele remained calm; his breathing almost undetectable in comparison to the now heavy panting that could be heard on the other end of the line.

'So long, Michele. Look forward to meeting you soon.'

The call came to an abrupt end before Michele was allowed any chance to respond. Not that he had anything further to say. As far as he was concerned, actions always spoke louder than words. But there was one thing that was clear to him right now:

This was the beginning of a new war.

Michele had woken up from one nightmare only to be dragged into another. He stood up from the bed and pulled on his pants, picking up his 9mm pistol from the bedside cabinet before making his way into the kitchen. He was in need of coffee and a cigarette. He was still perspiring heavily from another night of torment; visions of hurt still at the forefront of his mind.

He took a welcome drink of the hot beverage before stepping out onto the balcony, which overlooked the vast area of the Tyrrhenian Sea. He leaned over the railing and put a cigarette to his mouth, the flame shaking erratically as his hand trembled from the merest suggestion of anxiety. Michelle took a deep draw from the cigarette and then blew smoke into the morning air. The sea was calm and a vision of red as the Sicilian sun started its ascent on another day.

His attention turned to the matter at hand and the phone call that he had received on his brother's cell phone only a short time ago. Giovanni hadn't made the call. So, who had? And why? There would be no reason that his brother would be caught up in any business matters or anything of a nefarious nature, so *what the hell was going on?*

But more disturbing was the knowledge that both Giovanni and his wife, Aliana, were dead. Brutally gunned down in cold blood. It mattered little as to the numbers of those involved in the crime that had just taken place; as for every action, there was one criminal mind behind it. One person alone who had given the order.

And Luigi. His younger brother.

He feared the worst.

Michele picked up his cell phone and called Luigi, only for the dial to hang on until handing him over to the answering machine. Without leaving a message or calling him back, Michele looked up his uncle Gianluca and made the call.

'Michele,' Gianluca said before reaching the second dial tone.

'Gianluca. We need to talk.'

'You still having those dreams?'

'Yeah, some things never change. This is something different.'

'At this hour, I guess this must be important?'

'As important as things get,' Michele said.

'On my way.'

As he waited for his uncle Gianluca to arrive, Michele took a drink of the black coffee and then lit up another cigarette as he stood watching the sun rise steadily on the horizon. In a world that brought only sadness and tragedy, the rise of the Sicilian sun brought hope on the dawn of each day.

Michele only wished that that day would arrive soon.

Chapter Two

While the code of silence (omertà) had finally been broken, the mafia's grip on the island was still very much alive. Their influence on Sicilian business owners ensured that they would pay their share of protection money, which consisted of restaurants, shops, hotels and even tourism businesses. La Cosa Nostra proved influential in any building construction, and as such, they would play their role in terms of contracts and machinery. The demands for their protection and influence were for the most part extortionate, which meant that many businesses suffered and were left bereft of any profit.

Michele La Barbara had taken over his uncle's role as Il Capo of the Giordano family, and over the last decade or so, it was now considered to be the most powerful mafia family on the island. Having introduced his nephew to the life of a mobster from an early age, Michele had been groomed specifically for a time when he would take over the family business. His skills as an efficient and ruthless assassin were matched only by his business acumen, and after his uncle suffered from a bout of ill health, his time to take over the reins as the boss of the Giordano family, came a little earlier than expected.

Gianluca's role as an advisor meant that the family had no need for a consigliere, and with his connections and weight of respect he carried from the islanders, he was still a formidable character and very influential with regards to his business activities.

Having left his home in Porta Del Vento around dawn, Gianluca made the short drive to Michele's home in Mondello, which was one of the more lucrative areas of the island and a popular beach resort. He knocked on the front door approximately thirty minutes after Michele had made the call, and after both men greeted each other with their usual embrace, Michele invited him into his home and poured him some coffee.

Gianluca entered Michele's home holding an amused expression.

'What?' Michele said.

Gianluca continued to stare at him. 'Have you looked at yourself lately? You look like shit,' he said.

'Grazie,' Michele said. 'And thanks for coming round.'

'Prego.'

'Here,' Michele said and handed him a cup of black coffee.

'Great, I could do with having something to wake me up.'

'Mi dispiace,' Michele said. 'I guess not everyone wakes up as early as I do.'

'So, that's the reason you look so rough. Are you still having nightmares?'

Michele nodded. 'Regularly… too regular for my liking. What I would give just to have one night's peace without waking up in a pool of sweat.'

Gianluca put his hand on Michele's shoulder. 'I know it's hard, Michele. But give it time. Trust me. Things will get better.'

'Sure.' Michele smiled.

'Anyway, what is so important that you had to wake me at that godforsaken hour of the morning?'

'Come on,' Michele said. 'Let's go outside.'

Gianluca listened intently as Michele brought him up to speed with the morning's events: an unwelcome phone call and the atrocity that had followed. Gianluca was of medium height and stout in appearance. At sixty-three years old, he was moving a lot slower these days, not that he had any reason not to, spending most of his time sitting in his garden, while content to sleep uninterrupted in the shade of the afternoon sun. His hair was now grey and he wore a broad moustache, which he had had for as far back as Michele could remember. Exposure to the sun might have been responsible for his wrinkled forehead, but that aside, he looked healthy nevertheless.

Gianluca put a cigar to his mouth and Michele raised his lighter.

'You're certain they're dead.'

'As certain as I'll ever be.'

'And Luigi?'

Michele hesitated for a moment before responding.

'He didn't answer my call.'

Gianluca took a puff from his cigar as he looked out to sea. He stroked the stubble on his chin and then turned to face Michele.

'This just doesn't make any sense.'

'I agree.'

19

'Who else would have known that Giovanni and his wife were travelling to New York?'

'No one other than us, and Luigi of course.' Michele gave a brief thought as to his brother's state of health right now, and then quickly returned to the present.

'What about Aliana's family?' Gianluca asked.

Michele almost smiled. 'They're simple people if you know what I mean. I don't think they know anyone outside of Sicily, or many on the island, to be precise. I'd rule them out.'

'But we can't discount the possibility, nevertheless.'

'Not when we have so few to go on, however, I'd still rule them out of the equation.'

'Do you have a theory of your own?' Gianluca asked.

'No, not yet. If I had to reflect on every hit I've made, I'd be hiding in the shadows all my life.' Michele paused.

'What is it?' Gianluca asked.

Michele lit up a cigarette and continued to gaze out to sea as the sun made its steady rise above the horizon. 'I don't know for sure,' he said. 'Giovanni didn't make the call. That much is clear.'

'So who did? And why?'

Michele shook his head.

'And Luigi. You're sure he's dead, too?'

'I'm not certain of anything right now. But there was no answer from him when I called. I'll go and check up on him myself.'

'You're sure that's a good idea? What if he is dead and whoever is responsible are waiting for you to show up?'

Michele looked at Gianluca. 'Then they're in for a bad day.'

'Do you want me to come with you?'

'No,' Michele said firmly. 'So far you've been kept out of this. I want it to remain that way. Capisce?'

'Capisco,' Gianluca said.

'Anyway, I need you to do something for me.'

'Anything, just name it.'

'I need you to book me a flight to New York—one-way ticket.'

Gianluca smiled nervously. 'You're kidding me, right?'

That look told him all he needed to know. 'You are serious.'

'That goes for my passport and visa.'

'Same name as before I take it?'

'Certo.'

'When do you intend to leave?'

'Tonight.'

Gianluca raised his thick, dark eyebrows. 'Okay, leave it with me. I'll see what I can do.'

'One other thing,' Michele said.

'What is it?'

'I need a contact. Someone who can meet me at the airport. We have associates in New York City?'

Gianluca nodded. 'We have associates everywhere,' he said proudly.

'Then make it someone who I can trust.'

'Consider that done, too.'

'Grazie. I'll call by later this afternoon. After I've been to check in to see my brother. First, I need to say goodbye to my wife.'

Gianluca placed his hand on Michele's shoulder. 'No matter where you go, Michele. Mary will always be with you.'

Michele held the locket and allowed himself to smile. 'If only she would let me sleep.'

Michele watched as Gianluca drove away and then went back inside where he caught sight of himself in the oval mirror that hung on the living room wall. Curious as to his uncle's words regarding his appearance, he made his way over toward the mirror, stroking the stubble on his chin, which was now three days old and had added years to his appearance. Now at thirty-seven years old, Michele was in as good physical shape as he had ever been in his life. Although, he had to admit that he looked a little worse for wear, knowing that a shave, a shower and a good night's sleep would be the perfect remedy. *If only*, he thought.

Those blue, piercing eyes gazed back at him, cutting through him in an intimidating fashion. He swept his hands through his thick, dark hair, noticing strands of grey that he had failed to recognise until this day.

Michele withdrew his gaze and opened the locket around his neck to reveal Mary's picture of beauty. He studied it admiringly and smiled as if it was the first time he had set eyes on her. After closing the locket he took another glimpse at himself through the mirror and then made his way to the bathroom.

It was time to go and say goodbye to his wife.

Having made his appearance more presentable that morning, Michele had stopped off at the market to buy a single red rose for Mary. Her favourite flower. Now kneeling at her gravestone, he closed his eyes and smelt the rose, reflecting on times long gone, when he would bring his wife flowers and watch her face light up with joy. Despite the subsequent nightmares that had followed since her death, such fond, vivid memories could never be taken away from him.

Michele held on to the rose as he thought carefully about the words that he would say to her this time around. He would speak to her on each visit he made. It comforted him somehow. It made him feel close to her. And it was at her graveside when he would think more about their unborn baby, comforted at least that *they* were at peace and together for all eternity.

He looked up at his wife's headstone and took a deep breath and then smiled. 'I've got to go away, Mary,' he said. 'I don't know for how long… days, perhaps weeks, but I guess you know that already, don't you?' He laughed gently.

The thought of leaving her left him with a sense of guilt. But he knew that he was presented with no other choice. This was something that he had to do.

Michele placed the rose gently on the base of her headstone and then reached into his jacket pocket and took out a piece of folded paper. He felt the heat of the midday sun beating down on him and took off his sunglasses and swept his brow with his hand. This was no time to be out in the Sicilian sun, yet he would tolerate the heat of the day in order to be at her side.

Slowly, Michele unfolded the piece of paper. It was a poem he had written for Mary in his moments of solitude, words that—at least for him—portrayed some of the most beautiful times that they had shared together. He was nervous; his mouth had gone dry and, already engulfed in emotion, his eyes had become glazed and brilliant in appearance.

'I've written you a poem,' he said. 'I hope you like it.'

Sheepishly, Michele raised his head from the poem and discovered that he was now in another place. He was with Mary, sitting on the jetty that he had enjoyed many days' fishing, accompanied by the smell of sea air and the sound of the waves as they gently crashed against the side of the wooden pier. Mary was just how he remembered her: ageless and beautiful.

'Well, come on, Michele. I'm waiting,' she said in a soft tone.

His expression was lost and aimless, and for an instant, he had forgotten why they were there.

'The poem,' Mary said.

Dumbstruck, Michele looked down at the paper in his hand. 'Of course. Sorry,' he said, 'I was someplace else.'

'You're not going to back out on me, are you?' she asked.

'No way,' he said. 'But that doesn't stop me from feeling nervous.'

Mary laughed and then closed her eyes, waiting for her lover to read her his words of poetry. Michele had written many poems throughout his life, yet he couldn't recollect why he had chosen such literary verse, only a feeling that he had had at that time. He had never told anyone of his interest in poetry, only Mary, who was simply enchanted by the prospect of being able to hear her man recite some of his prose.

Nervously, he held the piece of paper up in front of him with one hand and held on to Mary's hand with the other. He was ready to begin:

'In grief, I stand, on this solid land, the earth now my prison, because you're missing; when will this torture end? I still see your face. I still feel your warm embrace. The memories are so real, but when I reach out to feel, I touch only emptiness and vast open space.

'I could never have dreamed that someone as beautiful as you could ever have deemed, my soul could connect with yours so perfect, and I would feel redeemed. So perfect I guess it was destined not to last, all my dreams trashed, your death so unnecessary undertaken with such intentionality—it all happened so fast.

'Penance I always knew I would pay, but never in this way. The cruelty of losing you has given to my torment every second of every day. There is no respite; grief and guilt mine to fight, but it was worth it to experience; your love so intense, forever you will be my light.

'Yet blessed am I and every day I pray; your memory will never fade. I will never be afraid when death comes my way. For then you and I will be together again.

'So for now I say amen, for I know your love way beyond and above, and life will eventually transcend. Your beauty will forever stay with me; your radiance so open and free, you taught me compassion and love in wild abandon. Indebted to you I will forever be.'

As the words began to fade into obscurity, Michele felt Mary's grip on his hand tighten for a moment, before finally releasing itself from his hold. Mary was smiling. 'Thank you,' she said. Her words were but a whisper. But they had been spoken nevertheless.

Michele watched as her image of beauty began to fade away. He was alone once again. He looked at the poem another time, wishing he could revisit those last few precious minutes of his life, but alas, their brief time together was over.

Michele was alone once again.

But, as for their brief exchange, it had been priceless.

She was there.

'You really liked my poem, Mary?' he said smiling. 'Grazie.'

Finally, Michele stood up, kissed his fingers and then placed them on top of her headstone.

'Addio per ora, mia cara.'

Chapter Three

It was 12.43pm when Michele pulled over to the side of the road. The engine purred gently as he studied his brother's apartment block. Something wasn't right. That much was clear to him. He caught sight of his eyes glaring back at him through the rear-view mirror. Studying him almost, he felt a sense of unease as he noted the caution in his eyes, a look that was urging him to turn the car around and get the hell out of there. Both brothers—one on the other side of the world, and the other, several blocks away from his own home in Mondello—*allegedly* murdered.

Michele turned the car around and parked into a lay-by and then turned off the engine. He glanced through the rear-view mirror, angling it so that he could see Luigi's apartment. There was no movement; in fact, the entire area was devoid of a living soul. The afternoon sun ensured that many stayed indoors or in the shade. But there was something more disquieting. There was a stillness that suggested more than just the local town folk concealing themselves from the torturous heat of the day.

Michele opened the glove compartment and took out his gun. He then snatched the car keys from the ignition and then stepped out of the car, tucking the 9mm into the waist of his trousers. The glare from the sun's rays made him squint, so he lowered his shades and then slowly made his way forward towards his brother's apartment.

Luigi was a loose cannon—he knew that. He had matured over the years, yet Michele understood that there was a part of his brother that refused to change. He was loyal to the core, but he was arrogant and relished the limelight. People feared him more than they respected him. And Michele knew only too well that he had seen many come and go who shared that mentality and erratic behaviour.

Michele scanned the roofs for snipers, curtain movement or even a raised blind from an apartment nearby. He turned sharply at the sound of a dog barking, almost reaching for his gun before deciding to venture forth.

Luigi's apartment was on the second floor of a modern complex that he had purchased only recently in Mondello. It was in a relatively quiet location away from the coast, but as Michele understood, if someone was after your blood, then there was no safe haven. They would find you no matter what.

Michele entered the complex slowly and stood at the foot of the stairs, raising his glasses up onto his head, he observed his surroundings. Everything was quiet, and as he had noted already, too quiet. He withdrew the gun from his trousers and then steadily proceeded up the stairs, the quiet, too unobtrusive for his liking. *If you're alive, I'll kill you*, he thought, regretful of thinking it the instant it had entered his mind. The thought that he was being watched, or that he was expected to turn up at his brother's apartment was predictable. Upon entering, he would have to be ready for any eventuality, and ready to open fire, should he have to.

Michele stood on the balcony facing the front door of Luigi's apartment. Slowly, he placed the side of his head to the door, listening intently before deciding to knock. After three successive knocks, he waited. Nothing. So he placed his hand on the door handle and slowly turned it. It was unlocked.

Michele turned the handle cautiously and then opened the door. He stood for a moment before entering the apartment. 'Luigi,' he called out. Nothing. The room was dark due to the blinds being closed, however, at a glance, there appeared to be no force of entry or anything to suggest that anything untoward had occurred. Michele closed the front door enough to avoid any observation from attentive neighbours and then called out his brother's name once again.

There was a smell in the air; a dank, rancid aroma that signalled death. The open plan room consisted of a small living room and kitchen and, despite the smell, looked relatively clean. Luigi—notwithstanding his nonchalant characteristics—insisted on cleanliness, while ensuring everything was in its place. He was almost obsessive about it.

His home would be free from dust or grime, photographs and portraits, albeit in small numbers, were strategically placed on the walls. The TV was the main feature of the wall, carrying a fifty-inch screen, it cast nothing more than Michele's reflection as he stood in front of it, carefully searching the room for something that would give him a lead as to his brother's whereabouts.

Michele walked carefully across the laminated flooring and made his way to the hallway. For a man who weighed just under fourteen stone, he was silent in his approach. He heard a murmur and paused. And then nothing, but he had heard something nevertheless, and he knew he wasn't alone. The bathroom door was open, and with two bedrooms at the end of the hallway, he cautiously approached the bedroom to the right, and slowly opened the door.

Luigi lay on his bed, gazing at Michele in a disorientated fashion. His body had been beaten badly, and even in the faint light; it was clear that Luigi had lost a lot of blood. Michele held back for an instant, almost refusing to accept that this was his younger brother. And then he walked over to him, reaching for his wrist, he felt the faintest pulse of life.

'Luigi,' he called out. 'Can you hear me?'

Luigi murmured, but he was unable to speak. His face was puffed and bruised, and he was far from recognisable. 'Luigi. What happened? Who did this to you?' Luigi coughed, and blood seeped from his mouth in abundance. And that was when Michele realised the full extent of his injury. He leaned forward and held Luigi's head, gently opening his mouth, he discovered that his tongue had been cut out.

By the way, be sure to check in with your other brother Luigi. I hear he's not feeling so hot today. Kind of lost his tongue, if you get my meaning.

'Come on, Luigi, let me get you help.'

Luigi mumbled again, but to no avail. Instead of any words coming out of his mouth, blood and drool continued to engulf the lower part of his face. Michele could almost hear him calling out to him, *Kill me, brother, please! Kill me!* If it had been him lying there instead of Luigi, he would have implored him to do the same.

Suddenly, Michele picked up the 9mm and pointed it at his brother, the barrel of the gun only inches away from his face. He watched as Luigi glared back at him with an air of acceptance, urging him to put him out of his misery. Those eyes of his, still hypnotic and intimidating, even while he lay there helplessly at the point of death.

Michele drew back on firing the one shot that would finally end his brother's life and went to help Luigi get off the bed. 'Come on,' he said hastily. 'We have to go.' But it was no good. The refusal to shoot him had merely presented Luigi with a few more agonising breaths. And with one last cough followed by a spit of blood, Luigi looked at his brother for the final time, and then died in his arms.

The boy whom he had raised to become one of the most feared men on the island had now—along with Giovanni—gone from his life.

Michele stood up from the bed. 'You're coming with me,' he said, and then picked his brother's lifeless body up and hoisted him over his left shoulder. With his gun in his right hand, Michele walked out of the apartment with only one thing on his mind.

Roberto Del Panucci was the local undertaker. Once a member of La Cosa Nostra, he had decided a long time ago that he could become as profitable burying people than actually being hired to kill them. His profession had proved just as sombre; yet he believed that his decision to move on had been a prudent one. However, if he had known that one day the most respected and feared mafia boss, Michele La Barbara, would come to him as a matter of urgency, and one that would require him to follow a code of silence, then he might have given his profession greater consideration.

Standing at five-foot-five, Roberto was as wide as he was tall. Of course, he hadn't always been that way; in his day as a Mafiosi, he had kept himself in shape. The coffins that adorned his building were not designed to carry someone of his bulk, yet, he had already made the necessary arrangements for such a casket to carry him to the grave when that fateful day arrived. He hadn't considered that that day might be sooner than he had originally anticipated.

Roberto's office was located in Il Capo, which had a host of traversed streets and blind alleys. This was a perfect location for his business, and despite his gloomy appearance that matched his profession, he was a popular character with the locals, who would stop and engage him in conversation whenever he frequented the Market del Capo.

The day had been a quiet one so far in terms of business; in fact, he hadn't had a phone call all day, which was quite unusual but suited him nevertheless. Arranging for people's funerals had been all too common to him throughout his life, and during his time as an undertaker, he had seen some all too familiar faces lying on a slab in his mortuary. Some of them had been ex-associates, and given his vow to their loved ones to give the dead a ceremonious send-off, he was more revered than reviled. It seemed that his decision to walk away from the *life* had been rewarded in as much as he felt needed more than people wanted him dead.

He was sitting with his feet up on his desk when Michele walked into his office carrying his dead brother in his arms. Roberto instantly jumped up to attention, his behaviour indicative of someone who had been caught off the job as opposed to someone who actually owned the business. Those *eyes* of his were glaring at him, cutting through him almost, in a rage of torment. This was the second time that he had come face to face with Michele La Barbara.

Their first meeting had come after the murder of his beloved wife when he had been given the task of arranging her funeral. And now, with Michele holding on to his brother's dead body, it was clear that he required his services once again.

'Don Michele,' he said. His bottom lip trembled as words failed him.

'Signor Panucci. I need your help.'

'Sì, Don Michele.' The undertaker glanced at the dead body, swallowed, and then looked back at Michele in a state of wonderment.

'This is my brother Luigi.'

Roberto made the sign of the cross and then sprang to Michele's aid, taking control almost as he ushered him into the next room where they could lay Luigi's body down where so many bodies had been laid to rest before him. He helped Michele to ease his brother's body from his arms, feeling his resistance to letting go of him, he spoke to him softly, urging him to release him.

The undertaker was nervous. Michele la Barbara was now Il Capo di tutti capi (the Boss of all bosses), and he had had his own Caporegime when he was only twenty-five years old. He was different to most bosses, and he wasn't the kind of guy who paraded himself around town to ensure that the townsfolk were aware of his presence. That wasn't his way.

In many ways, Michele lived two lives: the simple life, and the life of organised crime. Roberto had heard many stories of his exploits, along with the tragedy he had suffered some two years ago... the last time their paths had crossed.

The younger man in his arms had been nicknamed "The Fiend", because of his sadistic ways of murder. And even in death, Roberto felt unnerved by his lifeless body.

He looked cautiously at Michele as he considered the demands that were yet to be spoken. *Who had done such a thing?* he wondered, knowing that he dared not ask in fear of reprisal. The man would let him know, when or if he wanted him to know. For now, it was simply important that he followed Michele's instructions to the letter.

'There is some business I need to attend to,' Michele said, without taking his sights away from his brother. 'I need you to let my brother rest here until I return. Do you understand?'

The undertaker nodded, 'Sì, Don Michele.'

'You are to speak to no one about this. Understood?'

'Understood.'

No one had ever laid such demands on him before. The man who had called him only two years earlier had been a very different Michele La Barbara. And as he looked at him, he reflected on that day when he, too, had had a heavy heart.

Roberto Del Panucci reflected silently on Michele's orders not to discuss his brother with anyone. That meant, if anyone called to see him at any time, or whether they had a gun pressed against his head, or even his wife held at gunpoint, he would have to deny having any knowledge of what he had witnessed on this day.

'We will give my brother a decent burial on my return,' Michele said.

'As you wish, Don Michele,' Roberto said. Any thoughts on how long his absence would be, he refrained from asking.

'Restore his body the best way that you can. On my return, I will see to it that you are well rewarded.'

'I'll see to it personally, Don Michele,' he said.

Michele nodded and then turned to make his way out of the room when the undertaker called after him, causing him to stop at the doorway.

'Don Michele. Mi dispiace.'

Michele paused for a moment longer and then left without uttering another word. Roberto let out a deep breath, relieved as he heard the main door to the building close. He was sorry, however, more so for his own personal wellbeing than anything else. What if they came here and questioned him? He knew that those behind this heinous crime would go to any lengths, and with Michele La Barbara on their trail, they would be making every attempt to keep ahead. No, he decided. Michele had made a request and he would honour it.

The undertaker made his way into his office and locked the main door, before going to his desk and retrieving his shotgun from under the table. It was loaded and had been loaded for some time. The familiar saying that *it is better to have it and not need it, than not have it, and need it* was something that he had bought into after making the decision to leave the mob, just on the off chance that they came calling.

Of course, there was never any way out from that *life* that he had chosen. He knew that, yet had chosen to ignore it nevertheless. Roberto entered the room where Luigi lay, ready to protect him now more than he would have ever needed to when he was alive.

Chapter Four

The violent murder of his brother Luigi had been no regular hit. If it had, then the assassin would have put a bullet through his head and then moved on. No, this was something much more disturbing, and given the extreme violence that had taken place, Michele figured that there had been three, perhaps four men in his brother's apartment at that time. He would have put up a fight for sure. And it would have taken more than two guys to hold him down while one of them had pulled out his tongue.

But who had given the order?

Michele had a theory. A crazy thought that had entered his mind earlier that day, but one that had now manifested into something much more credible. He had tried to push the notion away on a number of occasions. But it had been impossible for him to shake off. The pieces of the jigsaw were now starting to fit together.

Someone had been watching, waiting patiently for the moment in which to strike. Invariably, the assassin would be someone who was known to the victim.

Had Giovanni and Luigi known who their killers were?

Michele was certain of it.

Having begun the day like so many others, waking up after a brief, traumatic night's sleep, the unthinkable had happened. Life had become too comfortable for all of them, and they had forgotten the most fundamental rules of the game that they had abided by for so long.

Michele turned over the engine and after a brief look through the rear-view mirror to check that he wasn't being followed, he drove slowly away from the undertaker's. His next stop—the home of Uncle Gianluca.

The heat from the sun was menacing at this time of the day, and up on the mountainside, there was very little breeze to accommodate any weary traveller. With Gianluca's home in sight, he turned off the narrow stretch of road that wound its way up the mountainside of Porta Del Vento, and then pulled over onto the grass verge and turned off the engine. Michele took a deep, almost deflated breath, and then picked up his gun from the passenger seat.

With no sign of anyone around, he got out of the car and walked toward Gianluca's home. Anticipating that his uncle would be in the garden and sitting in the shade as he was so fond of doing, he cautiously made his way to the back entrance. They—Michele, Giovanni and Luigi—had enjoyed many occasions here at their uncle's home. He was a great host, always making his family welcome and over the years had nurtured them into the force they had become. But these were troubled times, and such fond recollections of family gatherings now seemed to Michele to be nothing more than a distant memory.

As he walked by Gianluca's beaten red Ford Ranger pickup, Michele reflected on his uncle's arrival at his home earlier that morning and the discussion that had followed. Had it not been a close family matter, then it would have been likely that Michele would have missed the part that had been eating away at him for much of the day.

Never had he had to question his uncle's business activities, or more significantly, his loyalty to the family?

But as with all things, there was a first and last time for everything.

Gianluca was sitting in the shade on his wicker-style chair with his head leaning back over and his arms stretched out, which gave the impression he was in deep slumber. Sat at his feet was his loyal companion Lupo, his ageing Alsatian. Lupo (meaning wolf) was indicative of the beast that held savage, predatory instincts, despite its docile demeanour.

It looked at Michele in the same manner a human being would look at him: with caution and in deference. The garden, if it could be described as one, was small and quaint, however, captured the scenery of a vast area of the Sicilian Island and beyond.

Seeing his uncle sitting restfully in the shade, Michele walked slowly over toward him, all the while cautious of any movement inside his small dwelling or indeed any sign of life from the surrounding hills. The possibility of a lone sniper concealed only a short but safe distance away was a possibility, yet somehow Michele believed that he was destined for much more than being simply taken out by a marksman.

'Michele,' Gianluca called out. He was surprised to see him, even though he tried not to show it. He was about to stand up to greet him when Michele waved his hand for him to remain seated.

'Can I offer you something to drink?'

'No,' Michele said bluntly.

Gianluca sat back comfortably in his chair and looked at Michele quizzically. 'Any further news?' he asked.

Michele pulled up a chair and sat down facing his uncle. 'I have heard nothing more from Giovanni. He's dead.'

'You sound so certain.'

'As certain as I'll ever be,' Michele said.

'And Luigi? Has he been in touch with you yet?'

Michele held his nerve as images of his battered lifeless body engulfed his mind. 'Luigi's dead.'

For a moment, Gianluca remained silent. Then, he raised his head slightly and then sat up slowly. 'Dead?'

'Sì.'

'How…'

'I went to his apartment and there he was, lying in a pool of blood with his tongue torn out of his mouth.'

'Good God,' Gianluca said.

Michele looked deep into his uncle's eyes, which returned a solemn look. 'You know,' Michele said standing up, 'I remember when we were younger—boys rather than young men—we learnt the art of killing. But the thing I remember most was that you taught us never to become complacent. Not even for a moment. I have allowed myself to drop my guard on two occasions: two years ago, and now.

'Fear and respect only last for so long. There's always someone waiting, hungry to take over and create their own regime. You can either maintain the grip of fear or relent. Death comes to us all, eventually.' Michele smiled, but his expression was earnest. 'Life has become too easy and as a result, we've forgotten who we are.'

'I don't follow you. What are you saying, Michele?'

'Giovanni, Luigi… on different sides of the world and both murdered in one day. No, this is not the work of a lone assassin; this is something that has been very carefully thought out. And whoever is pulling the strings, knew exactly when and where the attacks would take place.

'How did you know Luigi was dead?' Michele said bluntly.

Gianluca's dark, piercing eyes gazed fixedly at Michele. And then he turned his attention to the gun that was now pointing straight at him.

'You're suggesting that I had something to do with this?'

'When we talked at my home this morning, you asked me if I was certain that Luigi was dead.'

Gianluca shrugged. 'What about it?'

'I made no mention of Luigi.'

'You must have done. How else would I have known?'

'Save it, Gianluca. You set us up.'

Gianluca made no attempt to respond; he just gazed back accusingly at Michele, as if it was he who was holding the gun.

Gianluca had taught him the ways of La Cosa Nostra. And that nobody in that *life*, even those who were closest to you, could be trusted. Michele had always found that hard to take, and even as he pointed his gun at his uncle, he could hardly believe what was he was doing.

'I taught you well,' Gianluca said. He smiled, which was more out of respect than derision.

'Too well. Why?'

Gianluca shrugged. 'For what purpose will it do to tell you now?'

'Call it for old time's sake. And more importantly, I'll let the dog live,' Michele said gravely.

Lupo looked up at his owner as if he understood what was going on.

'And I have your word,' he said.

'Certo,' Michele agreed, yet inside, he was hurt that he had not displayed the same compassion for his own nephew. Hurt that he—*they*—had been betrayed by the man whom they had come to love and honour. But that seemed to be many years ago. In Michele's eyes, the world was now a very different place.

Michele sat opposite Gianluca, pointing his gun at the man who had been in his life for as far back as he could remember.

'What do you want to know?' Gianluca said.

'Everything,' Michele said. 'But you can start by telling me who knew that Giovanni and his wife would be in New York for their honeymoon? And more importantly, why they would have them killed?'

Michele watched as his uncle put a cigar to his mouth and then lit it with a series of puffs before blowing a cloud of smoke into the dead calm of the afternoon heat.

'The Calabrese family.'

'What?'

Gianluca nodded.

'They discovered that you were responsible for the murder of Amadeo Calabrese, the man who was responsible for—

Gianluca saw Michele's pain and paused. 'You know the rest.'

'How? Did you tell them?'

'No,' Gianluca said, holding up both hands while holding his cigar in his mouth. 'I swear to you, Michele. I never uttered a word.'

'Then who was their source of information?'

Gianluca sighed, and then steadied himself to stand up. He then waved for Michele to follow him, and both men walked across the garden, stopping to gaze at the open scenery.

'They were on to you, Michele. Right from the very beginning. The source of their knowledge remains a mystery to me, and that's the truth.'

Michele continued to hold the gun at his uncle. 'So, exactly what role did you play in all this. And why take out Giovanni and Luigi? Why not just come after me?'

'My role?' Gianluca raised half a smile.

'What's so funny?'

'If I'd had my way, I would have told you to forget the whole thing.'

'So why didn't you?'

'Because I knew how headstrong you were when you made up your mind,' Gianluca said raising his voice. 'Nothing you could do was ever going to bring Mary back. All you did was to make matters worse—for all of us!'

'Answer my question, Gianluca?'

'Several months ago I received a call from Benito Calabrese who informed me that they had discovered who was responsible for the death of Amadeo. Initially, I denied any knowledge of this…'

'Benito Calabrese?'

'Underboss and eldest son of Alberto Calabrese.'

'Go on,' Michele said.

'I played a game of bluff with Benito, that was until he stated that he knew the whereabouts of my son and daughter, and what would happen to them if I didn't give them what they wanted.'

'There's always an alternative.'

'Not this time around.'

'You could have come to me,' Michele said.

'And make matters worse than they already were!' Gianluca exclaimed. 'Benito requested that I call both Mary and Anthony to confirm that he was being serious. After he hung up, I called them. My children, both on different sides of the island, and held at knifepoint. I had no choice, Michele. So when Benito called back a short time after, he asked me if I got the message. I got the message all right. And there was nothing I could have done about it.'

'So you told him everything he needed to know.'

'Sì,' Gianluca nodded. 'They knew exactly when to make their move on Giovanni and Luigi. With them out of the picture, you had no other backup.'

'You mean they bought out our men, too?'

Gianluca nodded. 'Luigi never saw it coming.'

'So why am I still alive? Why didn't they just take me out when they had the chance?'

'As I said, there's only so much I know, and want to know for that matter. As far as I was concerned, I did what I had to do, and for the right reasons. I simply had no choice. Believe me when I say that I wish things had been different.'

'Me, too,' Michele said. His expression was sombre, however, feeling more emotional than he had at any time in his life.

'Even now I favour your odds over theirs.' Gianluca smiled, as if out of admiration. 'But they'll be following your movements, nevertheless.'

'I'll be ready.'

'If you manage to stay alive long enough to make it off the island, then I'm sure you'll find what you are looking for in New York. You'll find your tickets and documents on the table, just as you requested. If you make it that far, you will be met by an associate of the Calabrese family called Franco De Blasi. He has been instructed to take you straight to the Calabreses.'

Michele stared at his uncle. 'You told them what they needed to know. What I want to know is, who sold me out?'

'I've told you everything I know, Michele. If I had sold you out, you would have known by now.'

Michele considered Gianluca's words to be true.

'Well someone did,' Michele said.

'Mi dispiace, Michele.'

'I'm sorry, too. More so to discover that you're not the person I thought you were.'

'It's the life we chose, Michele.'

'No,' Michele said. 'It's the life that you chose. I chose to look after my family.'

Gianluca nodded and then turned his attention to the majestic view of the island. He took a deep drag of his cigar and then closed his eyes, knowing that his time had finally come to an end.

As the sound of gunfire echoed around the surrounding area, Lupo watched from a short distance away as his owner's body slumped to the ground.

You don't deserve a burial, you murderous traitor, Michele thought.

But he couldn't leave him this way.

He had to bury him.

And he would bury him where he had fallen.

Like a loyal companion, Lupo followed Michele back to the car and at the command of its new owner, he jumped onto the back seat without any hesitation. Michele got into the car and then looked through the rear-view mirror, his gaze meeting the dog's eyes without either one of them flinching. In a strange sort of way, it was as if the dog understood the life and the consequences of betrayal.

The Calabrese family? Michele thought.

Gianluca may have told him everything he knew—but there was more, something far more sinister going on. The murder of Mary's killer had evoked an all-out war between two families from different shores. They had discovered that Michele had been the man responsible for the death of a Capo's son. And after hearing his uncle's declaration, he remained convinced that Gianluca had not been that source of information.

So, he pondered. *If it wasn't you who gave me up, then who the hell did? And why?*

After taking a final glance at his uncle's home, Michele turned the key in the ignition. 'Come on, Lupo,' he said. 'Let's get the hell out of here.'

Chapter Five

With very few people on the island that he could put his utmost faith in right now, Michele took Lupo to the home of Rosa Rossi. Mary had introduced him to Rosa not long after they had been going out together. In fact, Rosa had given them their blessing to wed so, given that his wife had held so much trust in the old woman, then it was only fitting that he would hold such confidence in her, too. Rosa was now seventy-six years old.

On the outside, she appeared frail. She was hunched over more now but taking nothing away from the old lady, she was as smart as a fox and as strong as a lion. Silver hair and a host of wrinkles on her sun-beaten face gave people the impression that she was living on borrowed time. Michele knew different, and he understood perfectly that she would be well enough to look after Lupo and be around for a long time after he returned from foreign shores.

At least that was the plan. After all, he had his brother's body to lay to rest, too. And that would be the time when he could finally grieve.

Rosa lived in La Kalsa, which was one of the city's most notorious neighbourhoods, however, one that she had lived in for most of her life. She was a familiar face with the locals, and seemingly treasured, given her friendship with Michele La Barbara.

At first, Rosa didn't ask him why he was going away or when he would return. She would look after Lupo just as Michele had requested, and just as the fine beast had warmed to him in an instant, he sat by the old lady's side with a look that suggested he would care for her as much as she would for him.

'Let me make you something to eat before you leave,' she insisted.

Michele hadn't had much of an appetite since he had woken that day; in fact, food had been the last thing on his mind. But now that the old woman had mentioned it, and given his knowledge of how great a cook she was, his appetite had returned.

'Grazie mille,' Michele said. He lit up a cigarette and felt his lungs burning as he inhaled deeply.

'You will never reach my age if you continue to smoke that way,' she called out to him from the kitchen.

Michele looked dumbly at her as the cigarette lay loosely from his mouth. 'I'll be lucky to live to be your age no matter what,' he said. 'Anyway, which other way is there to smoke?'

'Don't get smart,' she laughed. And for a moment she looked serious. 'Cut back on them or quit.'

Michele looked at her as he released the smoke from his nostrils. 'And how often do you smoke, Rosa?' Michele smiled. 'Come on, you tell Michele the truth.'

'Four a day. If that,' she said flippantly.

'Sure,' he said, 'anything you say. Okay, I'll make you a promise to quit when I return home. How's that?'

Rosa laughed. 'Sure, Michele. Anything you say.'

Rosa sat at the dinner table with Michele while he enjoyed the pasta al forno that she had made for him. Michele could feel the old woman's eyes pressing against him quizzically, watching him with wonder as she contemplated what it was he was getting himself into.

'What is it?' he asked, without taking his eyes away from his plate of food.

'Why are you going to America, Michele?' she asked.

'Just some business I have to take care of, Rosa. I'll be back soon enough.'

'What kind of business?' she asked. And now Michele noticed that she did look serious.

He paused for a moment before continuing to eat his meal. 'I never could keep anything from you, could I,' he said.

'Why would you want to?'

'You've just given me one good reason—you worry too much, Rosa.'

'So, this is something bad?' she asked.

'You could say that.'

'But you don't want to tell me.'

'No.'

Michele picked up a piece of bread and wiped the remainder of the sauce from his plate before putting it into his mouth. He wiped his mouth with a napkin while he continued to chew his food, watching the old lady watching him, her expression of curiosity now one of concern.

'You're a fine cook, Rosa.'

'The locket,' she said, 'let me see it.'

Michele nodded and then released the chain from around his neck and then leaned across the table and handed it to her. He watched her as her frail hands trembled as she opened the silver locket and observed her reaction on seeing the face of the young woman who had been stolen from their lives. The eyes that looked back at Rosa were dark but beautiful. Her long silky brown hair hung loosely over her shoulders, and her smile, infectious.

'She will always be beautiful,' Rosa said.

Michele nodded. 'I went to see her today.' He laughed.

'What's so funny?' she asked.

'I had written her a poem and decided today of days that I would read it out to her.'

'Do you have the poem with you?'

'Sì.'

'May I see it?'

'Certo.'

Michele picked up his jacket and then reached inside his pocket for the piece of paper and then handed it over to Rosa.

'I didn't know you were a poet,' she said.

'I suggest you read it first before you decide if I'm a poet or not.'

The old lady smiled at him, picked up her reading glasses from the table and put them on, and then turned her attention to the poem. Michele watched her facial expression as she read from the paper, feeling as nervous as he had done earlier that day when he read those words out loud while he knelt in front of Mary's headstone. He thought of what Rosa had just said, 'Mary would always be beautiful,' something that he had told himself earlier that day, and many times before that.

Rosa smiled as she looked up at Michele with glazed eyes. 'That's beautiful,' she said.

Michele retrieved the poem from her and then put it back safely into the inside of his jacket pocket. 'Thank you,' he said.

'Here,' she said and then handed him back the locket.

'I'll return, Rosa. I promise,' he said.

'Promise me something else,' she said.

'What is it?'

'When you return, you take me to see her.'

Michele smiled. 'You got it,' he said.

Having said their farewells, Michele instructed Lupo to take good care of the old lady until he returned. His own self-doubts of returning back to his homeland had been removed given he now had more than one reason to make it back alive.

Michele wondered how much Rosa understood about him. How much of his secret life she knew about. She was a wise old lady, and Michele respected her too much to involve her in such matters that she was better off not knowing.

And now that he was alone again, his thoughts drifted back to how the day had started, and a bizarre sequence of events that had seen his only living relatives murdered in cold blood. Gianluca had ordered the execution of his brother Luigi, who had had his tongue ripped from his mouth and had been beaten so brutally, and then left to die in a slow agonising death, as his blood slowly oozed from his body.

Suddenly, his sixth sense detected danger.

Roberto Del Panucci.

On the assumption that *they* had already been to his home to discover he was not there, then the undertaker would be their next point of contact.

It was 5.15pm when Michele arrived at Il Capo. Having parked a block away from the undertaker's office, he got out of his car and made his way through the almost empty marketplace, holding his gun in his hand whilst inside his jacket pocket. Despite his surety of the situation, he was also aware that those who had murdered Luigi, might have been and gone by now, which would leave him being the hunted, instead of the hunter.

With Roberto Del Panucci's office in sight, there was no sign of any break of entry, no one standing guard outside, or anything that looked untoward, just as it had been only hours before when he had arrived there carrying his brother's body. Michele walked carefully along the narrow lane and made his way around the back of the building, where he discovered a black Golf and an old pick-up truck parked outside. A sure sign that even at this late hour of the day, someone was at home.

Michele tried the handle on the back door. It was unlocked, so he opened the door carefully and then entered the building. He could hear voices coming from Panucci's office where he had entered earlier that day. With his gun in hand, Michele moved surreptitiously along the dark corridor toward the office, listening intently at the man who was interrogating the undertaker.

Standing in front of the open doorway, was a man of medium build, holding a gun at his side as he watched the interrogation taking place. They were Gianluca's men for sure and having anticipated that he would have brought his brother's body to the undertaker's to arrange for a burial, this was—after his own home—the obvious place in which to search for him.

Roberto Del Panucci was sitting calmly behind his desk while one of Gianluca's soldiers stood in front of him, gesticulating with a gun in his hand, and barking orders for him to own up to where Michele had gone to. Luigi's body was there, lying on a slab in the mortuary, which meant that there was no way he could deny that he had not seen him that day, but that did not stop him from refusing to acknowledge anything more.

The interrogator had been one of Luigi's closest friends. Fitting that he would have been the man to have called at his home earlier that day. A friendly face that had been invited into Luigi's home, shadowed by a number of his crew who, until this day, had followed his orders to the letter. Attilio Regio had that cheeky look that held a constant smile, which people considered made him look more untrustworthy than happy-go-lucky. His hair was greased back and his dark eyes were barely visible through a constant squint.

Attilio had watched as they dragged Luigi, kicking and screaming, into his bedroom, where they closed the door and beat him to within an inch of his life. Attilio had stood watching with a feeling of superiority over a man who he had feared more than he respected.

As Attilio continued to question him, Panucci kept his hand on the trigger of the sawn-off shotgun that sat under his desk, ideally located at arm's length, should he ever need it. Right now, he needed it and would use it, just as he had done in the past, however, with three men in the room, it was unlikely that he would come out of this alive. Not that facing death was a problem to him. He had faced death all his life, one way or another. His main concern was that he had made a promise to Michele that he would guard his brother's body until he returned to give him a decent burial.

He would keep that promise, even if it cost him his life.

A shriek from the man standing in the doorway alerted both men to turn toward him, including a soldier who was standing guard in front of the main door to the office. They watched in dismay as they witnessed Michele La Barbara moving slowly toward them, his gun pressed against the back of their colleague's head. Panucci responded hastily, raising the shotgun from his side, he aimed it at Attilio who was standing in front of his desk.

Firing from less than three feet away, the hole was big enough to see through him. Attilio's body was blown across the room with such force, it propelled off the back wall, and then finally slumped to the floor.

The last man standing at the doorway pointed his gun from one man to the next, hesitant to commit himself in case he was shot by the other. He watched anxiously as his associate was gunned down by Michele. By the time he looked up, Michele fired twice, the bullets entering his chest in rapid succession, he fell against the main door with force, and then slowly slid to the floor.

Still holding the shotgun, Panucci looked at Michele and nodded appreciatively. 'You trying to keep me in business,' he said.

Michele smiled. 'It was never my intention to do so.'

'How did you know they would come?' Panucci said as he set his shotgun onto the desktop. His behaviour had changed since he had last spoken to Michele, reminding him more of days long gone—"the life", as they called it.

'Call it intuition,' he said.

'Grazie,' he said. And a relieved looking Roberto Del Panucci held out his hand.

Michele took it. 'Prego,' he said. 'I have to go.'

'Don't worry, Don Michele. I'll clean up back here.'

Michele nodded to show his appreciation.

'Until you return,' the undertaker said.

Michele left the way he had arrived, refusing to even look in the direction of the room where his brother's corpse lay to rest. He would allow the undertaker the time he required to make Luigi partially resemble the brother he once knew, and on his return to the island, he would give him a respectable burial.

Just as he had vowed to do so.

With only three hours to go before he needed to check in at Falcone-Borsellino Airport, Michele drove back to his home in order to pack up what he needed for the long journey ahead of him. The possibility that there would be at least another traitor on his trail or waiting for him at his home was something that he had considered, but with Gianluca dead and his treacherous band of thugs who had murdered Luigi now disposed of, there was no one left to pull the strings, so any further threat seemed unlikely.

At least while he remained on the island.

The greatest threat to his life existed over four and half thousand miles away.

With one exception.

He would be a stranger on the streets of one of the most heavily populated cities in the world—an unknown entity, which would make him elusive to those who sought him, while allowing him to remain under the radar of law enforcement.

He was wanted in New York City, in a world very different from his own.

Part II
Michele La Barbara

Chapter Six

It was 8.32pm when Michele boarded the flight for Milan. Having returned to his apartment later that afternoon, he had collected several items for the journey: a leather flight bag, in which he added his phoney passport and visa to the US (which Gianluca had been able to obtain for him), and a bank card—all under the name of Marco Barone. He added a few items of clothing, binoculars, two packets of cigarettes and a lighter. Other than his cell phone and some loose cash, anything else, he would pick up in New York City, including a gun, which he would require sooner rather than later.

The short drive back to his home in Mondello had been uneventful, which was just as he had hoped, and just as he had suspected. Nevertheless, he remained attentive as he approached his home, acknowledging that much of the crisis that had unfolded had been due to *them* letting *their* guard down.

Fortunately, there had been no sign of a break-in. Gianluca's men had taken the opportunity to visit the undertaker first before making his home their final port of call. They had been out of luck. Michele had intercepted their next move and one that would be their last. A reminder that there would never be a moment when he would be allowed to drop his guard.

It was during the short drive to the airport when he felt that sudden sense of loneliness. His wife, his brothers, and now his uncle—all gone from his life. Other than the local undertaker, who he had broken bread with that same day, he was more alone now than he had ever been.

Michele had lit up a cigarette and tried to shake off the voices and images that were crying from inside. He knew he had to remain focused and composed if he was to get through this alive. Mourning of the dead would have to wait until he returned home. Right now, the Calabrese family were waiting for him.

He wasn't about to disappoint them.

Michele placed his flight bag safely above in the baggage hold, and then took his designated seat at the window. After sitting down he put on the seat belt, and while he had once laughed at the thought of a mere strap being able to save one's life in the event of a plane crash, it would remain locked in place until the plane had landed safely at its destination and had finally come to a halt on the tarmac. Michele loathed air travel. Statistics were fine and a comforting reminder that travelling by air was—and had been for some time—the safest form of transport. But to have one's life in the hands of a stranger, he found particularly disquieting.

As the sun started its descent on the horizon, the sky radiated a brilliant red. Michele squinted as he looked out the window and then pulled down the hatch, something he would do anyway before the wheels left the ground. As the captain's voice came over the speaker, Michele sat back against the chair and could feel the steady vibration of the plane as the engines began to roar and turn. The journey to Milan would be a short one, which would then make way for a much longer flight to the United States of America.

Michele closed his eyes and any thoughts of an aviation disaster drifted away from his mind as he reflected on a day that had cost him his family. What had taken many years to build up had been swept away in less than a day. By those he had loved, and by those who had yet to be identified.

Michele reflected on the conversation that he had had with his uncle, and once again, came to the conclusion that there was something more disquieting going on that he was yet to discover. Gianluca was never a man to show all his cards, and even in the face of death, Michele believed that to be no exception. But on this occasion, he was convinced that his uncle had told him all there was to know. Gianluca had lived his life as a man of honour, but one who would betray his *family* to save his family. Gianluca had known all the while that death was coming for him. Even when the gun was pointed at him before the trigger was pulled, he had looked into Michele's eyes with sorrow as opposed to hatred or anger.

As the 737 made its charge down the runway, Michele braced himself for take-off, and any thoughts of treachery and the brutal demise of his family were, for now, held firmly at the back of his mind.

***

It was a joyous time; news of Mary's pregnancy had spread throughout the family, which called for an immediate celebration. When the proud couple arrived at Uncle Gianluca's home, his brothers along with their girlfriends, Mary's parents and even her old friend Rosa Rossi, were there to greet them. Michele had never felt so happy. *So, this is what it feels like to be a family*, he thought. Many might have deemed this setting to be normal. And if this was what being "normal" was supposed to be, then it was clear that Michele has misjudged the "simple life".

'Complimenti!' came the roar of excitement.

'Did you…?'

Mary shook her head holding a tight grin.

'Then who…?' Michele looked at his uncle and then nodded. 'Who else,' he said. Gianluca returned a smile and then hugged and kissed his nephew. 'Grazie,' Michele said.

'Prego,' Gianluca said.

This was followed by a word of celebration from each of the guests, who took their time with both of them to express their delight at the great news. Mary's parents, who were now a pivotal part of Michele's life, were sincere in their excitement. Michele had warmed to them both from the instant he had been introduced. He remembered how nervous he had been and how important it was that he made a good impression. Fortunately, he had done so. And then later they had given their blessing for them to marry.

The smell of food from the kitchen was divine and the table was set for a grand banquet. This was a happy time. Gianluca was a great host and a splendid cook. Having relinquished his role as the head of the family, he was now afforded the luxury of having more time on his own. Such free time allowed him to enjoy his favourite pastime: cooking. However, such a fondness for exploring his culinary skills had resulted in him being overweight and, as a result, lacking physical condition, which his nephews were so fond of reminding him.

While Mary drank water, everybody else enjoyed copious glasses of red wine that Gianluca had personally selected to go with their meal. As the family conversed around the table, Michele would glance around, observing their behaviour and how at home each of them appeared to be. He looked over at Giovanni, who acknowledged him with a nod, before turning his attention back to his future bride.

Michele wondered how long his brother would remain in the family business. He had appeared to be distracted of late and watching him sitting at the table looking into the eyes of his woman, he was under her spell. Not that she was in any way bad for him; however, she was a distraction, and that always spelt danger. Luigi, on the other hand, was far from settling down with a woman. He loved the women and they swarmed around him at every opportunity.

He was confident and laid back... perhaps too easy-going at times, but nevertheless, when the bell went, he only saw red, which, unfortunately, Michele had determined would lead to his eventual downfall. There was no middle ground with Luigi; he would shoot first and ask questions later. Casual and lovable he might have been to some, yet a renowned psychopath to others. But Michele loved him nevertheless.

Gianluca looked over the table toward Michele and, without even so much as saying a word, Michele nodded and both men excused themselves from the table. Having stepped outside, both men lit up a cigar each and remained silent for a moment while they exhaled smoke into the stillness of the night air.

'She's a fine woman,' Gianluca said.

Michele smiled. 'She is at that.'

'I must say, you never struck me as the marrying type, nor one to have children.' Gianluca laughed, which took away any gravity that might have been intended.

'Doesn't change who I am,' Michele said. 'But I must say it feels good. Something I never knew existed.'

'And no doubt you will both make splendid parents.'

Michele smiled. Seldom had he heard his uncle talk with such compassion. More often than not, he would remain guarded over personal affairs, even amongst his own family. He was a man who showed little emotion about anything.

'What are you both hoping for? And don't tell me you don't mind as long as the baby's healthy.'

Michele shrugged his shoulders. 'I... *we* really don't mind,' he said.

Gianluca exhaled the remainder of the cigarette, and then flicked the butt to the ground. 'What's going on with your brother?'

'Which one,' Michele said curiously.

'Giovanni. I've never seen a man so loved up as he is. Not even you for that matter.'

Michele shrugged his shoulders once more. 'I guess he's just discovered the right woman, that's all.'

'But is she?' Gianluca asked earnestly.

Michele studied his uncle's stern expression and wondered what was going on in his mind. And while Michele had been observing his brother and wondering the same thing only moments ago, he refrained from making any opposing judgement.

'Are you concerned he's going to walk away from it all?' Michele asked.

'He's his own man. He'll do what's right for him, no doubt.'

'That's not what I asked,' Michele said.

Now it was Gianluca's turn to shrug his shoulders. 'My guess is that you want willing soldiers,' he said.

'Come on, Gianluca. I've known you all my life. What's going on?'

'I don't know, Michele. Times are changing. I'm watching you all moving on with your lives now, and while this is a time for celebration, perhaps I'm just being selfish and thinking of my own interests.

'You know, I've nurtured you all from being young boys into men and now... not that I am expecting any form of gratitude of course,' he said sarcastically.

Michele laughed and then placed his hand firmly on his uncle's shoulder. 'You want to know what I think,' Michele said.

'Yes, I do.'

'You think too much,' Michele laughed. 'That's what I think. Come on. Let's go back inside.'

When both men entered the dining area, everyone was in full voice, even Giovanni, who now appeared to have settled into the evening's celebrations. Michele returned to his seat and his wife kissed him on the cheek, holding his hand as if to demonstrate he was her prized possession. He glanced over at Gianluca, who too, appeared to be more at ease, so much so, he was conversing with Rosa who seemed to be hanging on to his every word. Convinced that Gianluca had shaken off the negative energy that he had been exposed to regarding the future of the family, Michele relaxed and joined in the conversation with everybody around the table.

It was a perfect evening.

And a time of joy for all.

As the wheels of the jumbo bounced and then screeched on the runway, images of happiness that were once so vivid and alive were now starting to fade. Michele fought for a moment in which to return to that other world, a place where he was at ease and, as far back as he could recollect, happy. But it was over.

The captain's voice came over the speaker to announce their arrival at Milan-Malpensa Airport. For Michele, another journey lay ahead. But he would sleep and wonder for much of the next flight—New York City awaited him.

Chapter Seven

Flight time from Milan to New York City was approximately eight hours and thirty-six minutes. On arrival at JFK Airport, Michele would be met by his contact and assassin Franco De Blasi, a valued and trusted member of the Calabrese family who had been instructed to ensure that he was delivered to them safely in one piece. Despite the danger that lay ahead, the current arrangement suited Michele. On the surface, everything would appear to be normal and as arranged.

Even if De Blasi or any other member of the Calabrese family had made attempts to get in touch with Gianluca since his untimely death, it would seem unlikely that they would have made the decision to retreat from their arrangement. If Michele turned up in New York, then everything would go ahead as planned. It was that simple.

Of course, Michele would play along with things and behave in a manner that befitted all members of the mob. That is he would greet him with a warm embrace, kiss him on each cheek and then deliver a warm smile that would suggest they were long, lost brothers. Naturally, Blasi would be ordered to behave in a similar fashion; playing the role as the good guy, he would ensure that the man from Sicily felt at ease in his company. Either way, under no circumstances was he permitted to harm him.

They wanted him alive.

It was 6.35am when flight #103 left Milan bound for JFK Airport in New York City. Michele had spent many hours at the airport resting, thinking little of the war ahead, instead, saving his energy both mentally and physically for when the time was needed. Patience and timing were crucial to his survival.

Flight #103 was full of passengers, leaving Michele sitting next to a mother and her young daughter. The window seat had been taken by the child, who remained awestruck as she observed the sights from above, refusing to withdraw her gaze until there was nothing to see but blue sky. Sat in the middle seat, her mother made several attempts to awaken her from her hypnotic trance, which caused Michele to chuckle and therefore diverted the mother's attention toward him.

'I'm sorry,' Michele said. 'I'm just curious.'

'As to what,' she said politely.

'I tend to close the hatch the moment I take my seat,' he said. 'Call it a state of nervousness or superstition, I do it anyway.'

The woman's expression changed to one of astonishment and concern. 'I'm sorry,' she said. 'I didn't realise that you were afraid of flying. You certainly don't look—'

'The type,' he cut in.

She smiled and looked at him with interest. Her eyes were bright green and dazzling in appearance; her skin tone was typically Mediterranean and she had long black, wavy hair. She was slender and wore a short white and blue flowery dress, exposing her knees, yet her smile was warm and genuine, which charmed him. He noticed she was wearing a wedding ring which, in a strange kind of way, eased him. Not that he was sexually attracted to her, however, it made things a hell of a less complicated all round.

Her smile said it all. 'I suppose so,' she said. Whatever else she had been thinking (and she sure wasn't letting Michele in on it, at least just yet), she kept that to herself.

'I don't fly that often,' Michele said. 'I guess I don't like the thought of my life being in somebody else's hands.' Michele grimaced as soon as the words left his mouth, anxious that his concerns of flying had been acknowledged by her young daughter, who was quite clearly at ease with the thought of being on an aeroplane.

'I've never quite looked at it that way before,' she said. 'I enjoy it—and so does Mary, don't you, darling.'

Michele watched as the girl withdrew her gaze from the window, looked at her mother, and then returned her observation to the outside world. She looked very much like her mother, and her name "Mary", made him think of his beloved wife accompanied by a feeling of guilt, knowing that he had left her behind whilst embarking on a journey far away from where she now slept.

'I'm Michele,' he said without thinking, holding out his hand.

'Pleased to meet you, Michele,' she said. She studied his huge hand for an instant before accepting it. 'I'm Chiara.'

Michele smiled and thought that that was a beautiful name, yet decided against saying so. 'So,' he said, 'are you and your daughter off on vacation?'

'Something like that. My husband spends much of his time working in New York City, so sometimes it's easier for us to go to him. Plus, I just love America.'

Michele considered asking about her husband and then decided against it, thinking that maybe, he was getting too involved in her own family affairs. In fact, although he had never considered it until now since his wife had died, any conversation with women had been minimal, to say the least.

'And you?' she asked.

'Visiting,' he said matter-of-factly. 'My brother and his wife live in New York. They recently got married and, well… I guess I failed to turn up on their big day.' Even to a stranger, Michele felt uneasy speaking untruths. However, given that the alternative was *I'm off to New York to find out why my brother and his bride have been murdered*, his initial response had been a worthy one. Besides, as he had noted with a previous response, there was a young child sitting close by, and as with all young children, they would listen in, even when they looked uninterested.

Michele settled into his chair for the remainder of the flight, glancing around from time to time, and other than one toilet break and food service, he did little else in terms of movement. The mother and daughter had drifted off to sleep; their heads touching one another, they looked at ease as they remained in deep slumber.

Michele glanced at his wristwatch, which he had set six hours ahead shortly before boarding the 747. It was 6.03am, leaving a little over three hours until the plane was due to land at JFK Airport. He had managed to sleep for several hours already. But now, and probably for the first time since he had left Sicily to fly to Milan, he was contemplating the mission before him.

The Calabrese family, he wondered. Michele glanced out of the window and could see the sun beginning its ascent on the horizon. There were many questions to be answered, and when the timing was right, it would just be a matter of how much his contact would be prepared to tell him.

***

Michele made his way along the wooden beams of the jetty; a glorious day demanded the need to enjoy his favourite pastime as he pursued an uninterrupted day of fishing. The Tyrrhenian Sea held a green tone as the sun's rays shone down with relentless force. A scene of paradise to many, and one he never grew tired of looking at. As he withdrew his attention away from the sea, he noticed a young woman sitting up ahead on the jetty. Unaware of his presence, she continued to paint the scene in front of her.

Cautiously, Michele moved closer to the young woman but was careful not to get too close so as not to startle her or interrupt her doing her work. Having settled at the side of the pier, he set down his fishing tackle and rod on the old wooden boards and then began setting up his gear, ready for a day's fishing. As he prepared his rod and line, he would occasionally glance over at the curvaceous brunette who, up until now, had made no attempt to acknowledge his presence.

Michele cast out the line and waited for a moment until the lead weight made contact with the calm water, the sound of which was enough to disrupt the silence, and sufficient to arouse the young woman away from her hypnotic state. As Michele reeled in the excess line, he turned to see the woman glancing in his direction.

'Buongiorno,' he said.

'Buongiorno,' she replied smiling.

Michele was mesmerised by her beauty, and unknowingly he gazed at her in an almost stupefied fashion. Her brown eyes displayed a warmth about them that he could not explain, but if there was such a thing as falling in love with someone at a glance and without understanding anything about them, then this was it.

Why don't you just go over and talk to her, he uttered in silence.

'Sorry,' he said softly. 'I didn't mean to stare.'

'That's okay,' she said and smiled. As she turned away to continue with her painting, Michele had noticed that she had blushed slightly, which in a way, reduced the tension that he had felt since he had set eyes on her.

Michele reeled in a little of the loose line, glanced over at the slender brunette who was now fully engaged in her work, and then nodded to himself in agreement that this was that one woman who he was not going to allow to get away. *Okay,* he thought, *here goes! It's now or never,* and with that, he placed the rod down on the wooden beams and made his way over toward her.

'That's beautiful,' he said.

The woman jumped slightly from her folded outdoor chair, almost smudging her painting with the tip of her paintbrush.

'Mi dispiace,' he said, apologising more in the time he had met her than at any other time in his life.

The nervous tension between them was broken as they both erupted in a state of laughter.

Michele stuck out his hand. 'Michele,' he said.

'Nice to meet you, Michele,' she said, holding his hand for longer than she would have done when meeting a man for the first time. 'I'm Mary.'

'Mary,' he said. 'That's a beautiful name.'

'Thank you,' she said and smiled.

'Do you mind if I take a closer look at your painting?' he asked.

'Please do,' she said.

'It is as perfect as the scene itself,' he said, much to her delight.

'Thank you,' she said, and as the gaze deepened between them, Mary found herself blushing even deeper than before.

'Do you live nearby?' Michele asked.

'Mondello.'

Michele raised his eyebrows. 'Funny I haven't seen you around, Mary. Look,' he said, and moved closer to her as her gaze followed the direction of his finger. 'You can just see my home from here.'

'How fortunate you are to live so close to the sea,' she said.

The couple remained silent for a short while as they were both deep in thought.

Mary jumped from her seat as she witnessed Michele's fishing rod bending ever closer to the edge of the wooden pier. Observing her animated behaviour, Michele looked over at the rod and ran over to grab it, followed closely by Mary, who could not contain her excitement.

Michele picked it up and then waited patiently for the fish to bite once more. Only then would he make his strike.

Mary stood by his side—closer than she would have anticipated, but she was comfortable nevertheless.

As the line tugged furiously, Michele whipped the rod back in one swift motion and then started to reel in the line. Turning to face Mary, he stopped and offered her the fishing rod. 'Would you like to give it a try?' he asked.

'Oh, I couldn't. I don't have the strength.'

'Sure you do. Here,' he said, and placed the rod in her hands, and then located her hands on the spool, and together they started to reel in the line.

Michele withdrew slightly as he allowed her to reel home the fighting fish, his hands guiding her own, she giggled childishly, embroiled by the moment and elated by her newfound experience. The fish flapped hysterically as it was pulled out from the water, and then Michele carefully took the rod from her hands, and then guided the fish toward the wooden beams of the jetty. Mary's excitement was cut short as she immediately felt sorrow for the tormented fish; understanding what would now become of it, her expression told Michele all he needed to know.

'Would you like me to put it back? If we do it soon, it will live… at least for another day.' He smiled.

'I would like that,' Mary said warmly.

Michele carefully removed the hook from the fish's mouth, his huge hands taking extra care not to do it any further harm. He estimated the fish to be around three pounds, and with a resigned shake of his head to signify the loss of a meal, he dropped it back into the calm water, leaving Mary to watch intently as it scurried away down into the depths of the vast sea.

'Sorry, Gianluca,' he said.

'Gianluca?' Mary asked.

'Yes, my uncle. He promised to cook dinner this evening.'

'I won't tell him if you don't,' she said smiling.

'It will be our secret,' he said.

'I have to go now. I enjoyed meeting you, Michele.'

'Nice meeting you too,' he said.

And then came that uncomfortable silence, however, this time, Michele was determined not to allow it to linger.

'I would like to see you again, Mary.'

'Me, too,' she said.

'Come to think of it,' he said looking out to see, 'I think I'll call it a day.'

'What about your uncle?'

'He bet me I wouldn't catch anything. I said I would. So I guess I'll be cooking us dinner this evening.'

'You really liked my painting?' she asked changing the subject.

'Very much so.'

'Would you like to take it home with you?'

Michele smiled. 'I'd love to.'

Mary laughed.

'Would you like to walk me back to my car?' she asked.

This time it was Michele's turn to laugh.

'Let's go,' he said.

Their fortuitous meeting was one that would lead to their undying love for one another. For the first time in his life, Michele had experienced the true meaning of love and affection; for Mary, she had given him his heart the moment he had entered her life. In a world where Michele had experienced only tyranny and violence, Mary had shown him the meaning of love.

It was from that moment on that they were to remain inseparable.

***

It was 8.30am when the captain's voice came over the speaker to announce that the plane was about to begin its descent. His voice was a wake-up call for most of his passengers, who having been woken up with such a start, looked around aimlessly after having slept peacefully for much of the transatlantic flight.

While a vast number of tourists arrived in New York each day, the month of August was particularly busy with holiday-makers, keen to engage in the countless attractions that the city had to offer. For many on the flight it was their opportunity to visit and explore "the city that never sleeps", whereas, for one man, he was there to shake the "Big Apple" down to its very core.

Michele slowly opened his eyes; he had slept soundly for over two hours and now felt refreshed as a result. Sleep was the one thing he was devoid of in his *normal* life. To slumber meant being pulled into that world where he would be subject to visions of torment. But for the short duration he had been asleep during the flight, he had felt at peace.

Ironic it was that having left his homeland he had also left behind the horrors of his past. For how long, he did not know, but he woke up feeling more invigorated than he had done for some time. His time with Mary might have been nothing more than memories, but they were real nevertheless.

As he reflected on the dream, he was distracted by movement as both mother and daughter who were sitting beside him had woken up. 'Good morning,'

Michele said, waiting for Chiara to finish yawning before she was able to respond.

'Please, excuse me,' she said, laughing almost. 'Good morning. Did you sleep any?'

'A little,' Michele said. 'I can't sleep when the person sitting next to me is snoring.'

Chiara was aghast and held her hand up to her mouth, her eyes wide and gazing at Michele in horror. 'No,' she said.

Michele smiled. 'I never heard a word.' He laughed. 'Nor from you,' he looked over at Mary.

Mary yawned and raised her hand to signal good morning, which caused her mother and Michele to laugh further.

'Will your husband be waiting for you at the airport?' Michele asked.

He had considered the possibility that he would be accompanied by mother and daughter as they left the plane, however, cautious that their farewell would take place before being exposed to prying eyes. The enemy would use any tool at their disposal. They would search for any weakness and inflict pain and suffering on anybody to accomplish their motives. Even if that meant the abduction of a young woman and her daughter. So, with that in mind, it was necessary for him to make his departure alone.

'Yes,' she said, waking him from his thoughts. 'And you? Will there be someone to meet you?'

'Yes. There will be someone there to meet me.'

'Good,' she said, *however, sad that it is unlikely that we will ever meet again.* She wanted to tell him that. A stranger he may be, yet she felt a warmth towards him that she could not explain, and a feeling that she had known him for some time.

As if reading her thoughts, Michele observed her for a moment longer and then said, 'Your husband is a lucky man. He has a fine family.'

'Thank you,' she said.

As the seatbelt sign came on, the captain's voice interrupted any further conversation as he announced that they would be landing in approximately ten minutes.

Ten minutes, thought Michele. *And then it's time for some answers.*

When flight #103 landed on the runway and then finally came to a halt, Michele stood up from his seat, grabbed his flight bag from above, and then made his way to the exit, his view obscured by the rest of the passengers who were eager to depart the plane.

As for the mother and her daughter, they would never see or hear of the Sicilian again.

After making his way through passport control with relative ease, Michele headed to the nearest men's restroom in order to freshen up. After doing so, he caught sight of a small teashop that was surprisingly desolate at this hour, so asked the waiter for a large coffee, and then pulled up a stool at the edge of the bar where he could see without being seen.

To avoid walking into the enemy's hands, Michele's first move on this foreign land would have to be a measured one. There could be no margin for error.

Franco De Blasi would be outside, waiting for his man to exit the airport. Then, he would act as a delivery boy and take Michele to see those who had acquired his services. He had been shown a photograph of Michele and told what he needed to be told before pickup. He had performed that act on numerous occasions and was in no doubt that this task would be no different.

Naturally, he had been told to be cautious, but his own ego would not permit anyone—no matter what their reputation might be—to undermine his authority. And, as Michele finally made his appearance from the airport, their eyes met for the first time, holding their gaze for several seconds, before smiling to signify their meeting.

Michele studied De Blasi from afar before making his way toward him. He was standing next to a black Chevrolet waiting to greet him. He was short in height, about five-foot-six, and wore a black suit, white shirt and tie which made him stand out from the crowd. He was stocky in appearance, which give him the guise of being a powerful man.

Okay, here goes, he thought to himself, and then crossed the road to meet his contact.

De Blasi held his arms open to greet Michele and both men embraced one another as if they were lifelong friends. 'Welcome to New York,' Blasi said. 'Gianluca has requested that I take care of your every need.'

'Piacere,' Michele said holding his gaze. 'I have heard much about you.'

'All good, I hope.'

Both men laughed.

'Certo,' Michele said. 'My uncle chooses his friends well.'

De Blasi opened the passenger side door to allow Michele to get into the car, and then casually made his way round to the driver's side. He got into the car and closed the door. By the time he turned to face Michele, he felt a brief blow to his lower jaw and then slumped forward against the steering wheel. Michele gently pulled the dead weight of his body back a little and then reached into De Blasi's jacket pocket and pulled out his gun. By the time De Blasi came round, he could feel the barrel of his own gun pressed against his right temple.

'Drive,' Michele said.

Chapter Eight

Franco De Blasi had been caught off guard and had paid the price for his arrogance. Not for a single moment had he considered that Michele would have been aware of his treachery. And why would he? It had been less than twenty-four hours since Gianluca had made the call and set up the arrangements to have him picked up at the airport. The once-powerful and trusted mob boss, now dead and buried in his own garden.

De Blasi was one of the most reliable members of the family and had proven himself to be a ruthless assassin. His role had been a simple one: to pick up the Sicilian from the airport and then take him directly to underboss Benito Calabrese, who would then hand him over to his father and head boss, Alberto Calabrese.

That had been his instruction.

No questions asked.

Nothing could go wrong. In fact, for Franco De Blasi, it had all become too easy. And as Michele had learnt only recently, complacency spelt only one thing: disaster.

Still dazed from the blow to his lower jaw, De Blasi did as he had been instructed, but with little idea as to where he was heading. The gun pointing straight at him was enough to tell him that he would be killed once he had fulfilled his passenger's instructions.

Michele watched the driver as the vehicle occasionally drifted from side to side of the road; the impact of the blow to his jaw, which had left him dazed and to some extent, confused.

Despite being in a foreign land, the principles of attack were the same. Interrogation and murder had become more than just a part of his life—it had occupied him since as far back as he could remember.

De Blasi glanced at Michele and caught the eyes of a trained assassin gazing back at him.

'Do you mind telling me where we're heading?' he asked nervously. He was in unchartered territory, and having given every ounce of his loyalty to the Calabrese family, it was now a fight for his own survival.

'Just drive,' he said. 'We'll get down to business soon enough. In the meantime, I suggest you start thinking about what it is I need to know, and whether or not you value your life more than your allegiance to the Calabreses.'

He looked at Michele and then turned his attention back to the road ahead. 'What difference does it make,' he said. 'Either way, I'm a dead man.'

De Blasi understood that his failure to succeed in his mission would now have serious ramifications; he would either die at the hands of the Sicilian or he would be hunted down by those that had once upon a time embraced him and welcomed him as one of their own. As one of the *family*.

'That choice is yours, my friend.'

De Blasi caught his eye once again. Death wasn't something that frightened him. That threat existed day to day. It was part of the *life*. It was the thought of betrayal that bothered him more so, wondering for the brief moment that he had to himself, whether or not he could turn an informer as opposed to a soldier with so little influence.

Neither the gun pointing at him nor the man holding it were sufficient to change his ways. He was in unknown territory. As it was, it was the men who had used him when they had needed him that was now at the forefront of his mind. Those who had sent him on a mission, knowing full well the danger that existed, and one that he might never return from alive.

Betrayal was part of the *life*, too. And despite the code of silence, such rules had been broken for some time. Rats or informants were either hiding away on some witness protection program, or they were dead. But for Franco De Blasi, there was no protection.

Other than the man at his side.

The man who held him at gunpoint.

De Blasi took a deep breath and then sighed: 'So,' he said. 'What do you want to know?'

'Everything,' Michele said.

De Blasi took a turn off the highway and then made his way over the Ed Koch Queensboro Bridge, taking them over the East River and toward Manhattan Island. He glanced over at his passenger who remained poker-faced and pointing

De Blasi's own gun at his side. This was the man who he had been ordered to pick up at JFK Airport and deliver to the Calabrese family.

Having never been one to question an order by the underboss, Benito Calabrese, he had followed his instruction to the letter. Other than offering a generous word of caution, Benito had never expressed any danger, so De Blasi made no assumption that this mission would differ from any other.

It wasn't the first time that he had had a gun pointed at him, but in such cases, he had always maintained the upper hand, holding his own gun and being more confident of the outcome than his adversary. There were times when he relished such a challenge, confident in his capabilities that he would kill before being killed.

But this was different. There was something about the guy in the passenger seat that made any form of retaliation seem futile. Whoever he was, Benito wanted him badly.

'Have you been to New York before?' De Blasi asked casually.

'A city is a city as far as I am concerned,' Michele said. 'Do you have more weapons?'

'Yes,' De Blasi said. 'They're at my apartment.'

'Good. We're going to need them. Do you live alone?'

'Yes.'

'Even better. Let's drive to your place and then we'll take it from there.'

'That's the first place they'll look.'

'Have they called you yet?'

De Blasi checked his cell phone.

'No, not yet.'

'Once you're overdue, they'll call. After which they'll follow your movements to the airport, and by the time they call on you, we'll be long gone. And just in case you're wondering whether I'm going to kill you'—Michele looked at him—'You're merely the messenger. You're not the brains behind this operation. If you were, trust me, you'd be dead already. I have a car and a gun, what need would I have for you?'

'Thanks,' De Blasi said. He had been belittled to some extent, but at least he knew where he stood.

So far, the Sicilian had it all worked out.

Michele maintained his eye on the road and held his gun pointing at the man who he had asked to trust him. This may have been city life and a world apart from the small island that was his homeland, however, the tactics were the same.

The wait for a new war had already begun.

Franco De Blasi's apartment was located in Fort Greene, Brooklyn. Having undergone a major renewal over a number of years, it had long been at the centre of African-American life and business. It was a modest location in terms of the money he had accumulated over the years, and strangely enough, made him feel comfortable, as it had afforded him the luxury of keeping a low profile in terms of any potential harassment from law enforcement.

With little to show of his fortune, his operations went undetected, along with any connection to the *family*. He knew of others who showcased themselves and their families, living in the most luxurious areas of the city, more or less flaunting themselves in the public eye without considering the ramifications of their actions. Others, however, held legitimate businesses throughout the city, which enabled them to conceal their illicit dealings from the possibility of any police or FBI investigations.

As De Blasi turned into Clinton Avenue, he looked around nervously at his surroundings, and for one single moment, he wondered whether he would be gunned down the instant he stepped outside the car.

This was his neighbourhood, but somehow, right now, he felt that he was looking out on foreign territory.

'You expecting someone?' Michele said.

De Blasi turned to face him. 'Once they realise I'm overdue, they'll come looking for me. I guess I'll feel a lot safer for the both of us once we get away from here.'

'Then let's go,' Michele said calmly.

De Blasi led the way and got out of the car with a look of authority and composure which, given that this was his neighbourhood, was important to maintain. He was respected but only by way of fear. Even for those around the neighbourhood who had turned to a life of crime, they knew he was a man to be reckoned with. It had been rumoured by many that he was connected to the mob.

Nobody knew for sure, but the fact that the whispers were strong and his movements were covert, there was a mystery surrounding him that naturally made others cautious.

Michele followed him into the building and up the stairs, the sound of De Blasi's footsteps echoing around the staircase. The stairway held a smell of urine and disinfectant, a distinct aroma that De Blasi had become accustomed to, however, one that made Michele feel a sense of nausea from the pit of his stomach. Once again, he was reminded that he was not in Sicily.

De Blasi stopped outside of his apartment on the third and top floor of the building, and Michele waited patiently as he took out his key to open the door. Michele looked around casually, yet listened intently for any uninvited visitors. He observed De Blasi who had begun to perspire, wiping his brow with the back of his hand before inserting the key into the lock, he glanced at Michele with a worried expression.

'You okay?' Michele asked.

De Blasi turned the key and then opened the front door to his apartment. After releasing a deep sigh, he looked at Michele with an obvious expression of relief.

'Sure,' he said. 'I'm fine. Come in.'

Michele stepped inside the apartment and watched as De Blasi closed the door and locked it immediately after. He went over to the window, closed the curtains and then took a surreptitious look outside below. 'We'll have to move fast,' he said.

'How long before we are considered to be overdue?' Michele asked.

'I'd say that time has elapsed.'

That was the moment when De Blasi's cell phone rang inside his jacket pocket.

He looked at Michele with an expression that said it all.

'Keep them guessing,' Michele said, lighting up a cigarette. 'It will buy us more time.' He offered one to De Blasi, who took it with a shivering hand.

'I guess you're right.'

Michele took a deep drag from the cigarette. 'Relax. They'll think you're dead anyway.'

'Well that's reassuring,' De Blasi said.

Not that he felt he was going to be alive much longer.

'Okay,' Michele said. 'Grab whatever you need and let's get out of here.'

De Blasi paused for a moment as if undecided on whether to speak up.

'What is it?' Michele asked.

'I have a friend who lives at Queens. If anybody can help us out, he can.'

'Is he a man we can trust?'

'I'd trust him with my life.'

Michele nodded approvingly. 'Good. Does he live alone?'

Blasi hesitated for a moment. 'Yes,' he said cautiously. 'He's—'

Michele looked at him for an instant and then nodded. 'Okay, I get it,' he said. 'But the fact that he's your lover doesn't make him anymore trustworthy?'

'As I said, I'd trust him with my life,' De Blasi said defiantly.

'Good, because that's exactly what's at stake. But understand this,' Michele said. He stepped closer to De Blasi and looked him directly in the eye. 'Now that you have become their enemy, they will burn everything and anyone in your life to get to you. Do you understand?'

After a moment's hesitation, De Blasi nodded. 'I understand.'

'Other than you, nobody knows of my private life. To the outside world, I'm a loner. I've lived this way for so long now it seems, but it's had its advantages. Up until now, I have been able to come and go without any unwanted surveillance from law enforcement agencies.'

De Blasi made his way toward a large mahogany cabinet and opened up a top drawer; rummaging around some clothes, he pulled out two revolvers and a knife that had an eight-inch jagged blade. Desperate to confirm his loyalty to Michele, he handed him one of the revolvers and then opened one of the cabinet doors that revealed suits and other items of clothing. Ignoring the clothes he reached inside and then pulled out a shotgun and rifle, along with a small bag.

'Expecting someone?' Michele asked humorously.

'Better to be prepared than not, I say.'

'And the bag?'

De Blasi opened the bag to reveal the contents. 'Silencers and ammunition,' he said proudly.

Michele nodded to show his approval.

'Is that everything?'

'Yes, the clothes can stay. I have what I need over at Queens.'

'How will your friend feel when you turn up at his place with a stranger and a bag of weapons and ammunition?'

De Blasi smirked. 'I'll tell him what he needs to know. Where my work is involved, he simply doesn't get involved. That's the deal. As for the weapons, I'll figure that out when we get there… if we manage to get that far.'

'Okay,' Michele said. 'Let's go.'

Before they reached the front door, De Blasi's cell phone rang once again.

It was Benito Calabrese.

The name on the screen brought the former Calabrese crew member back to reality.

Michele sensed his anxiety and held out his hand. 'Give me the phone,' he said.

De Blasi handed it to him without question.

Michele answered the call and then waited.

'Franco?' Benito said. 'Where the hell are you?'

'I'm afraid Franco can't talk right now.'

After a brief pause, Benito said, 'Michele La Barbara. I commend you on getting this far. My father wishes to discuss business with you. You would be wise not to disappoint him.'

'Oh, I won't disappoint him, Benito Calabrese. Nor you for that matter. You can expect to see me soon enough. In the meantime, you might want to give your father a message from me.'

Benito didn't answer.

'You can tell him that it won't be too long before he gets to spend eternity with his son. As for you, Benito. You'll be joining them.'

Michele ended the call and then handed the cell phone back to his ashen-faced companion.

'I'm a dead man,' De Blasi said.

Michele nodded. 'That is what we want them to believe.'

'So, what next?'

'Tell me what I need to know and then we can go our separate ways.'

De Blasi met his gaze. 'What if I want to help?'

'That is your choice. However, you will be putting your friend in harm's way. Take my advice, Franco. Grab what you need and you and your friend get as far away from the city as possible and start all over again.'

'I've never run away from anything in my life. And I'm not going to start now.'

'Okay,' Michele said. 'You know once you're in, there's no way out.'

De Blasi raised a smile. 'That's the way it has always been, my friend.'

Chapter Nine

Alberto Calabrese was sitting at a table at a café on Broadway, holding a teaspoon and stirring his coffee. It was the second cup he had put in front of him since he had entered the small espresso bar, and he had tasted neither one of them. The sign on the door was turned to "closed", ensuring that he would not be disturbed.

Right now, his presence was simply to give him the space he required until there was some news he wanted to hear. Franco De Blasi had been sent on a mission and so far, there had been no news of his whereabouts, and more importantly, that of the Sicilian.

He had watched without an ounce of remorse as Michele's brother, Giovanni, had pleaded for his wife's life to be spared. The couple were sat tied up and facing each other, close enough to be able to see the expression of torture being imposed on each other. As the call to Sicily had been made, Alberto had approached the bride and stroked aside the tears from her face. He smiled at her and then stepped behind her.

Alberto nodded to one of his men, who handed him a loaded gun and then stepped back. As he pressed the barrel against the back of her head, he looked at her husband, whose screams could be heard over four thousand miles away.

The sound of gunfire was immediately followed by fragments of his wife's skull and brain particles showering over him. It would be only moments later when Giovanni would suffer the same fate as Aliana.

When the call had come to an end, Alberto turned to his son, Benito.

'That should be enough to grab his attention. You say the other brother has been taken care of?'

Benito nodded and smiled. 'By the time our Sicilian friend turns up to save him, he'll find most of his organs lying on the outside of his body.'

'And our lead?'

'As long as he knows his son and daughter's life are hanging in the balance, he'll play ball. He'll have his men ready to make a move when the time is right.'

'No!' Alberto exclaimed. 'He is answerable to me, and no one else. Is that clear?'

'Certo,' Benito said.

He refrained from adding that it might be too late to call off any hit on the Sicilian boss, feeling confident that if he was as good as his lead had made known, then he would get by them without too much difficulty. Besides, the least men left from his crew, the better, he thought. A risk that the underboss was prepared to take.

Alberto Calabrese's youngest son had been murdered in cold blood. And for that, he would live up to the ancient tradition by tracing each and every loved one as far back and afar, and ensure that there wasn't an ounce of blood left to inherit the name of Michele La Barbara.

Alberto Calabrese was still gazing deep into the past when the café door opened. Standing in the doorway was Lorenzo Esposito, consigliere to the Calabrese family, and Alberto's most trusted advisor. The owner of the café came from behind the bar to see who had dared to intrude at this time, but upon seeing the familiar face of the consigliere, he acknowledged him with a nod and then returned to his duties.

His boss had been waiting patiently for some news as to the arrival of the Sicilian, and it was Lorenzo's responsibility to keep him informed of the situation—good or bad. But today he looked agitated, and as much as he tried to conceal his mood from his boss, those eyes had a way of motivating one to speak up. Lorenzo glanced over at Alberto and then slowly made his way over to his table. He could see that he was not about to get up to greet him, so he waited for his boss to signal him to sit down.

As always, Lorenzo was smartly dressed in a black suit, white shirt and tie, which made him look more like a city lawyer than a member of the mob. Around six-foot-two inches tall, at fifty-five years old, he was younger than his Capo but a worthy advisor to the family. He wasn't afraid to question his boss and, if necessary, confront him if he felt that he and his underboss—his son Benito Calabrese—were making the wrong decisions.

But today was different. His advice was not wanted and neither would it be appreciated. No news was considered to be no better than bad news; in fact, as far as Alberto was concerned, he found the not knowing even harder to take.

Alberto Calabrese looked up slowly at his consigliere and nodded for him to take a seat.

'I trust you have some news to tell me,' he said. He hadn't taken his eyes away from his consigliere since allowing him to sit down, and the expression on his face was enough to suggest that he was in no mood for excuses.

Lorenzo felt his throat tighten and his mouth dry up but managed to call out to the owner to bring him a glass of water, all the while feeling his boss's eyes pressed against him. For a man of fifty-five, he was devoid of a single white grain of hair on his head, which was spectacular given the day-to-day stress that he was under. His black, silky-smooth hair matched his dark, thick eyebrows and blue eyes. A handsome man of Sicilian blood, he had a wife of forty-five years, and a strong appetite for younger women, who he had no problem picking up when he was in the mood to do so. He was father to five children, four sons and a daughter, who were all well-educated and career-minded.

For most people, they would have found his life too dangerous and too complicated to handle. But for him, he was able to deal with having separate lives and went about both his personal life and business in an almost casual manner. Yet, on this day, he was feeling the full weight of the *life* pressing down on him.

Lorenzo glanced up at the owner as he placed his glass on the table in front of him, and then watched briefly as the little man scurried back behind the bar.

'Franco has failed to return,' he said. 'He should have been back more than an hour ago.'

His boss shrugged his shoulders. 'So, what are you doing about it?' he said firmly.

'Benito has ordered some of the guys to go to the airport, to search the area and see what they can find. In the meantime, he has gone over to Franco's apartment, just in case. He said he'll come here directly after, to report to you.'

The Capo gazed fixedly at his advisor, a man who he had trusted for many years. The old man was looking a lot frailer these days, worry etched on his face that had been there since he had witnessed his son's murder in Sicily. His years as a mob boss had taught him to deal with the death of a friend or even a loved one. But to watch his youngest son being gunned down on the day of his wedding, to be with the woman he loved in the hope of a new beginning, had been too much for him to bear.

If his motives had been dishonourable or if he had been involved in something nefarious, then perhaps, he could live with his death knowing that that was the life that he had chosen. A loyal son and trusted caporegime; he had more business acumen than anyone else in the family, including the Capo, who felt a sense of pride more than envy. Along with his elder brother and underboss Benito, and a steady consigliere, the family was a dominant force in times when the FBI considered the mob to be a spent force.

Alberto had aged since that fateful day and had trouble getting to sleep each night. On the outside, his body looked more dishevelled, which made him look shorter in appearance. His hands and face held more wrinkles, and his hair, at least what was left of it, had turned grey almost overnight. But he was as astute and determined as he had been since the day he had become a made-man, many, many years ago.

Now, sitting in a rundown café on Broadway, Alberto Calabrese looked his consigliere in the eye and demanded answers. Only yesterday had he shown his true ruthlessness when he murdered a man and his wife in cold blood. He had made it abundantly clear to all that he would not rest until Michele La Barbara was in his custody. In fact, he would refuse to die until he had dealt with the man who had murdered his son.

Still, something just didn't sit right with Lorenzo.

'This operation was supposed to be full-proof,' Alberto said. 'Franco was supposed to be a friendly face, someone who could be trusted.'

Lorenzo looked at his boss in a stupefied fashion before nodding.

'Make your point,' Alberto said.

Lorenzo was about to say *I don't know* and then thought better of it. 'There is the possibility that the Sicilian knew what to expect.'

'Meaning?'

'Meaning he was one step ahead of Franco before he even met him at the airport.'

'Guesswork?'

Lorenzo raised a hand to indicate the possibility. 'Perhaps?'

'Or it could be that Franco has become a traitor.'

'Franco?'

'With the barrel of a gun pointed at your head, you can be persuaded to betray your own mother,' Alberto said. 'Even you, Lorenzo. My faithful consigliere. Let me ask you: would you risk losing your family?'

Lorenzo felt himself being dragged into an interrogation that he did not want to be part of. Nothing—including his ageing boss—could make him betray his own family. The women in his life, yes, but not his family.

'You are my family,' he said convincingly. He didn't know where it had come from, but he felt a sense of relief as soon as the words had left his mouth.

Alberto nodded approvingly.

Lorenzo felt a build-up of sweat on his brow, nonetheless, he was now relieved that his boss had approved of his response. Times like these had been rare, and for the most part, the boss took the word of his most trusted man as gospel.

'Still, I thought that Franco was a man we could trust,' Lorenzo said.

The Don moved his hand as if to signal an end to the discussion, and then called out to the owner for more coffee.

'Make that two,' Lorenzo called out before returning his attention to his ageing boss. 'So, any further instructions at this time?'

'For now, we sit and wait for Benito to return with some news. Then and only then will we know what to do next.'

For the first time that morning, Lorenzo Esposito was feeling more relaxed. He was far from being let off the hook, yet the time had come for Benito Calabrese to come under his father's questioning. Lorenzo despised Benito more than he was willing to show it.

Not that he was too fearful of reprisal from Alberto but rather cautious as to when the underboss would eventually become the overall boss of the Calabrese family. For Benito, the feeling was mutual, and he had no problem showing it, and therefore tolerated Lorenzo knowing that his days as consigliere were indeed numbered.

Some time ago Lorenzo had advised his boss to hire an assassin in Sicily to take Michele out. To him, it seemed more logical and in the family's best interest to deal with matters overseas than to invite unnecessary trouble on their own soil. Life in Sicily was so different to city life, and despite their covert operations, law enforcement would always remain a threat.

Alberto had refused his request without any consideration. He wanted Michele alive. And that had been the one and only time that he had made such a plea to the Don. Whether his boss had been right or wrong made little difference, he had made his decision, and that was final.

When the café owner placed the cups of coffee on the table, a jingle from the doorbell made the three men turn to face the doorway.

It was underboss, Benito Calabrese.

Benito Calabrese was a shape-shifter. A brute of a man, his men didn't know what kind of a mood he was going to be in from one day to the next. They were loyal to him through fear rather than respect. He knew how to be a best friend and the worst enemy.

So for the men, they joked with him and accepted his praise when he was in the frame of mind to give it; when he turned on them, they held their silence and did his bidding without any contradiction. Only Lorenzo and his father—Alberto Calabrese and head of the most powerful crime family in New York—had the balls to question him, argue with him, and even belittle him without any retribution.

Standing at six-foot-two, he had grown up in the streets of Brooklyn as an amateur boxer. Long-ranged and lethal punching made him a knock-out specialist. His hands were lethal yet it was the ease at which he could pull a trigger that made people fear him. His facial expression and dark eyes made him look intimidating.

His nose was crooked from the numerous fisticuffs on the streets and he had a four-inch scar on his left cheek from a knife attack many years ago. The faint, pink line down the side of his face was a constant reminder of the knife attack, however, unlike the assailant, he was alive to tell the tale.

When he stepped foot into the café, he was dressed in faded denim jeans, black leather boots, a white T-shirt and a black leather jacket. Suits were for businessmen, lawyers and bosses. He was neither, and he made no pretence of being anything other than what he was.

Benito picked up a double whisky at the bar and then made his way over to the table and pulled out a chair. Without any invitation, he sat down and then drank back the whisky in one go, and then called out to the owner to bring him another drink, before even acknowledging both men sitting at each side of him at the table.

His lack of respect was noted by both men, and while the Capo held a poker face, his consigliere looked at him holding an expression of disdain.

'Well?' Lorenzo asked. It was his time to ask the questions. 'Did you find them?'

Benito shook his head while his eyes searched behind the bar. 'Not exactly,' he said. He paused for a moment until the owner brought his second drink to the table, and then turned his attention to the Capo and consigliere. 'The flight arrived on time and there was no sign of them at the airport. We turned his place upside down and even spoke to some of the neighbours. But nothing. It's like that fucka just disappeared without a trace. I've left some of the guys back there just in case; two in the car and two in the apartment, see if he comes back. However…'

His father looked at him without saying a word.

'I called Franco on two occasions before heading out to his apartment. No answer first time around, but on the second call…' he trailed off again.

Now he felt both his father's eyes and Lorenzo's gazing back at him.

'The Sicilian answered,' Benito finished. He drank back the whisky and then placed the glass firmly on the table before almost lying back in his chair.

'And what?' Alberto said.

'Franco's dead and now the Sicilian is after us,' he said simply. Almost too casually for either man sitting at the table.

'What next?' Lorenzo said, turning to his boss.

'We file a missing person ad, what do you think,' Benito said.

'You think that this is some kind of joke, Benito,' Lorenzo said.

'No, but I'd be interested to hear any advice that you have to offer, consigliere,' he said.

'Basta così!' the Don said. 'Benito. Get back over there and talk to Franco's neighbours.'

'Done that already—'

'Do it again. However, Benito'—the Don said, holding his gaze with intent—'this time you don't come back to me until you have some news that I want to hear. Capisce?'

Benito held the glass of whisky in his hand before taking a drink. 'Sì,' he said finally and then threw back the drink in one go.

'If Franco has been back to his neighbourhood, then it's likely that someone has seen him. If they still don't remember anything, then ask them again, until they do remember something.'

Lorenzo was sceptical about this, yet remained reticent throughout the conversation between father and son.

'How do we know for sure that Franco isn't dead?' Benito asked.

'Trust me,' the old man said. 'He's alive.'

Chapter Ten

After leaving his home for what would likely have been the final time, Franco De Blasi kept his eyes on the rear-view mirror for any sign of pursuit. He was thinking about the goings-on and conversations that were taking place now that he had been listed as either dead or overdue.

And then he wondered how long it would be before Benito and the rest of the crew would catch up with him and his most sought-after companion, who was sitting shotgun and seemingly composed as he smoked on a cigarette. He was looking out of the passenger side window and watching the world go by as if he was on a tour of the city.

For Franco, part of him was still battling with his conscience. The voices in his head echoed only cowardice and treachery to the family that he had once sworn his allegiance to. Those that would now swat him like a helpless fly if he wasn't dead already. The days of being a valuable commodity were now over. It had now become a matter of survival.

De Blasi pulled over to what he considered to be a safe location under the Brooklyn Bridge—a spot where he had visited on many occasions: either to discuss business or dispose of someone. With the mob on your trail, the city offered few places or options for protection—so this would have to do, he thought. Michele had been fortunate so far to have obtained the services of the former member of the Calabrese family. Still, a man who could be turned that easy was not a man that he would trust with his own life. De Blasi was looking after his own interests right now. And number one was to stay alive.

De Blasi switched off the engine and then turned to face Michele. This time without a gun pointing straight at him. 'So,' he said. 'Where would you like to begin?'

'Do you know who I am?'

It was a simple question, but how he responded would tell him everything he needed to know.

De Blasi sighed, 'I got a call this morning from Benito Calabrese to go and see him straight away. You know how it works, right? I didn't give it much thought. I get the call, I do what they ask me to—I get paid and go home.

'I was shown a photograph of you and then told to pick you up from the airport. To play host'—he smiled—'and then take you directly to them. I hadn't given it much thought at first as to why they would call me to pick somebody up. It was something they hadn't asked me to do before. When I get the call, I know I have to whack someone.

'So, other than your name and where you had come from, they told me nothing about you, and therefore I didn't feel the need to ask.'

Michele maintained eye contact, but remained silent as if processing the information he had just heard.

'So,' he approached carefully. 'Who you are? And why you are so important to the Calabrese family?'

'My name is Michele La Barbara. Two years ago my wife was shot and killed in Sicily as she was shopping in the marketplace. She was carrying our first, unborn child.'

De Blasi waited for a moment and then said, 'I'm sorry.'

'The man who was responsible for her death was Amadeo Calabrese.'

'Oh, fuck,' De Blasi said. He leaned forward and lowered his head against the steering wheel.

'You've heard the story, then?' Michele said.

De Blasi sat up and reached into his jacket pocket for his packet of cigarettes. He took one out before holding the packet toward Michele, who held out his lighter for his shaken companion.

De Blasi took a deep drag and then exhaled smoke out of the open window.

'I know only that the Capo's son had been murdered at his own wedding in Sicily around a year ago. As you might expect, word had quickly travelled around, and that the boss was out for blood.'

De Blasi hesitated and took another deep drag from the cigarette before flicking the butt out of the window.

'Did you kill him?'

'Yes,' Michele said matter-of-factly. 'I killed him.'

Michele observed De Blasi's confused expression.

'What is it?' Michele said.

'I just can't help but wonder why Amadeo would get involved in affairs overseas? He wasn't a hitman. If he had wanted someone killed, then he would have made the order himself, not carried it out.'

Michele looked fixedly at him. The question as to whether he had indeed killed the man responsible for his wife's death had been one he had asked himself time and time again since the moment he had pulled the trigger. Even earlier than that if he had to be honest with himself.

He had been so desperate for a name that he had neither questioned nor reasoned with how that information had been delivered. He had hoped that by punishing Mary's killer, then life would become more tolerable. As it was, he had closed one door and opened another.

'You're not so certain you killed the right man, are you?' De Blasi said cautiously.

Michele met his gaze. 'The information came from a reliable source, so I had no reason to question it. Just as Alberto Calabrese is bent on revenge by his own hands, I was intent on taking his son out singlehandedly. If it had been a hit from an enemy on the island I would have understood it fully. But not this. The question as to why has haunted me as much as my loss. But there's more.'

Michele went on to inform De Blasi of events spanning the last twenty-four hours, and the trail of death that had followed.

'You didn't feel like telling me any of this before I agreed to help you,' he said.

Michele didn't pick up on the humour, and even if he had heard it, he failed to acknowledge it.

'So why you, Michele?'

'How do you mean?'

'I mean no disrespect, but what did they have to gain by killing the wife of a soldier?'

Michele took a final drag on the cigarette and then threw the remains out of the window. 'I'm not a soldier,' he said.

'Oh shit,' De Blasi said.

'Now are you getting the picture,' Michele said.

'Yeah,' De Blasi returned. 'I'm getting the picture.'

Having heard everything that Franco De Blasi had told him, Michele felt safe in the knowledge that what he had heard was the truth. He knew what to look out for. And having heard his uncle Gianluca make a mistake that had cost him his life a mere twenty-four hours earlier, he was certain as he could be that he had not missed anything.

Franco De Blasi had shown no signs of deception; in fact, he had looked more clouded about the events that had taken place than Michele had, in terms of whether he had taken out the right man. De Blasi was merely a soldier. He was told what to do and when to do it. No questions asked. He had proved reliable, however, he was expendable, like many others before him.

'What next?' De Blasi asked.

'This friend of yours…'

'Vincenzo,' he cut in.

'Are you sure it's a good idea to have him involved in all this?'

'I see little choice—I'll tell him what he needs to know.'

'There is always a choice.'

'Forget it,' De Blasi said more bravely than he had intended. 'I've held enough back from him over the years. He's in or I'm out.'

Michele sighed. 'Okay, but understand one thing, Franco. If and when they discover that you are alive, it will be the one you love who they will come after.'

'I know. And if it comes to that, I'll take care of us both.'

'You might not have that choice to make. I'm sure my brother Giovanni would have said exactly the same thing. As it was they killed her first—just so he could watch no doubt, and more importantly to them, so I could hear. I want you to know that you have a choice. Go to Vincenzo, and pack up and leave. It should be some time before they trace your steps, and by then, the two of you will be many miles away from danger.'

De Blasi looked at Michele.

'I don't intend to run away from something, only to keep having to look over my shoulders. That's no way to live.'

'So, you're in?' Michele said.

De Blasi held out his hand.

'I'm in.'

Michele took his hand. 'Okay, let's go.'

Franco De Blasi briefed Michele as to the whereabouts of his friend and lover Vincenzo Conti, as they made their journey toward Queens. The anonymity or their relationship had been concealed from the family, a tactic that he had employed to avoid any unnecessary complications. Now, that had proved to have been a wise move. Knowing Benito Calabrese the way he did, he would systematically kill anyone in his way, and he enjoyed murdering the innocent in order to get to his main target.

Vincenzo Conti was such a person and a far cry from his homicidal lover. De Blasi had ensured that he had remained an unknown entity for his own safety rather than a feeling of shame, his only admission falling to the hands of the Sicilian, Michele La Barbara.

Other than displaying his concern over Vincenzo's safety, Michele had remained reticent over De Blasi's declaration that he was a homosexual. It really was of no interest to him. But this was a dangerous time. And as Michele was reminded each night, it was the innocent ones who would pay dearly with their lives.

'Vincenzo?' Michele said.

'What about him?' De Blasi said curiously.

'You said he doesn't ask questions about your business activities. Does he have any idea what you do for a living?'

De Blasi sighed. 'He knows as much as he needs to know. For the early part of our relationship, I had him believe that I was a debt collector, which wasn't far from the truth, except…'

Michele looked at him.

'He wasn't aware as to what measures I would go to, to collect such debt,' he said.

'You mean you didn't tell him that you murder people?'

He took his eye off the road as he turned to face Michele. 'Something like that. He asked me one day what I meant by "debt collecting". I told him that I collect money from people who owed money. He asked who they owed money to, and I told him "don't ask". Till this day he has never asked me what I do for a living.'

'Not the most romantic tale I've ever heard.'

De Blasi laughed. For now, it seemed at least that the two men had grown comfortable with one another.

'And what does Vincenzo do for a living?'

'He owns a salon.'

De Blasi could see the confusion on Michele's face.

'He cuts people's hair.'

'I see,' Michele said. 'And how will your friend react once you've introduced me?'

'He'll be just fine. And when he holds you firmly by your shoulders and kisses you on both cheeks, please, don't get offended.'

Michele smiled nervously. 'I'll try to remember that.'

'So, how did you ever get involved with the mob?' Michele asked.

So much for the casual stuff, while it lasted, De Blasi thought. 'A friend of mine introduced me to Benito Calabrese some years ago.'

Michele looked at him curiously.

'Not that kind of friend. He was always eager to tell me of his involvement with the family, what he got up to, you know… boasting about his exploits and how much money he was making.'

Michele smiled. 'Whatever happened to the code of silence?'

De Blasi took his eyes off the road ahead for a brief moment and turned to face his passenger. 'Yes, I'll get to that.'

'So what happened?'

'I was out of work and eager to earn some money, so much so, I was barely days away from being on the breadline. I thought of what it would be like to have a career but figured that such a venture would take too long, and I needed money fast. In the end, it came down to whether I was prepared to take a chance and enter the world of organised crime or risk living on the streets.

'Even now I can recall thinking and wondering how the hell those guys make it out alive living on the streets, begging for the odd buck that will get them a cup of coffee, or spilling their way through trash cans to pick up some scraps of food in order to stay alive.

'Those people are tough—far tougher than I could even possibly imagine. They live day by day, whereas I, would end it.' He looked over at Michele. 'I mean it. Life has to have some purpose, right?'

Michele thought of his own life, and how he had basically lived day by day since his wife's demise.

'So I called him up and asked him if he could get me any work. He made arrangements for me to meet up with the Calabrese family, and that was when I was first introduced to Alberto Calabrese. Benito was there too, along with the consigliere—'

'Was his other son there?'

'Yes. He wasn't a captain at that time, but he later went on to have his own caporegime. He was smart, just like his father, but more charismatic, and certainly more intelligent than his brother Benito.' De Blasi raised a smile.

'And he didn't strike you as a killer?'

'As I said, he didn't strike me as the soldier type. No doubt he would have made his hits as he made his way up through the ranks, but my guess would be that he would order hits as opposed to carrying them out. He was certainly no mercenary from what I understood.'

'I see,' Michele said. 'So you were sworn in?'

'Yes. It seemed that my initial introduction had been a success, so much so, I was welcomed into the family with open arms.'

'But you were owned from that point on, right?'

'Right,' he said, glancing over toward his passenger. 'They pricked my finger and then dropped the blood on the picture of a saint. "As this saint burns in my hands, so will burn my soul if I betray the family in any way. I enter alive and will have to get out dead".'

De Blasi held that thought for a moment.

'What became of your friend?' Michele asked, breaking the silence.

'Funny you should ask.'

'Well, I figured if he was such a good friend, we wouldn't be running short of options right now.'

'Right again. As you pointed out earlier, he couldn't help but talk. He wasn't a rat by any means, but he loved to talk. He loved the life, but he never anticipated for a single moment that the life he had chosen would somehow seal his fate. One day, he was in a bar and got chatting to some guy about football. As the drinks went down, so did the conversation, and during the entire time they were together it hadn't dawned on him that he was speaking to a rookie police officer.'

'Was he arrested?'

'Yes. By the time they walked out of the bar together, there was a police car waiting outside for him. They took him to the station and questioned him.'

De Blasi shook his head. 'He refused to comment and denied all that he had said in the bar. But it was too late. When he was picked up outside of the police station the following morning, he was never seen or ever heard from again.

'From that moment on, I understood the harsh reality of the world I had become involved in. When I made my first hit I remember thinking, *kill or die on the streets.* The fear of living in some alleyway on the cold winter nights in the city is what kept me alive. With that thought in mind, I was able to pull the trigger without shedding an ounce of remorse.'

Franco De Blasi had drifted off into a past he had fought so hard to forget, and as such, had told Michele only half a story that was engulfed in shame and treachery.

'Interesting,' Michele said.

'So, how did it all start for you?'

'You had to ask.' Michele smiled. 'A story for another time,' he said.

'Then let's hope I live long enough to hear it,' De Blasi said as they reached their destination. 'That goes for you, too,' he said.

Chapter Eleven

When the two men entered the apartment on Queens, Vincenzo was at home and eagerly awaiting his partner, who had failed to respond to any calls he had made that day. He had been worried about what might have become of him. Content to acknowledge Franco's plea not to make him answerable to his business activities, he remained concerned that one day he would fail to show up at his home—their home.

So, when Franco De Blasi opened the door to their apartment, Vincenzo hastily made his way toward him in an over-excited fashion, holding his arms out ready to grab him in an emotional embrace. Excitable at the best of times, his emotional tendencies made him more possessive toward his lover, and he was eager to show it.

'Franco!' he sniffled, holding on to him firmly.

Michele stood in the doorway, his eyes meeting De Blasi's, he could sense his embarrassment of the situation. Vincenzo continued to hold on to his lover as if it were their final moments together, and at which time, Michele coughed, and while it was not intentional, it had the effect of releasing the two men from their embrace.

'Vincenzo, I'd like you to meet Michele La Barbara.'

Vincenzo looked at him curiously before reaching out his limp hand, which fell into Michele's large hand with a certain amount of grace and delicacy.

'Hello,' Michele said, and then smiled.

'It's a pleasure to meet you,' Vincenzo responded. He looked the Sicilian up and down, caught sight of the flight bag he was holding, and then turned his attention back to his partner. 'Would your friend like to join us for dinner?'

Both men turned to face Michele who, for the first time since arriving on foreign soil, was reminded of how hungry he was and gratefully accepted. The smell coming from the kitchen was inviting to say the least.

'Bravo,' Vincenzo said. 'In the meantime, please make yourself at home.'

Michele entered the living room and took a seat on the brown leather sofa. He could hear the two men in the kitchen having a conversation about matters relating to his uninvited appearance in their lives. And while there was nothing but murmurs, he didn't hear anything that suggested Vincenzo was uncomfortable with having him around—at least for now. Michele wondered about the two men with greater interest; Blasi, five-foot-six and intimidating in appearance, while Vincenzo was at least five-foot-ten, slender and feminine in his entire demeanour.

Without a single hair out of place he was a good-looking guy and the complete opposite of the man in his life. *Perhaps opposites do attract,* thought Michele, which made him think about Mary. And despite the many differences that separated them, he considered that they had been so compatible in every way.

Strange but true, he thought.

***

Michele reflected on the conversation he had had with De Blasi on their way over to Queens and thought back to how he had made his way up through the ranks of La Cosa Nostra, to become the island's *Capo di tutti Capi* (the boss of bosses). A time when his Uncle Gianluca would finally consider giving up the reigns that he had held on to for so long and hand the family business over to his nephew. Of course, Gianluca's role as Capo existed only with his own *family.*

At that time, there was no boss of all bosses.

Even for those who had dared to consider it, nobody had the nerve to make any attempt to accomplish it. That was until one day when two of the bosses of the most notorious families in Sicily decided to make their move toward greater dominance: taking over the remaining four families and gaining control of the island.

The De Luca and the Lorenzo family.

Gianluca had tipped Michele off that there was unrest amongst the two family members, and with their number of members growing, so were their numbers in caporegimes. Together, they were taking over some of the families' businesses on the island, pushing their weight in an attempt to overthrow them. This spelled out trouble. And while they remained no threat in the present day, it was clear that one day they would take control over the whole island.

Gianluca was concerned.

Michele was calm.

Which only spelled danger.

At least, for the other families involved.

For the heads of any family, they were considered to be untouchable. But, as Michele had discovered, nobody was untouchable.

Matteo De Luca or Don De Luca as he was accustomed to, controlled the surrounding area of Agrigento, while the Lorenzo family controlled Syracuse. In time, they had vowed to take over the entire island, but making their move against the Giordano family in Palermo, would be a means to the downfall of the other families, who would have little or no power to take a stranglehold of the territory that they had held on to for so long.

Michele had made the decision to drive alone to Agrigento, and to the territory of Matteo De Lucca, who he had met once before in the company of his uncle and the other head members of each of the families. He was typically arrogant, always had a cigar in his hand, and had no business acumen other than his right to control the men beneath him.

Agrigento was an old city overlooking the Mediterranean Sea, with a population of circa 60,000, it was a major tourist attraction because of its archaeological legacy. Two hours' drive away from Palermo, Michele set off early that morning, knowing from his source of information that Don De Luca would be sitting having an espresso sat at his usual table outside of his local restaurant.

He goes there every morning, he was told.
He's closely guarded at all times.

The Ficus Bar

Michele had arrived in the city around nine o'clock that morning and parked up around two hundred yards from the café. He looked through the rear-view mirror and observed his facial features; now looking into the eyes of an old man, with a complexion of patchy skin tone and wrinkles from too many years of being exposed to the sun, he ensured his grey overgrown hair, white eyebrows and fake moustache were firmly in place before getting out of the car.

Walking stick in hand, he opened the car door and climbed out gingerly, using his stick to aid him to stand up, he looked up at the morning sky and squinted as he caught the full beam of the Sicilian sun. Typically overdressed as elderly people do no matter what the season, he made the slow walk forward toward his destination, walking stick to guide him on his way, and a gun and attached silencer, carefully located on the inside of his heavy coat.

As he made the slow walk toward the café, he observed a vehicle pull up outside, and watched as the driver got out and made then his way round to the back passenger side and opened the door. After several moments, the unmistakable figure of Don De Luca climbed out of the car, looked around and then placed a cigar in his mouth. As the other car doors opened, he was followed to the café by three other men, who remained close by him as if they were protecting the President of the United States.

Michele smiled beneath the make-up, curious but praiseworthy as to Gianluca's sources that had provided him with such accurate information. Now, it was just a question of whether his presence would be accepted if he sat at a table outside in the company of the other men.

As he watched the obese frame of the unkempt Don take his seat before the other men, Michele slowly edged his walking stick to the wooden steps leading up to the dining area, and with one foot trailing the other, he made his way to a table that was sufficient distance away as not to encroach on their privacy or listen in on their conversation.

One of the men stood up and stared at the old man as if to question his temerity to invade their privacy. But the Don waved his hand, showing compassion for the elderly man who was clearly in need of some refreshment.

Michele slowly sat down at the table, and after the men had been taken care of by the waiter, he came over to serve the old man.

'Quello che posso ottenere, signor?'

'Succo d'arancia fresco, per favore,' the old man said.

'Certo,' the waiter said, and then went inside the building.

Michele sat back in his chair and looked around, taking in what was going on at the table—three tables away from him—but cautious not to raise any suspicion. A short time after taking his order the waiter returned with his glass of fresh orange on a tray, and he placed it on the table in front of Michele.

'Grazie,' the old man croaked.

'Prego,' the waiter said, and then went about his duties.

Michele welcomed the cold drink and noted that the men sitting at the table had been served and were enjoying their morning breakfast. The Don, who was sat sipping on his espresso and taking the occasional puff from his cigar, glanced over toward the old man, before returning his attention to the discussion in hand.

Michele took another drink from the glass and then placed it on the table.

It was time to make his move.

The old man put his right hand in his pocket and pulled out a five-euro note, and placed it on the small silver plate in front of him. Then, he grabbed his walking stick and slowly got to his feet. With his coat pocket already open, he made his way across to the other table with greater stealth, and as he flicked the walking stick, a sharp blade ejected from the base.

In a vicious assault, Michele thrust the blade from the end of the walking stick into the side of the man sitting nearest him, and then pulled out his gun with rapid motion, leaving the other three men helpless to respond in time. Michele opened fire on the two men, and, with the other bleeding to death from the knife attack, he aimed the gun at Don De Luca.

'Don't shoot,' he said, dropping his cigar to the floor. 'Who are you? What do you want? Tell me what it is and I'll make you a deal.'

'Who is the boss on this island?' Michele asked.

'I am,' Don De Luca said.

Michele fired a shot into the Don's left shoulder, which made him scream out in agony, causing further pandemonium from inside the building.

'Wrong answer,' Michele said. 'Your people work for me now. Do you understand?'

'Who are you!' the Don yelled.

'My name is Michele La Barbara, and Don Lorenzo is next.'

Michele watched as Don De Luca's expression went from confusion to horror, and then he fired a bullet in the centre of his forehead.

Michele placed the gun back inside his coat, picked up the walking stick and then made his way from the café far quicker than how he had arrived. When he got back to the car, he took off his heavy coat, wig and pulled off his moustache, and then drove away leaving a chaotic scene behind him.

'One down,' he said to himself, and then looked through the rear-view mirror and observed the heavy prominent grey eyebrows that were still in place. Beyond the thick layer of make-up, he managed to break a smile and then turned his attention to the next part of his mission.

***

As Michele recalled memories from his past, he was woken from his reverie as De Blasi called him into the dining area. 'Come, Michele. Let's eat.'

The atmosphere over dinner had been far more relaxed than Michele would have expected; Vincenzo playing the charming host, and his lover making light-hearted conversation as if they had all been friends for a long time. Meatballs and spaghetti with a bowl full of crusty bread ready to dip in olive oil gave Michele a taste of home. One of his favourite dishes, and plenty to go around.

'Franco tells me you're here on vacation?' Vincenzo enquired.

Michele nodded as he held up a forkful of spaghetti to his mouth. 'Just for a few days or so. I'll be heading back home after checking in with a few friends.'

He was grateful that his host didn't pry any further; if he was curious how he and De Blasi had met, he didn't ask, at least not at the dinner table.

'Do you have a place to stay while you're here in New York?' Vincenzo asked.

Michele met De Blasi's eyes for an instant, before Vincenzo added, 'Because there is room for you here if you'd like to stay.'

De Blasi looked at Michele and raised his hands slightly, as if to gesture that it was okay with him, too.

'Thank you, but it's okay. I'll be spending most of my time in the city, so I'll check into a hotel this evening.'

De Blasi wiped his mouth with a napkin while still chewing his food and then took a sip of red wine. He looked at Michele but remained silent, wondering what their next move might entail. And as the man from Sicily and his partner continued to make light-hearted conversation over dinner, De Blasi took a moment to reflect on how things had changed so radically in a matter of hours. He had had little time to consider how the hell he had made it this far, knowing full well that he should be out there lying dead on the streets.

Dangerous times lay ahead, though. That much he understood. The man sitting at their table was no regular hood; he was a Sicilian crime lord, and from what he had acknowledged so far, one of the most dangerous and capable men he had ever come across in his life.

Michele wiped his mouth with a napkin and then pushed the empty bowl in front of him. 'That was delicious, Vincenzo.'

De Blasi stood up from the table. 'Come on, Michele. Let's go into the living room.'

'I'll make coffee,' Vincenzo said as both men made their way into the next room.

'Take a seat,' De Blasi said, and then closed the door to give them the privacy that was needed. 'I thought—'

'No,' Michele cut him off. It's much too dangerous for me to stay here.'

De Blasi took a seat and then nodded. Despite having questioned him, he understood.

'I can recommend some good hotels in the city.'

'No,' Michele said. 'I'll find my own way.'

'You don't want to tell me where you're going to be staying?'

'No,' he said firmly. 'It's far too dangerous, and you know it. Wait for my call. When I need you, I'll call you.'

'I'll be ready,' he said.

The door opened and then Vincenzo appeared holding a smile and carrying two cups of coffee. The charming host placed both cups onto the oval-shaped smoked-glass coffee table, and then returned to the kitchen.

Michele took a drink of coffee, his eyes meeting De Blasi's as he looked over the rim of the cup.

'I know what you're thinking,' De Blasi said.

'Then allow me to say this only once,' Michele said. 'If you want to help me, then you need to let Vincenzo go.'

De Blasi leaned forward in his chair and placed his coffee cup on the table in front of him. 'Give up Vincenzo,' he whispered. 'Never.'

'If you are correct in saying that they know nothing of your private life, then this the time to leave him. If you love him, then let him go.'

'It's just out of the question, Michele. They come for him, then they'll have to take me out first.'

'You might not get that opportunity. Just think about,' he said.

He could not help but think of anything else, yet there was nothing that would ever make him give up his lover and best friend. Not the mob. Not Michele.

'When do you expect to get in touch with me?' he asked, changing the subject.

'Soon.'

'Please stay and freshen up before you leave.'

'Thank you,' Michele said.

The two men were interrupted as Vincenzo walked into the room holding a glass of red wine.

'Thank you,' Michele said. 'And thank you for the meal. You're a perfect host.'

'You're very welcome,' Vincenzo said, and then sat down on the arm of the chair next to his lover. And it was at that moment when Michele looked deep into Franco De Blasi's eyes, and without the need to say anything further, De Blasi knew what he was thinking.

I won't ever give him up, he thought.

Chapter Twelve

Michele waited until nightfall before leaving the apartment in Queens in search of a safe place to stay. Having showered, he had dressed casually in denim trousers and wore De Blasi's maroon hooded sweater which, despite the Italian's size difference, fit him perfectly.

In spite of the danger that now existed, Franco De Blasi had offered to drive Michele into the city, which Michele had refused without any consideration. If De Blasi was relieved he didn't show it but accepted the Sicilian's decision nevertheless. Benito and his crew would be searching for them no doubt, and they would have every source at their disposal to locate them.

Vincenzo remained unaware as to the extent of the danger that was lurking in the shadows, waiting for the single opportunity to strike. While he was in no doubt that his lover and newfound friend were in some form of trouble, he was unaware as to the scale of the threat that existed. They had discussed little over dinner, leaving business until after when they were able to retire to the living room. And while Franco had protected his lover from the nefarious world that existed outside their cosy environment, he could conceal the truth from him no longer and would have to level with him soon enough.

As it was, Vincenzo had been stood close to the door that separated them, listening in to their conversation. He couldn't be sure as to the level of trouble that they spoke of, however, had heard enough for him to shed a tear.

Both men made their way out of the apartment block and to the car, where De Blasi opened the trunk so he could give Michele the ammunition that he needed. De Blasi kept the shotgun, which he felt he would need to use sooner rather than later.

'I'll be in touch, Franco.'

'I'll be waiting.'

Both men shook hands and then he watched as the Sicilian made his way out onto the streets of Queens, where he would locate a cab that would take him into the city.

It wasn't long before Michele spotted a yellow cab that De Blasi had told him to look out for, which he waved over and then got inside.

'Where to?' the driver asked.

'Take me into the city.'

The driver laughed and met his eyes through the rear-view mirror. 'It's a very big city, my friend.'

Michele wasn't familiar with names or places in New York, however, he thought back to when he had been sitting next to Chiara on the flight over, and she had been reading through a magazine. He hadn't been interested in the magazine but remembered the name "Fifth Avenue", for whatever reason that might have been.

'Take me to Fifth Avenue,' Michele said.

'Okay,' the driver said. 'Fifth Avenue it is.'

***

The day after the assassination of Don Matteo De Luca, Michele made his surreptitious move on his target, Don Lorenzo, who was sitting inside a dilapidated restaurant at the foot of the hills in Syracuse. Two men had sat outside, soldiers, their rifles hanging loosely over their shoulders as they concealed themselves in the shade as the sun shone its merciless rays on the island. Disregarding the merest suggestion of any threat, they remained oblivious of the eyes that observed them as they slumbered through the stifling heat.

Their day-to-day duties to protect the one man whom they displayed their total allegiance to, had become one of ease and boredom, regardless of the need to be on guard at all times. Beyond the doors of the building, the room was faintly lit, allowing only a small margin of light to pass through the wooden hatches. The bartender remained behind the bar; a slender, middle-aged man, who went about his duties in a manner that created an impression of all-round activity.

In the corner of the room, an elderly, rotund man sat at a table stirring his coffee and reading a newspaper. Above the pages, a stream of dense smoke from his cigar spiralled up towards the old wooden panelled ceiling. Occasionally, he would take a mouthful of coffee followed by an uncouth slurp, signifying the only sound of his existence.

Outside, the two guards continued to slumber, their only movement was to squat aside the occasional fly, flinching momentarily before resuming with an uninterrupted and emphatic snore. At their side stood the assassin. His movements had gone unnoticed, both men, oblivious to the danger that now existed.

Holding an eight-inch knife with a jagged edge, the stranger approached the man sitting nearest him, and placing his left hand firmly around his mouth, he guided the blade with precision from his left ear to his right, opening his throat as if gutting a helpless fish. The merest suggestion of anguish from the stricken man did little to distract his colleague, who continued to sleep through the heat of the afternoon sun, however, only moments away from suffering the same fate. As the assassin sliced his throat in a similar fashion, the man looked up at his killer with grimacing terror.

The barman glanced over at the stranger as he entered the restaurant, nodded, and then disappeared from behind the bar. The assassin made his way over toward the ageing Don, moving with stealth, he sat down at the table facing opposite him. Don Lorenzo paid no regard to the person sitting opposite him, refusing to acknowledge him, he continued to sip his coffee and read his newspaper.

The stranger raised his gun toward the newspaper and fired a single bullet, which cleared a small hole in the centre of the old man's forehead, gorging out fragments of his skull and showering blood against the wooden panels behind him.

As the assassin stood up from the table, he left the building as casually as he had entered it. For Don Lorenzo, his years of tyranny had finally come to an end.

Michele La Barbara had now become Il Capo dei Capi—the boss of bosses.

***

When the cab driver pulled over next to the Museum of Modern Art at 53rd Street on Fifth Avenue, he called out to Michele who had drifted off into an uncomfortable slumber and informed him that he had reached his destination. Initially unaware of his surroundings, Michele looked outside the window and onto the streets of New York, where he could see that the city was alive and far from the life that he was accustomed to back in Sicily.

'Quanto?' Michele asked.

'If you mean how much, that'll be thirty-five dollars.'

Michele reached inside his trouser pocket and pulled out a bunch of notes, and then handed the cab driver a fifty-dollar note. 'Keep it,' he said, much to the driver's delight, who told his passenger to take care as he opened the back door and stepped out onto the streets of New York.

Well, he thought, *here goes.*

Mesmerised by city life, the heavy flow of traffic, people including families with young children crowding the walkways, Michele made his way down Broadway in awe of the spectacle. The show of skyscrapers that lit up the city was a sight to behold, and in a faraway land, Michele was a stranger, and above all, a loner.

For no apparent reason, he crossed the busy road and headed toward 46th Street and Broadway in search of a place to stay. Money was no object; he just wanted a place to rest his head, someplace where he could take some respite without holding a gun in his hand.

Just as he crossed the road, he was met by a young woman who, strangely enough, had appeared out of nowhere. Michele had disregarded her approach, and even when she spoke to him, he was determined to push by her as if he was ignoring a beggar on the street.

'Hey, good lookin',' she said. 'You looking for a good time?'

Michele stopped in his tracks and turned to look at her. She was small and pretty and possessed a curvaceous figure. As he looked at her, he considered that she could indeed be young enough to be his daughter. The young woman was wearing black high-heeled boots and a short white dress, which exposed her slender legs and her shapely figure. Her hair was short and blonde and her blue eyes glistened even in the fading light.

'How old are you?' Michele asked.

'Twenty-six,' she said, which surprised him, yet made him wonder if she was telling him the truth. 'What's it to you anyway?'

'Just curious,' he said.

'You're not from around these parts,' she said.

'No,' he said softly, and then turned to walk away, regretful that he had not done so from the moment she had called out to him.

'Hey,' she shouted, 'please don't go. We were just gettin' to know one another.'

'Were we indeed,' he muttered to himself as he kept on walking. But the girl continued to call out to him, hurrying her pace up she quickly caught up to him, and then linked his arm with hers as if to claim that she had caught her prize.

Michele stopped and looked down at her, and gazed deep into her blue eyes. 'What's your name?' he asked. 'Your real name?' He wasn't in the habit of speaking to prostitutes, yet he was aware of their behaviour and the methods that they would go to in order to get themselves some business.

And just as Michele turned away for the final time, she called out to him in earnest: 'Beth,' she said. 'My name is Bethany, but I'm known as Beth.' There was a friendly, almost sincere tone to her voice that Michele recognised.

'It's not safe out here on the streets, Beth. I think it would be best if you go home.'

'The streets are my home,' she said.

'Sorry, Beth. I have to go. So either go to wherever it is that you come from, or go find someone else.'

'I don't have anyone,' she said.

Michele stopped but didn't look back. For a moment he wondered whether he alone had invited her into his life or whether she adopted the same approach with every man she attempted to lure. 'You're not my problem,' he said coldly, and then walked on for what he had determined would be the final time.

The sound of a car pulling up at the roadside caused Michele to stop and turn round. A black man of medium build, wearing grey jogging bottoms and a black hooded sweater got out of the passenger side and approached the young woman, holding her firmly and shaking her, he slapped her face and then punched her in the stomach.

'Hey,' Michele called out. 'Leave the girl alone.'

'What the fuck is it to you, mister?'

At that moment, the driver side door opened, and another black man stepped out of the car. Taller than his associate, and wearing a black suit that gave him a wider look than he was, he held his position with just a glare of intimidation to ensure that Michele understood the threat that awaited any possible intervention.

'I don't want any trouble,' Michele said. 'So why don't you just let the girl go.'

'My girl not good enough for you?' he asked. 'This bitch not good enough for you, Dago?'

Michele made a steady approach toward the man while maintaining his sights on his colleague, who remained in position outside of the car. Beth was kneeling on the ground and holding her stomach. It was not the first time that she had had to endure a beating, yet each punch or kick would be inflicted on the body to ensure that her face was not damaged in any way. At least while she was making money.

'Yes,' Michele said (and to Beth's surprise, if not his own). 'She is good enough for me and too good for you. So why don't you do the right thing and let her go.'

Both men laughed, and then the man standing over Beth kicked her in the stomach without even looking at her. He then stepped forward toward the stranger and pulled out a flick knife from his trouser pocket. 'Come on, Dago,' he said, as he flicked open the blade and waved it in front of him. 'You want to dance?'

Michele watched him closely as he cast the knife from one hand to the other, taunting the Sicilian to step forward. And then he made a fatal mistake. In a state of fury, the pimp launched himself at Michele. His right arm extended too far out in front of him, Michele evaded the strike with ease. As the man stumbled forward, Michele grabbed his head with both hands. And in one swift motion of brutality, he broke the man's neck and then watched as his lifeless body fell to the ground. Having witnessed the assault, the pimp's colleague scrambled back into the car, the sound of tyres screeching on the tarmac as the vehicle sped away.

Michele turned his attention to Beth and held out his arm for her to grab on to, which she accepted without the slightest hesitation. With little effort, he pulled her up from the ground and waited until she caught her breath.

'Are you okay, Beth?' he asked softly.

'Yes,' she said. 'Thank you. Thank you so much.'

'Prego,' he said. 'Friends of yours?'

'Best a girl could have,' she said sarcastically.

Stood just outside an alleyway, it was fortunate that nobody had witnessed either assault that had taken place. It had all happened so quickly.

'I think we better get out of here before the police arrive,' she said.

Michele quickly weighed up his options: walk away on his own, or accompany Beth. For now, he decided to go with the latter.

'Do you want to go for a cup of coffee?' he asked.

Beth smiled. A man who wanted her company instead of using her for sex. 'I'd like that a lot,' she said.

As the couple began the walk down 46th Street on Broadway, Beth stopped for a moment and looked up at the stranger who had saved her from certain death.

'I never did get your name?' she said.

'Michele,' he said. 'My name is Michele.'

'You saved my life, Michele. I don't know how I will ever be able to repay you?'

Michele smiled through the darkness. 'You can start by buying me a coffee, and then we'll talk, Beth. Okay?'

'Okay,' she said and smiled.

Beth held on to Michele's right arm and then led him toward their destination. She had never felt so safe in her life.

Beth had met Michele La Barbara, and it was from that moment that her life was about to change.

Chapter Thirteen

Franco De Blasi was feeling less confident about matters since Michele's departure earlier that evening. Despite having made every attempt to block out the advice that he had been given, he was beginning to consider the prospect of life without his partner Vincenzo. Convinced for the moment at least that the Calabrese family were unaware of his private life—and that he was still alive for that matter—he acknowledged why Michele, a stranger from a foreign land, had strongly suggested that he let his lover go.

While Vincenzo was aware of his partner's involvement with the mob, he was unaware to the murderous extent to which he *had* gone about his business. He had never dwelt too much on De Blasi's covert operations, and while he had considered the possibility that he might be involved in something nefarious, he assumed that it was in the form of money collecting or racketeering. Anything else, he simply did not want to know.

They had agreed at the start of their relationship that they would not discuss the life within the mob, and until Michele La Barbara had entered their lives, that's the way things had remained. De Blasi had briefed Vincenzo that Michele had just arrived in the country and needed someone to help and guide him around the city.

Looks like a man capable of helping himself, if you know what I mean, Vincenzo had responded. He had looked deep into his lover's eyes and remained silent about matters thereafter, however, De Blasi knew from the words he had spoken and the way he had looked through him that he hadn't bought his story. And that made him feel guilty in more ways than one.

De Blasi was sitting on the sofa watching the baseball game when Vincenzo called out to him from the kitchen doorway. He looked up and smiled. 'Sorry,' he said, 'I was miles away.'

'You were thinking about your friend, right?'

'Kind of,' he smiled. 'Vincenzo, we need to talk.'

He watched as Vincenzo's bottom lip trembled, and then he realised what his immediate thoughts were. 'And before you ask, no, I'm not in love with Michele.'

Vincenzo made the sign of the cross and said *thank the Lord*. 'I did notice his wedding ring, but...'

'Seriously?'

'Hey,' Vincenzo stood looking at his lover in a manner that was less than masculine. 'What can I say, he's hot.'

'Looks can be deceiving,' he said, thinking more of how he posed a danger to those who crossed him, but he raised a smile nevertheless.

Vincenzo made his way into the living area and then took his place on the sofa next to his lover. 'So,' he said softly, 'what did you want to talk to me about?'

'You know I would never do anything deliberately to hurt you, right?'

Vincenzo nodded, yet his eyes had already begun to glaze over. 'You're beginning to scare me, Franco. What's going on?'

'I'm in trouble, Vincenzo.'

'What kind of trouble?' he asked, holding on to his partner's hand as if this would be their final moments together.

'The people I've been involved with for so long... well, they're looking for me and I don't want you to get involved.'

'What do you mean looking for you? What have you done to betray your friends, Franco?'

Vincenzo had used the word *betray*. And without knowing the facts behind that betrayal, he was right. Franco De Blasi had sworn allegiance to La Cosa Nostra, and now he had betrayed that oath. A perfidious act that would not go unpunished.

'Franco? What have you done?' he repeated.

'I guess it's more what I haven't done,' he said.

'How do you mean? Does this have something to do with your friend Michele?'

De Blasi nodded. 'I'm afraid it has everything to do with Michele. The man who we invited into our home is a wanted man. He comes from Sicily, and I was ordered to pick him up from the airport and then take him directly to them.'

'Why? What do they want from him?'

'I really don't know, Vincenzo, and I didn't ask. I simply do what I'm asked to do.'

'So why didn't you?'

Tongue-tied, De Blasi blushed a little, causing his lover to become more curious as to why he had failed to hand over this man to his mob friends.

'He'—Blasi paused—'caught me with my pants down.'

'You mean he pulled a gun out on you.'

'You catch on fast,' and if the situation hadn't been as dangerous as it was, he assumed that it would have been a moment that would have been met with laughter.

'What have you got yourself into, Franco?'

'Michele could have killed me but he chose not to. In return, I agreed to help him.'

Vincenzo stood up and wandered around the room, before finally settling himself down on a chair facing opposite his lover.

'Vincenzo, listen to me. I gave my life and soul to the mob many years ago. I made a pledge to do their bidding when I took the oath, which meant I would be called on at any time to serve their needs.'

'But why, Franco, why on earth would you have done such a thing?'

'Because it was the life that I had chosen; a life that kept me off the street and,' he said solemnly, 'in lots of ways they were like a family to me. The only family I had ever had.'

'And now that *family* wants to kill you. Is that correct?'

'Yes,' he said, 'and that means that I have to protect you at all costs, even if it means…'

He couldn't say it.

But Vincenzo understood what he meant.

'I fear for your safety, Vincenzo. These people will stop at nothing to find me. And if they were ever to find out about us, then they would use you to get to me. I'm sorry I didn't tell you everything before, but I had to protect you from any possible threat that might have existed.'

Teary-eyed, Vincenzo stood up and quickly walked over to sit down on the sofa next to him. He sat closer to him this time, holding his hand tighter than before, and this time he was desperate not to let go.

'Now, you listen to me, Franco. We've been together for five years now, and we're more than just lovers. We're best friends and soul mates, which means that we don't just up and away at the first sign of trouble,' he said confidently. 'Now, they don't know about us and nor are they ever likely to. So, for now, we'll keep our distance from them and then move on and start a new life.'

'But what about your work here in the city?' he asked surprised.

'I can start again elsewhere. In fact, I quite like the sound of that,' he said enthused.

De Blasi let out a deflated sigh and shook his head. 'I'm worried—'

'Shush,' Vincenzo said, holding his finger against his lover's lips. 'This is the first time I have asked you to stand by me, Franco. We'll get through this together and then we can begin a new life and one that we can cherish. So, what do you say; are we still an item or not?'

'I guess so,' De Blasi said. 'But look, any sign of trouble and I want you to get as far away from here as you can, do you hear me?'

'Understood,' Vincenzo said, almost too casually for his liking.

'In the meantime, I've got some unfinished business to attend to, which shouldn't take more than two or three days.'

'And then what?'

'And then we'll take what we need and get the hell out of here.'

'Promise me you'll never leave me,' Vincenzo implored.

Franco De Blasi remained silent for an instant as he gazed deeply into his lover's eyes. Secretly, he knew that it was a promise that he would not be able to make, however, from this moment on he would do the right thing and protect Vincenzo at all costs.

'I promise,' he said.

Under clear instruction from his father, Benito Calabrese had paid another visit to Franco De Blasi's Brooklyn apartment. He had his boys turn the place over on two occasions already that day, and here they were again, rifling through every draw and cupboard in order to try to find some clue as to his whereabouts.

Benito had ordered the questioning of some of De Blasi's neighbours in the hope that they had seen something of him that day. Their presence at the apartment had not alarmed the police and nor was it ever likely to. The folk around the neighbourhood knew or at least suspected that De Blasi had been involved in organised crime, and while they were never certain as to their claims, it meant keeping their mouths shut about his alleged exploits, nevertheless.

'Come on,' he said to his men, 'there must be something around here that tells us where that rat went.'

Until they had arrived, De Blasi's apartment had been neat and tidy. The clothes that he had left behind were either folded or hanging up in the closet. There was food and fresh milk in the fridge, and on the surface, everything had seemed normal in that the place had not been abandoned indefinitely. But there was no sign of any weapons or money, and that alone was enough to tell Benito that his father had been right all along.

Franco De Blasi was alive and well, which meant that the Sicilian, Michele La Barbara, was out there, somewhere in the city. Whether De Blasi had aided him or he had been out-muscled, he was being held accountable for the family's current dilemma.

It was only a matter of time before they found him. That's just how it worked. It was always just a matter of time. They would run like mice, but in the end, they would have no place left to hide. They had their informants too, who as always were eager to help the family out when requested to do so.

But while Alberto remained impatient as to the Sicilian's whereabouts, Benito was more concerned that De Blasi, knowing the punishment for the crime he had committed, might have done the unthinkable and sought refuge with the FBI. Law enforcement had failed on every attempt to tie the Calabrese family with crimes such as murder and assault, bribery, protection rackets and racketeering. Their only hope was to get inside the family by way of an informant, but up until now, none had been forthcoming.

De Blasi had been a member of the family for so long, he would prove to be a vital resource for the FBI. The safety of the Witness Protection Program would prove to be a lucrative offer, and more importantly, one that would save his life and keep him out of prison.

Right now, Benito was thinking ahead of the game, anticipating De Blasi's next move and any possible ties with the Sicilian. Whether he had been apprehended, coaxed into joining him, or had decided to turn to law enforcement—he was a dead man.

'Hey, boss.'

Benito turned around and looked at one of his men, who was holding a small passport-sized photograph that he had discovered in one of the drawers, wedged at the back and almost folded into the flimsy panel of the drawer.

'Take a look at this,' Luca said and handed him the photo.

Benito looked uninterested at first, and then his curiosity grew as he studied the photo. 'You've got to be fucking kidding me,' he said. 'Who is that guy?'

'Non lo so,' Luca said smiling. He was a trusted soldier of the Calabrese family and wanted De Blasi's scalp as much as Benito himself. Until now the trusted assassin had been a faithful servant to the family. And with him out of the way, it would present Luca with an opportunity to move up through the ranks. But despite him being unaware as to the other man in the photograph, he had hit on something that had made his boss's day.

Benito studied the picture with an air of humour and fascination and then looked firmly at Luca. 'Find him,' he said.

Luca Rossi retrieved the photograph from his boss and then waved the rest of the men to follow him out of the apartment. He had been assigned with the task of finding their former crew member and his male friend, and he relished the opportunity. Someone must have seen them together. So where better a place to start than in his own neighbourhood.

And while they might have denied seeing him around that day, one look at the photograph and Luca would know by their reaction whether they had seen the other man before. It was a big city, and recognition of someone's face was not conclusive. But it might prove to be another step closer to finding their man.

Luca had Tommy Byrne stay with him, an Irishman who was six-foot-six and at forty-five years old, he was built like a professional wrestler. He was just the kind of guy you wanted to be with when you went calling or collecting. He was a prodigious sight. His jaw was obtruded, which looked like it had been the result of taking growth hormone, and his facial features were made up of scars and over protuberant eyebrows, which made him look more animal-like than human.

People either told him what he needed to know or if he went collecting, they paid up or they were beaten to an inch of their lives. If, however, he came looking for you on a more personal note, then the safest bet would be to run and jump out of the window, no matter which floor you happened to be on. He carried a gun but seldom used it. His main purpose for the family was to beat people to the point of death, but not quite, just enough to put them in hospital for several months and then go looking for them again when they came out.

Luca on the other hand was of medium height and build, Italian origin and handsome in appearance. For the most part, he dressed casual, yet he loved the limelight, especially when it was on him. His eyes were dark and mistrusting, a trademark that he didn't mind at all. He spoke quickly but articulately, and above all, he loved the action.

His love and loyalty toward the family had not gone unnoticed, and as such, there had already been talk that he would have his own caporegime in the not-so-distant future, which at thirty years old was not just an honour, it was a testament to his ingenuity and ability to make money for the family. The capture of Franco De Blasi and Michele La Barbara would almost solidify that claim. His slick-talking was a testament to the many business activities he was involved in, some licit others illicit.

From gambling and racketeering, he had developed a lot of money for the family, and when it came to him having to pull the trigger, he was as reliable and efficient as the notorious Franco De Blasi.

He called out to the other two men to keep close, just in case they needed to display the photograph to jog somebody's memory. Leonardo and Gianni Mancini. Identical twins with complete devotion to their boss. They had been groomed into the mob after being picked up from the streets as teenagers. They were orphans and had left their foster homes to be with one another, fighting on the streets for money, they had made the best of a difficult upbringing. They knew what it took to survive on the streets, yet they had no desire to return there.

Alberto Calabrese had had his driver pull up to them one day and then called them over. He had been observing them for some time before deciding to present them with a more lucrative lifestyle. He had watched as they were standing and chatting on the street corner smoking a cigarette, with an attitude that presented itself as if they owned the neighbourhood.

Alberto sat in the back of the car and watched as they pickpocketed several people who walked past, who remained oblivious to the fact that they had been robbed as they took turns either accidentally bumping into someone and then apologising, or asking somebody a question while robbing them in public view.

Alberto had chuckled in amusement as the scene unfolded and their nonchalant behaviour amused him further. After a short while, he asked his driver to move over to their side of the road, where he lowered the window and smiled. The two young men looked at him for a moment, turned to face each other, and then looked back at him. They were astute to understand that this was no ordinary member of the public.

Even at their young age, they knew that the stranger presented an opportunity, and when Alberto Calabrese got out of the car and offered the two boys a ride, they accepted his offer without any discussion. That was the beginning of the rest of their lives. The day that the Capo had offered them a ride they had been teenagers; ten years on, they were twenty-five years old and as determined as they had ever been to survive.

Luca knocked on the door immediately opposite De Blasi's apartment and waited patiently until the door was answered by a young woman who looked uninterested in both men as they stood in her doorway. The twins had called at the apartment earlier that day, but nobody had been home, or at least, nobody had answered. The fact that she had opened the door without even checking to see who was there told them she was far from streetwise. She was slender, half-dressed and untidy. Luca decided that there was probably a pretty girl underneath her slovenly appearance, but he was in no mood to examine her any closer.

'Yeah,' she said. 'What do you want?'

Luca held up the photograph while she glanced up at the giant of a man at his side. 'Do you know this guy?'

'Which one?' she asked.

'Both of them.'

'Yeah, he's the guy from next door.

'Smart,' Luca said and smiled. 'Let's try a little harder this time shall we. The guy standing at his side... the one with his fucking arm round him looking like he's wanting to take him up the ass, have you ever seen him before?'

He held the photograph closer toward her face and she studied the picture of the two men for some time before finally shaking her head. Luca wasn't certain as to whether she had done that just to build his hopes up and then deflate him, but he was becoming increasingly impatient nevertheless.

'Are you sure you haven't seen them together?'

The girl grimaced as if this was all too tiresome for her and said, 'No, I haven't seen the other guy before. What a waste, though,' she said. 'He's too good looking to be gay.'

'Okay,' Luca said, and with a final gaze at the young woman, he pulled the picture away from her face. He looked at Tommy, 'Let's go,' he said.

'He was here earlier,' the young woman called out. 'He came back to his apartment with some other guy. They stayed for only a short time and then left... they seemed to be in a bit of a hurry.'

Luca smiled and held his position in the doorway. 'Tell me more,' he said.

The girl explained that she had been sitting at her window and looking out onto the front street when De Blasi had pulled up outside in his car. She said she was curious as to the stranger, as this was the first time that she had ever noticed him return home with anybody. She had thought of her neighbour as a bit of a loner, and the most she had ever received in the eighteen months that she had lived in her apartment had been the occasional "hello" or "good evening".

She had held the front door ajar as they had made their way from the top of the stairs, just enough for her to see them without being noticed. She closed the door as they got closer to his apartment, but even a brief glimpse of the man at his side was enough to tell her it was not the other man in the photograph.

'Anything else you can tell me?' Luca asked.

'No,' she said, shaking her head. 'As I said, I heard them leave shortly after they had arrived. I guess they were in some sort of hurry to get out of here.'

Luca smiled. 'Yes, you could say that. Thank you,' he said. 'You have been most helpful.'

The young girl gave both men a bemused look and then closed the door.

'Bingo,' Luca said. 'Benito's going to want to know about this. In the meantime, let's see if we can find out who this other guy is.'

Benito was en route to see his father and consigliere when the call came. Luca had confirmed what they had already suspected, however, they now knew for certain that De Blasi had betrayed them, which meant that he was now a dead man for sure. The news was a step forward nonetheless. The Sicilian was out there too, and what better way to end the day but to find all three men together.

The pieces of the jigsaw were already coming together. Michele La Barbara had somehow managed to persuade Franco De Blasi to join him, and as such, betray the family. From leaving the airport, they had gone to De Blasi's apartment to pick up some things and had then left and were now hiding out with his boyfriend. An assumption but an accurate one Benito was led to believe, nevertheless.

The ransacking of the apartment had revealed his *other* life—his private life that had been obscured from the other members of his crew and his associates. And with good reason, for any knowledge of his homosexuality or at least his long-term relationship with another man could have major complications. He had heard the guys crack jokes about gay men and women, and whether they were revolted by their sexual tendencies or not, their need to raise the subject from time to time was enough reason for him to keep his private life concealed.

But the main reason for secrecy was to protect his lover at all costs. Life in the mob was always full of suspicion. Husbands told their wives what they needed to know; a man who could potentially end up being a jealous lover was just too great a risk.

But none of that mattered anymore; De Blasi's secret life was out in the open.

'All this time,' Benito said to himself. 'I wouldn't have believed it.' And he still couldn't, despite the picture of the two men holding on to each other and maintaining a loving gaze. 'Well,' he said, 'let's see how loyal your friend is when he's got the barrel of a gun instead of your cock in his mouth. I wouldn't miss that for the world.'

Benito had voiced his appreciation to Luca and then told him to carry on with the operation. This was a large city but a small world. And in their line of work, there were no hiding places.

Back at the apartment block on Brooklyn, the four men went from door to door with less success than their initial call. Nobody had seen the other man in the picture, and they were willing to swear to it, despite the obvious sign of danger that loomed over them. By the end of the day the four men had covered the entire block and questioned several other people in the same neighbourhood, but without a break forward.

De Blasi had been discreet and it had served him well. He had ensured that his friend remained anonymous and that had safeguarded his lover as well as provided him with a safe haven—for the time being at least. Oblivious to the picture that had now been discovered at his apartment had meant that his private life had been uncovered, but more significantly, his long-term lover Vincenzo had now become a target.

Even if the mob got to De Blasi before they discovered Vincenzo, they would still hunt him down for the inconvenience. Michele had expressed his concern and had laid it all out to him, however, the option of leaving him was just something he could never do, no matter the consequences.

Luca called the men together and they stood on the streets of Brooklyn discussing their next move. Agreed that it was unlikely that De Blasi would ever return to his apartment, the four men got back into the car ready to drive off.

'I guess it's time to put the word out in case anyone spots them. We just have to be careful that they don't get overanxious if they see anything and do something stupid,' Luca said. 'If anyone sees them or knows where they are, then we make sure they give us the information we need and then back off and let us take over from there. Benito has insisted that they remain alive until he gets there.'

'Who shall we call?' Gianni asked.

Luca looked at him through the rear-view mirror. 'Anyone we know or owes us a fucking favour.'

Gianni smiled. 'I guess that means everyone.'

Chapter Fourteen

Michele had followed Beth into a café about two streets down from where a murder had recently taken place. He had barely reflected on the brutality of the crime or the end result, and even the sound of police and ambulance sirens that resounded above the noise of the city's traffic and the population didn't seem to interest him one bit. He was more concerned that for no apparent reason he had crossed the busy road in one of the largest most populated cities in the world and had become involved in an incident that had opened up his anonymity.

He could have walked on the first time she had called out to him, but he didn't, and he asked himself *why?* He could have killed the guy and still walked on, but he didn't. He wasn't attracted to Beth in the sexual sense. But, despite his reluctance to stop and accompany her, in the end, he had been defenceless to her persuasion.

Beth had gone to the counter and ordered two coffees while Michele sat at a table away from the window. He preferred his privacy, especially when New York City's most notorious mobsters wanted him dead. He was, however, curious as to why anybody would want this kind of life—the fast life!

The tooting of car horns from bumper-to-bumper traffic; the hustle and bustle of New Yorkers and tourists, constantly on the move and scurrying around the city from place to place like mice. The high towers were a display of power, money and corruption. And despite a world that was contrary to the one he had left behind, the rules of life were exactly the same.

Michele glanced around the café looking at the customers who were of different nationalities. He found it uncommon, yet he was intrigued nevertheless. As he observed the people and his surroundings, he looked up and saw Beth standing over him with a cup of coffee in each hand. She smiled at him and then sat down at the table, facing him.

'Thank you,' he said. Michele looked at the paper-like cup curiously before picking it up, much to Beth's amusement. He looked almost afraid to drink from it, which made her giggle.

'What's so funny?' he asked.

'Don't they have coffee where you come from?'

'Yes. In a cup. What the hell is this?'

'New York City's finest coffee cups. The coffee ain't too bad either.'

Michele took a sip of coffee from the cup. 'Not bad,' he said. 'Not great, but not bad.'

'I'm glad you approve,' Beth said.

They sat in silence for a moment. Beth turned her cup on the table, her eyes drawn away from the man sitting opposite her as she loaded up her question. 'I know there's part of me that should be frightened, but I'm not,' she said calmly.

Michele shrugged his shoulders slightly. 'Should you be?'

'That guy. I've seen him bully and beat up girls my own age and even younger. He is,'—she paused—'I mean he was, a real thug. But then you come along and…'

'It was either him or me, Beth.' Michele had been cautious not to fill her mind full of wondrous claims that he had killed the man in her honour, even if, perhaps, that had really been the case.

Beth reached across the table and held both his hands. They relaxed to her touch, but she could see that they had been through so many wars, which told her there was a history to this man that was way beyond her own comprehension.

'You saved my life. I don't know what would have happened if you hadn't have been there.' She wanted to question him further, about who he was, why he was here and where he had developed such murderous instinct, yet she hesitated, and instead, felt compelled to show her gratitude for being alive. But despite having lived on the streets and taking a beating from time to time, she felt no sense of fear from the stranger sitting in front of her.

'Tell me, Beth, how did you get to be mixed up with a guy like that?'

'It's called survival,' she said.

'So is working in a coffee shop,' he said dryly.

'Oh, you disapprove of me being a hooker, is that it?'

'A hooker?'

Beth grimaced: 'A prostitute.'

'Oh. No. Why, should I?'

Beth laughed. 'Okay,' she said. 'How about we level with each other. I'll tell you about me and then you tell me about you?'

'I'm here on vacation, Beth, that's all,' he said casually.

'Sure you are.'

Michele shook his head and then took another drink of coffee. 'It's too risky, Beth. Trust me, there're some things in life you're better off not knowing.'

'Such as?' she persisted.

'Me,' he said bluntly.

'So where do we go from here?' she asked.

'We?' he asked. 'Beth, there is no we.'

'So, you're just going to leave me on the street, is that it?'

'I'm not responsible for you… or anybody else for that matter. We've just met, Beth. And for you, I just happened to be in the right place at the right time.'

Michele noticed that her eyes had become glazed, and before he had time to respond to her pleas for help, a tear had formed and then began to stream slowly down the side of her right cheekbone. He leaned over the table slightly and caught her tear with his finger, stopping it from rolling any further, he gently wiped it away.

That was the first time that Beth had caught sight of Michele's wedding ring. Many of the men she had known had been married, most of them in fact, but she felt there was an untold truth about this man that she was yet to discover. Behind his rugged exterior, there was a sadness buried deep behind those blue, piercing eyes.

'I thought you were tough,' he said, which woke her from her dreamy haze.

'Don't you ever cry?' she asked.

'No.'

'No, I guess you don't,' she said.

Michele sighed: 'Okay, Beth, here's the deal. I'm too tired to talk, so why don't we book into a room tonight and then we'll discuss matters in more detail tomorrow?'

Beth looked at Michele in a state of astonishment. 'Okay,' she said excitedly.

'No promises, Beth. Only that we'll talk.

'Understood,' she said.

'And one more thing.'

'What is it?' she asked.

'I sleep alone.'

Beth smiled and then giggled. 'Now, that's one chat-up line I've never heard before. Are you always this romantic?'

'Always,' he said.

Beth held on to Michele's arm as they made their way through the busy streets of New York City. She had asked Michele what kind of room he was looking for: a room with no more than a bed in it and a bathroom that would be down the hall and shared by many, or something more lucrative that had its own balcony, which stood proudly amongst the city's skyscrapers.

Michele didn't have to think too long for an answer. He just wanted to get some rest, though, preferably in an establishment that had not been one of Beth's local haunts where she might have entertained one of her many clients. Taking no offence, Beth laughed off the comment, while Michele continued to wonder how the hell he had ended up in this situation.

Since his arrival in the city, he had befriended an assassin, his *male* lover, and now a prostitute. What was next, he wondered?

So far in his life, he had discovered that he was more comfortable with murder than friendship.

It was decisive.

In response to Beth's question about what kind of room Michele was looking for, she considered the alternatives: *Then you want something a bit upmarket*, she had said. *I hope you have the money then*, she had added.

Having walked for almost a half-hour from the café on 42nd Street, they stopped abruptly at the entrance of The Benjamin on 50th Street at Lexington Avenue. Outside of the hotel, there was a huge American flag positioned above the entrance, with two beautiful large, decorated plant pots at either side of the foyer, which led to a glamorous entrance by way of two mahogany doors with rectangular sections of tinted glass.

After taking a quick glimpse at the building, Michele said casually, 'Let's see if they've got a room.'

Beth held him back before moving any further. 'You're kidding me, right?'

'Why?' he asked nonchalantly.

'Do you have any idea how much a place like this costs?' she said, shaking her head, and she tried to walk him on.

Michele stood his ground. 'You don't approve?'

'Have you ever been to New York before, Michele?'

117

'No.'

'Then believe me when I say that there's a lifestyle for the rich and famous, and then there's the poor.'

'Tell me a place where there isn't,' Michele said.

'Okay,' Beth sighed, 'but don't say I didn't warn you. One look at us and we'll be lucky to get past the foyer.'

Michele was going to ask her what she meant by that but decided not to pursue the matter.

'After you,' she said.

Michele let out half a smile and then the couple made their way toward the grand entrance of the hotel. Once inside the lobby, Beth stood and looked around, mesmerised by the extravagance of the building, she could only wonder how the other half lived.

'Nice,' Beth said.

Michele looked disinterested.

'You'd think you entered hotels like this every day,' she said.

'In what way?' he asked.'

'Never mind,' she said. 'Are you sure you can afford this? I mean, you, rather we, don't exactly fit in here.' Beth had already noted that some of the women in the foyer had looked at her with an expression of disdain, while the young guy behind the reception area—who had been attending to some guests checking in— was taking particular interest in their presence.

Unhurried, Michele took a look around at the luxuriously designed lobby and the enormity of the building. Despite his initial lack of interest, Beth was right, he hadn't seen anything quite like it, but still, he couldn't imagine swapping this life with the one he had back home. *Home?* It was the first time he had thought about his homeland since he had arrived in America, and he wondered what kind of life would be there for him when he returned. That was assuming he survived…

The head of New York City's most notorious Mafia family had summoned him over to his territory in what now appeared to be an act of vengeance for the murder of his son. The man he had murdered to avenge the death of his wife, Mary—

'Well?'

Michele returned from the world he had left behind and stared at Beth as if she had just slapped his face to awaken him out of a hypnotic trance.

'Sorry,' he said. 'I was someplace else.'

'Yeah, me too,' she said. 'Now, let's make our way to the desk and check-in before you change your mind.'

Humoured by her sharp tongue, Michele smiled.

'What is it?' she said unwittingly.

'Nothing,' but in his mind, he couldn't help but consider how uncommon she was. 'Come on,' Michele said. 'Let's check in.'

Stood at reception was a young man, who was smartly dressed in a grey suit and tie, with dark, silky hair that was swept back without a single strand out of place. His eyes were blue, his lips pursed, and with a brown skin tone, he looked Hispanic in appearance. He looked around the hotel foyer with a sense of pride, while holding a smile that over time had become a permanent fixture that was etched on his face.

As people entered and left the building, Michele and Beth made their way toward reception, and toward the young man whose expression of satisfaction had already turned to one of distaste. He looked at Michele and then turned his attention to the young woman, looking her up and down, before returning his focus back on the Sicilian.

'Can I help you, sir?' he asked almost condescendingly.

'Yes. I'd like a room with two bedrooms, please,' he said politely.

Michele observed the young man, who was tall and slender—too slender, Michele thought, and his mannerisms depicted a lack of masculinity about him. He had noticed his expression of contempt as they had approached him, a look which told Michele that this would not be straightforward. And now as he waited for the young man to respond to his request, he could sense Beth's level of anxiety of the situation increase, and a need to make her way to the exit at the earliest opportunity.

'Something wrong?' Michele asked him.

Beth grabbed Michele by the arm and he turned to face her. 'Come on,' she said, ready to turn away, 'let's go someplace else.'

'I think the young lady is right, sir, if you don't mind me saying so.'

Another couple approached the desk and stood patiently behind Michele and Beth. The young man looked over to them and signalled them to move forward, until Michele stuck out his hand, preventing the man and his wife from moving any further forward. The man didn't argue or even attempt to question Michele. Instead, he stood back and waited.

Michele returned his attention back toward the man at the desk. 'Now, where was I? Edward,' Michele looked at his name tag. 'Do you have a vacancy?'

The young man nodded. 'Yes, sir.'

'Good. Now we're getting somewhere.' His eyes met the young man with an unflinching gaze, which sent a cold shiver down his spine. 'Two bedrooms.'

'Yes, sir. Can I ask how long you intend to stay?'

'Two nights—for now, Edward,' he said firmly.

The young man nodded without looking. 'Very good, sir. And will you require room service or—'

'No,' Michele cut him off before he could speak any further. 'A room with two bedrooms, for two nights, and *no* questions.'

Almost too afraid to charge Michele for the room, he was relieved when Michele said, 'How much?'

'Thank you, sir. That will be eight hundred dollars. I'll just take your details, and then you can settle the bill when you decide to check out.'

Michele nodded. Seldom did he have to use a bank card, rather than preferring the method of cash. But he was in the city now, and city life was far different from the lifestyle that he was accustomed to back in Sicily. Here, handing a number of bank-notes over the counter would look so out of place, and would draw unneeded attention toward him.

Besides, his bank details and passport were bogus, and held the name of Marco Barone. After giving his details, he took two fifty-dollar notes from his bag and then placed them carefully in the young man's jacket pocket. 'You'll see to it that we are not disturbed, Edward.'

'Yes, sir.'

'By anyone.'

'Absolutely, sir.'

'Good. Now, if you can just give me the key, then we'll make our way up to our room.'

'Certainly, sir,' he said, and handed Michele his key card. 'Room 513. Would you like someone to help you with your bag?'

'No thank you. We can find our own way.'

'Very good, sir. I hope you both enjoy your stay.' This time smiling at Beth, who felt a sense of satisfaction after watching his arrogance dissolve in front of her eyes.

Michele looked at him for a moment, and then he and Beth turned and headed for the elevator. After a brief moment, the young man signalled for the couple who had waited patiently for assistance, yet he could not help but take another glance at the man whose eyes had cut deep into his soul.

He could have called for security or even his manager, who could have called a more senior manager, except he understood perfectly that some things were better off left alone. He took a final look at Michele who caught his gaze as he stood in the elevator. And as the elevator doors closed, Edward, whose initial behaviour toward the couple had been one of arrogance, shivered with anxiety.

'Four hundred bucks a night?' Beth said.

'Is that expensive?'

'Are you kidding me,' she said. 'I'd have to lie on my back for days on end to earn that much money.'

'I had to ask,' he said. But as he looked through her eyes and at her gentle soul, he felt a sense of warmth toward her.

'And I couldn't help notice that hundred bucks you slipped into his jacket pocket. Are you crazy?'

'It's just a security deposit in case anyone should come asking about us. I'm sure he'll keep his mouth shut.'

'I think he would have done that without you having to bribe him. It was almost funny to watch. Two nights?' she asked curiously.

Michele shrugged. 'I can't say for sure,' he said. 'Right now, I just need somewhere to get my head down and rest.'

'I guess that makes two of us then,' she said.

A ring sounded and the elevator doors opened slowly, revealing a majestic looking hallway, which was far quieter than the hustle and bustle of activity down on the ground floor.

Michele remained in the elevator and observed her curiously as she stepped out onto the hallway. Beth stopped and turned round to face him. 'Well,' she said teasingly. 'Are you just going to stand there or are you going to escort me to *our* room?'

Beth's words suggested that she was on a romantic adventure, as opposed to the sinister reality that awaited them on the streets of New York. And as Michele finally stepped outside the elevator, he and his new companion made the short walk along the hallway, and to their room.

'Wow,' Beth said as she stood in the doorway. Excited, she laughed rather than grinned at the spectacle. The living area was spacious and of modern design, with an ornate coffee table in the centre of the room, with a sofa and two chairs, and a modern TV. Beth made her way from room to room, exploring the dining area, bathroom, and each of the guest rooms.

Michele opened a window in the living area and then lit up a cigarette. 'You approve?' he said to Beth when she came back into the room.

'Yes,' she said excitedly.

Michele wondered how long her excitement would last once she discovered who he was, and why he was in New York.

'Thank you,' Beth said.

Michele took a deep draw from the cigarette and then blew smoke out into the humidity of the evening air.

'How little you know about me, Beth,' he said without facing her.

'You saved my life,' she said. 'What more do I need to know.'

Michele turned to face her. 'Who I really am.'

Beth walked over toward him and took the cigarette from his hand to take a draw. 'Well,' she said, 'I know one thing. You're not the kind of guy who takes advantage of a woman just because you've saved her life.' She took another short drag, and then handed the remainder of the cigarette back to Michele and then turned to walk to her chosen guest room. Before she walked out of the room, she turned to face him: 'I really didn't believe that a gentleman existed—until now.

'Goodnight, Michele,' she said. 'Sleep tight.'

Sleep, Michele thought.

How he longed for a night's sleep.

Since his arrival in New York, this was the first time that Michele had been alone. Beth had retired to her bedroom only moments earlier, and other than the noise of city life below him that came in from the open window, he was finally able to unwind. Even if it was only for a short time.

Now in the comfort of a hotel room, Michele took off the sweater that Franco De Blasi had given him earlier that evening and then walked over to the mini-bar, where he pulled out a small bottle of Glenfiddich Whisky. Giving little credence as to the cost of the small bottle of spirits, he grabbed a small whisky tumbler from the cabinet, and then dragged a chair over to the window, where he sat down and poured himself a nightcap.

He was tired, but the need for a drink and a moment of solitude was an opportunity for him to reflect on happenings that had led him to foreign shores. Forty-eight hours ago he would have been alone at his home in Sicily, far removed from the horrific events that were unfolding. And now… now he was on the other side of the world, away from the merest suggestion of familiarity, and being hunted down by New York's most notorious and feared crime family.

Michele lit up a cigarette and then took a drink from the glass, savouring the whisky for a moment before swallowing, he felt the heat of the spirit work its way down his throat. It tasted good, and if he had been at home right now, he would have thought nothing of grabbing a larger bottle and sitting out on the balcony where he could happily get drunk and sit there until the sun rose to signify the dawn of a new day.

He had enjoyed such an experience on many occasions, and over the past two years, he had done so more often than not, sometimes waking up where he had sat, other times waking up in bed, despite having little memory of how he had arrived there.

Michele took another draw of the cigarette and then turned to look at where Beth had been standing a short time ago. Just before she had said "goodnight". Transported from his homeland to one of the largest cities in the world, he had met a young woman who had needed his help. Fate had a funny way of showing its cards, and right now, Michele had no sure way of knowing what route his journey would take. He took another drink of whisky and then shook his head, almost in disbelief as to the situation he now found himself in.

For Beth, she had been in the right place at exactly the right time.

As for Michele, he could only wonder…?

Lives had now changed as a consequence of his arrival in this strange city. Lives that until he had set foot off the plane, had gone about their day-to-day activities—no matter how meaningless, banal, adventurous or dangerous— without risk and without the prospect of change.

With a journey of uncertainty ahead of him, Michele understood one thing, and that was when the sun rose the following day, it was inevitable that more lives would be lost.

The rules of mob life were simple.

Obey the rules or pay the consequences.

Either way, there would be no happy ending.

Part III
La Cosa Nostra (This Thing of Ours)

Chapter Fifteen

***

England

Less than three weeks after the unprovoked attack on an innocent eighteen-year-old boy, life continued without little thought of the atrocity that had occurred on that fateful evening. Early evening and crowds had already congregated in the city centre, many of whom had already made their way toward the most popular bar in town.

Outside the bar were three men, who were casually dressed for a summer evening around town, and who stood patiently as they waited for the queue to move steadily forward toward the building. Dressed in jeans and wearing a flowery yellow shirt, Luigi was content to converse with the females as he was so often fond of doing, while his brothers kept an eye on the route ahead, watching the doormen as they allowed or denied anybody into the building. Michele and Giovanni each wore jeans and a straight black leather jacket over a plain white T-shirt and black leather shoes.

As they drew near to the doorway, Michele made eye contact with the largest of the doormen who, after staring straight at him for a split second, returned his attention to bar control. Unaware of the sinister force that was ready to enter the building, the head doorman allowed the men to enter, refraining from making any further eye contact with Michele, daring only to observe his movements when his back was turned.

Michele made his way to the bar with his brothers following close behind him. Luigi danced his way through the crowds of partygoers, mingling in a conspicuous fashion as he waited for the signal that would launch him into a spate of violence.

Michele approached the bar as Giovanni stood at his side. Patiently, he waited for a member of the bar staff to serve him, and as a young man from behind the bar approached him, Michele ordered three bottles of lager. He gazed at the young man as he carried out his request; he couldn't have been any older than Roberto, and in many ways, he reminded him of his distant cousin, who was lying in a hospital bed and fighting for his life. Yet, despite his feelings of sorrow, he remained composed and ready for the undertaking that he alone had orchestrated with meticulous fashion.

Michele paid the barman and then handed his brothers their drinks. He then took his place on a stool at the bar and sat in a state of calm as he waited for his moment to arrive. Giovanni and Luigi moved away from his side, their actions unnoticed as they mingled in with the crowds while awaiting the signal from their brother.

Michele had observed that there were four doormen in the building: two standing at the doorway, and two at either side of the bar. It was at that moment that he decided to draw attention to himself, and taking a packet of cigarettes from his inside jacket pocket, he shuffled the pack, and took one out and placed it in his mouth. As he lit the cigarette, he placed the lighter back into his pocket and then inhaled deeply, before exhaling a thick cloud of smoke into the crowded room.

Michele remained composed as the largest of the doormen made his way from the right side of the bar toward him. As he got closer, his immense frame swaggered uncontrollably, and his shoulders began to widen in an attempt to intimidate the unwelcome victim of his presence. As far as he was concerned, this was all but a full gone conclusion, and as his colleagues looked on with savage amusement, the huge bulk of a man made his way past the crowd of partygoers and stood tall in front of the waiting Sicilian.

As Michele took another drag from the cigarette, the doorman stood in front of him, shoulders wide and chest puffed out, he stared fixedly at the stranger as a curious yet intimidated crowd moved to one side.

The doorman was now staring at the man half his size; however, his expression showed much to Michele, an undeniable truth that he was afraid. He remained seated, his eyes unflinching as he gazed back at him, he inhaled on the cigarette and then blew smoke at his face.

As doubt crept over the doorman, his colleagues increased their awareness of the situation that was unfolding and slowly but surely made their advances in order to support him.

'Put out your cigarette!' the doorman exclaimed.

Maintaining eye contact, Michele took a final draw from the cigarette, and then flicked the stub away from him, watching the doorman's eyes as he followed its trail to the floor. Michele reached into his pocket, took out another cigarette from the packet, and then lit it, leaving his opponent bereft of any other option than to safeguard his fearless reputation.

'Just in case you didn't hear me the first time, Dago! Put out your cigarette and get out, before I throw you out!'

The doorman had made his move. He was trembling. But as Michele noted, it wasn't out of aggression—he was trembling with fear.

As the doorman placed his huge hand on Michele's shoulder, with speed and stealth, the Sicilian hit the base of the lager bottle against the edge of the bar and then launched himself toward him, striking the jagged bottle deep into the side of the man's throat. As the gathering of partygoers went into a fit of hysteria, Michele stood back and watched as the man fell to his knees holding his throat, and as the blood oozed from his arteries, so with it came the realisation that his life was about to come to an end.

Before his three colleagues could assist him, Giovanni and Luigi had already made their move. As one of the doormen tried to push his way past the crowd, Giovanni met his path, and before he knew it, the barrel of a gun was pressed firmly against his forehead. The sound of gunfire was met with screams of hysteria by those in the immediate vicinity, whose faces were showered with blood and particles of brain tissue.

The sounds of screams intensified as the music finally came to an abrupt end, and the DJ cowered his way under his musical cove. In a frenzied state of aggression, Luigi had launched himself at the third defenceless doorman. The man screamed as Luigi bit into his nose, and after one fateful bite, he spat the torn flesh onto the dance floor, and then sat on the man's chest and holding his head in both hands, beat his head savagely against the floor. As the man eventually fell into a state of unconsciousness, Luigi looked up as the mass of people scattered in every direction to avoid being caught up in the violence that was taking place.

Amid the pandemonium, Michele had made his move on the fourth doorman. His face depicted an expression of extreme terror as he gazed down at the barrel of the 9mm that was pointed at his face.

'The bar owner, where is he?' Michele exclaimed.

'I don't know,' the doorman said, his body trembling with fear.

'One more time,' Michele said, pressing the barrel firmly against his head. 'Where is he?'

'I swear I don't know!' he yelled, and then fell to his knees in a last attempt to save himself from a similar fate to that of his colleagues. The man urinated before Michele had pulled the gun away from his temple. As Michele knelt down in front of him, he grabbed hold of his quivering chin and gazed into the eyes of a man who had witnessed a fury that until now, he had never known existed.

'I'm going to let you live,' Michele said. 'But you must do exactly as I say, do you understand?'

'Yes, yes,' the man said.

'Good. I want you to report exactly what you witnessed here tonight. And then inform him that his business and his life are over.'

The doorman nodded, 'I will, I swear, I will tell him.'

'Then you will live to see the dawn of another day.'

Michele calmly placed his gun back into his jacket pocket and then stood up ready to leave the building. As the three men left the bar and headed toward their pick-up, they could hear the sound of sirens as the police made their way toward the scene of the crime.

When the three men had made it safely to their waiting vehicle parked only a short distance away from the building, the driver calmly pulled away from the chaos that had unfolded, leaving behind hordes of panic-stricken onlookers who were traumatised from the massacre that they had witnessed only moments ago.

As the black BMW drove away without any observation, Michele turned to face Luigi who was sitting in the back seat of the vehicle, and searched his feelings as he looked at his blood-stained face and menacing eyes, which displayed only a desire for insanity.

He was a valuable asset no doubt, but there was craziness to Luigi that his uncle had warned him about. A desire to prove himself to be worthy of a homicidal maniac would one day be his undoing. And that was the moment that Michele had seen it in his eyes.

As Michele returned his attention to the road ahead, he glanced at Giovanni through the rear-view mirror, and as their eyes met, it was clear that they had been thinking the same thing.

***

Michele had slept deeply for almost ten hours before being roused by the distinct aroma of freshly made coffee. He opened his eyes gingerly to see Beth sitting on the edge of the bed dressed in a white nightgown (courtesy of the hotel), holding a cup of black coffee.

'Good morning,' she said.

Michele yawned and then slowly pulled himself up on the pillow. 'Good morning,' he returned. He took the cup from Beth, took a drink, and then thanked her by way of appreciative nod of his head.

'You snore,' Beth said smiling.

'Then you should have closed the door.'

'I did. I could still hear you.'

Michele was reflecting on the dream that had seen him and his brothers on missions assigned by their uncle, which had come at a time when he was awaiting news on the identity and whereabouts of Mary's killer. Days of long gone by, but they had been vivid nonetheless, especially the insanity that he had seen in his brother's eyes.

'What time is it?' Michele asked.

'Last time I checked it was nine-thirty. It must be ten o'clock by now. Why?'

'Don't ask,' he said casually.

Beth smiled. 'I tell you what,' she said. 'Why don't we get to know more about each other? You tell me about you and why you're here, and I'll tell you all you need to know about me. What do you say?'

Michele's eyes peered menacingly over the brim of his cup. He took a drink of the coffee and sighed: 'Believe me, Beth, you don't want to know who I am.'

'Try me,' she said.

'Are you always this lively first thing on a morning?'

'Sure,' she said.

'Of course, you are,' he murmured, and took another drink from the cup.

'So, do we have a deal?'

Michele sighed again. There was so much he wanted to say to her right now, but his initial thoughts were that Beth would not want to hear it. There was an excitement in her he hadn't seen in anybody before. A liveliness that was most uncommon. But behind that seductive smile and those dazzling blue eyes, Michele detected a sadness that he had yet to learn about. And while he could promise her nothing, he decided, albeit reluctantly, that the least he could do was to go along with her request.

'Okay,' he said, 'but only if you go first.'

'Deal,' she said and knocked her cup against Michele's as if to say *saluti*.

'I never knew my real parents,' Beth said.

'You're an orphan?' Michele asked.

Beth nodded. 'I was handed over to a foster home when I was less than six months old… at least that is what I was told. As a child, I grew up on the streets of Brooklyn, passed from foster parent to foster parent, I spent the early part of my teenage years being sexually abused.'

Michele grimaced as he envisioned her innocence as a child being physically maltreated. Sadly, the way she had spoken of her horrific experience, suggested that she had become accustomed to the ordeal. Beth took a cigarette from the packet on the bedside table, lit it and took a deep drag, and then placed it carefully into Michele's mouth.

'Have you heard enough already?' she asked.

'I've heard worse,' Michele said (Beth uncertain as to whether he was serious), 'but please, carry on.'

'As well as being raised in Brooklyn, I've grown up in some of the poorest neighbourhoods in New York. My last foster parents were really sweet at first and everything seemed to be okay,' she said sadly. 'I thought I'd finally discovered what it was like to be part of a loving family. But sadly it didn't last.

'My foster dad…', she paused, '…he would come into my room and…'

'You didn't tell anyone about it?'

Beth shook her head.

'Why?' Michele asked.

'I had considered talking to my foster mum, but she was smitten by her husband, to such a degree that she would have believed anything that came out of his mouth.'

Beth took another drag from the cigarette and then passed it back to Michele.

'So, what did you do?' Michele asked.

'Nothing at first… I mean, I had dreamt of being part of a real family and this had been the closest by far. *The closest thing to heaven*, as they say. However, I knew inside that this was just a pipe dream. My foster parents were church-going people, religious in every sense of the word to those on the outside, yet living in sin behind the walls of their own home.

'Eventually, the day arrived when I decided that I had had enough. So, I got my things together, stole what money and jewellery I could from the house, and then took my chances on the streets.'

'How old were you?' Michele asked.

Beth shrugged: 'Almost sixteen, I guess. On my first day on the street, I was befriended by a girl called Kimberley. She was eighteen years old but looked older, and had been working on the streets since she had been fourteen.'

'You mean she was a prostitute?'

'Right,' Beth said. 'As I said, she looked after me and I looked up to her in many ways… you know, she was the older sister I never had. So, I decided to follow her lead; after all, what did I have to lose.

'Kimberley introduced me to Marv, and from that moment on the streets became my livelihood.'

'Marv?' Michele asked.

'Yes,' Beth said. 'I seem to remember you breaking his neck.'

Michele nodded as he stubbed out his cigarette on a saucer on the bedside table. 'That Marv,' he said flippantly.

'Yeah. Anyway, that's my story.'

Michele was in unchartered territory. Discussing the *life* with a stranger who, by her own admission, had survived on the streets by way of stealing and prostitution. She didn't know what loyalty was—she had never been given the chance to understand.

How many other encounters had she had with other men who had come to her aid or at least pretended to? How many other men had she woken up with the next morning and had given them the same *show and tell* scenario? How long would it be before she was waking up next to another guy, bringing him coffee, and telling him about the night she had met the Sicilian. The man who had saved her life from the very people she had run back to.

Her story had been horrific in so many ways, and how she had made it this far in life, Michele could only wonder. Beth's words had been spoken so matter-of-factly; without anger, without remorse, without any feeling whatsoever. She had spoken the truth. And having listened to Beth's harrowing upbringing, he felt compelled to level with her—at least to some degree. He reflected on their encounter, and how he had turned to protect her rather than walk away.

She was alive for a reason.

At least for now.

Michele got out of bed wearing only his briefs and then made his way over to the window where he looked out onto the city. Beth sat on the edge of the bed to allow him his space, waiting patiently for him to go on.

He began his account with his early introduction to life as a mobster. He remained stood looking out of the window as he revisited his past; a life which now seemed so far behind him—much more than he could possibly have imagined. He talked about his rise from Mafiosi to a mob boss, the eventual demise of the *family*, and why he had travelled to New York City.

'So,' Beth said cautiously. 'You're telling me you're a Mafia boss?'

Michele looked at her. 'Yes, something like that.'

'Shit,' she said as she took another deep drag from the cigarette. 'Now he tells me.'

Michele returned his attention back to the window. He was holding on to the locket, something he would do unconsciously as he thought about his wife and the life that once was. 'Mary and I would wake up each morning to the view of the sun rising over the Sicilian waters,' he said.

As Michele began to talk about Mary, Beth noted the sadness in his voice, and as the story of her death unfolded, a tear ran down her cheek as she took pity on his tortured soul.

'I'm so sorry,' she said.

Michele turned to face her and witnessed an expression that held genuine grief.

'Me, too,' he said.

'The locket?' Beth asked. She had noticed him toying with it and wondered what emblem of beauty and sadness lay inside it.

Michele released the chain from his neck and then opened it carefully before handing it to her.

'Mary?' she said.

Michele nodded.

'She's beautiful,' she said.

'Thank you. There's not a day goes by that I don't think of her.'

Beth closed the locket and then handed it back to him. After a brief uncomfortable silence, Beth said, 'They say that time is a great healer...'

'I don't know about that,' Michele said. 'Has time healed the wounds of your childhood?'

Beth shook her head. 'Hardly, I am reminded of it every day. The only difference now is that I do it by choice. Or lack thereof. But life goes on, as they say.'

'Only on the outside, Beth.'

'Yes,' she said nodding. 'I guess you're right.'

Beth heard her cell phone ringing from her room, so she hurried from the bed before the call ended. She picked up the phone and noted that the caller was her friend, Kimberley.

Before she had the opportunity to return her friend's call, Michele snatched the cell phone from her and then threw it on the bed.

'What are you doing?' Beth said.

'You want in, then you do as I say. Understood?'

'It was only my friend Kimberly.'

'Your best friend, right?'

'Yes, the girl I was telling you about.'

'She's been asked to betray you.'

'What?' Beth said. She held her hands on her hips and looked at Michele in a way that demanded an explanation.

'They know you're with me,' he said. 'And now they're looking for you, too.'

'You're paranoid,' she laughed.

Michele grabbed Beth's cell phone from the bed and then handed it to her. 'Here,' he said. 'Call her.'

Beth took the phone and watched as Michele turned away from her and made his back into the living quarters. 'She's already dead,' he muttered.

Beth waited for a moment before returning the call. Her heart rate began to increase and a sense of anxiety swept over her. The words of certainty that Michele had spoken had sent a shiver down her spine. Beth closed her eyes and prayed as she waited for the call to be answered.

Please answer, Kimberley.

Not to prove Michele wrong, but to be reassured that her friend was still alive and well, even if she had decided not to be her friend anymore.

'Hello, Beth,' came a man's voice. His tone was deep and grave.

'Who is this?' she asked. 'Where is Kimberley?'

'Where are you, Beth?' he asked, dismissing her question. 'Let me know where you are and I'll send someone to pick you up. We're missing you, Beth.'

'I want to speak to Kimberley,' she said, almost pleading.

Michele appeared back at her side; he took the phone from her hand and then ended the call.

'I'm sorry,' he said.

And as Michele made his way back out of the room, Beth fell to her knees and wept.

Beth had paid the price for her disobedience and had been naïve to think that there would be no repercussions for her actions. Having made an approach to the stranger on 46th Street, she had just made that fatal step into a world of hurt.

And now there was no way back.

Michele put on his gown, and then made his way over to the open window. He lit up a cigarette and looked out at the enormity of the city, which was already alive with the sounds of impatient traffic and hasty commuters. A city that held a population of over eight million people, was where this battle would be won or lost.

The Calabrese family had no knowledge of Michele's location at this time, however, it would be merely hours before their paths would cross. They would have their informants around every corner of the city—it was only a matter of time before their whereabouts would be revealed.

Michele knew he had to keep on the move. Which meant that he would have to do one of two things: ditch Beth, or let her accompany him throughout his ordeal. She knew the streets, and she lived each day with little or no expectation. In many ways, she was ideally suited to assist him. She was streetwise and knew her way around the city.

As Michele pondered over matters at hand, Beth approached him with a cup of coffee.

'Grazie,' he said softly, taking the cup from her hand.

'Prego,' Beth responded.

Michele raised his dark eyebrows. 'You speak Italian?'

'Parlo un po di Italiano,' she said proudly.

'Molto bene,' he said.

'It doesn't get much better, I'm afraid.' She giggled.

Michele raised his finger and gently rubbed a tear away from her cheek. 'I'm sorry about your friend,' he said.

'Why kill her, though?'

Michele thought of the conversation he had had with Franco De Blasi, and wondered whether he had taken his advice. Unlikely, he thought. He had remained headstrong, just like Beth.

'That's what they do, Beth. They'll kill anyone in their way to obtain their objectives.'

'I guess that goes for you, too,' she spat.

Michele looked at her and then nodded. 'Yes,' he said.

'I shouldn't have said that. I'm sorry.'

'Forget it,' he said.

'So,' she sniffled. 'What next?'

Michele lit up a cigarette, took a deep drag and then handed it to Beth.

'Now I'm going to do what I came here to do,' he said. 'Are you in?'

Beth exhaled smoke from her lungs and then looked him in the eye.

'Are you saying we're partners?' she asked.

Michele nodded. 'Yeah, I guess so.'

'Then I'm in,' she said.

Chapter Sixteen

While Beth made her way to the bathroom to take a shower, Michele took the opportunity to call Franco De Blasi. He remained standing as he looked out of the window, observing the city beneath him, all the while on the lookout for anything or anybody that looked suspicious.

'Michele,' De Blasi said.

'Any news from the Calabreses?'

'Nothing. No further calls, either. Perhaps Benito bought your story? I take it you got yourself a place to stay?'

'Yes,' he said. He turned to face the bathroom as he heard the sound of running water. 'Yes, I found a room okay. Listen, I ran into a spot of trouble when I turned up in the city last night.'

'Really?' De Blasi paused. 'What kind of trouble? You should have called me. Are you okay?'

Michele wanted to say that he sounded like Vincenzo, however, decided against it.

'There wasn't time. Besides, I dealt with it.'

'I bet you did.' De Blasi smiled. 'What happened?'

'It's what led up to that and what happened afterwards that is important.'

'Okay.'

There was a pause in conversation as the sound of running water ceased and moments later Beth stepped out of the bathroom with a bath towel wrapped around her wet, naked body.

'I'll just go and get dressed,' she said and smiled before making her way into the bedroom.

'You hear that?' Michele said.

'I heard that,' De Blasi said. 'Now I understand what you meant by trouble. I'd be interested to know what you meant by "dealt with it", though.'

Michele could hear him laughing.

'Very funny,' he said, lighting up a cigarette. 'It's nothing like that. Beth…'

'Beth?'

'She was in a spot of trouble. I just happened to be in the right place at the right time.'

'I'll say. At least as far as she is concerned anyway.'

'Yeah.'

'There's more isn't there?' De Blasi said.

'Yeah. There's more. The guy I ran into, his name was Marv.'

'If it's the same Marv I think you're talking about, then he's an associate of Benito Calabrese.' Blasi waited a moment before speaking. 'Beth?'

'What about her?'

'Is she a hooker?'

'Yeah.'

'And have they tried to contact her?'

'Yeah.'

'Yes, it's the same Marv. Over eight million people living in New York City and you go and murder an associate of the family who's out looking out for us.'

It wasn't a telling off, but it felt like one.

'Anyway, good riddance. He was a piece of shit and the world is better off without him,' De Blasi said.

Michele sensed that he had something else to say.

'What is it, Franco?'

'This Beth. Are you sure she's worth the trouble?'

'Let's just say that some of the people you meet on your journey have been placed there for a purpose. Just like you, Franco.'

De Blasi didn't respond. He knew what Michele meant by that. To Michele, he was no more as trustworthy as the hooker he had picked up on 46th Street.

'What next?' De Blasi said.

'Since it's clear you didn't take my advice, I would suggest that we meet up sooner rather than later.'

'Sure,' he said and checked his wristwatch. 'How about we meet up at two o'clock?'

'That's fine.'

'Assuming that you don't want me to meet you wherever it is that you're staying'—De Blasi paused for effect—'I was thinking we could meet at the

Dairy Visitor Center and Gift Shop in Central Park. It's in a public setting but will afford us our privacy. I'll message you the address.'

'Grazie.'

Michele ended the call and stepped away from the window just as Beth entered the room. She was wearing her dress from the previous night, a transformation from the young woman who had awakened Michele that morning with a cup of coffee.

'You don't approve?' she said.

'When it's important that we remain below the radar, no.'

'Okay,' Beth said as she moved close up to him. She was close enough to kiss him, and if that was the first time that Michele's heartbeat had jumped since he had been in her company, she didn't notice it. 'Then why don't you get ready and take me shopping.'

Franco De Blasi was still sitting on the sofa and gazing at his cell phone after speaking to Michele when Vincenzo entered the room. He had been awake for much of the night with a gun under his pillow and it was likely he would sleep little that night too. It wasn't the first time he had slept with a gun by his side. However, it had been his conscience that had kept him from sleeping more than the danger that now existed.

When Blasi had finally succumbed to sleep, he was plagued by voices of the dead, who called out to him in anguish as their tormented souls wandered aimlessly in the dark. Their physical lives had come to a brutal ending, murdered by the barrel of his gun. He was compelled to look at each one of them, their gaunt, blood-soaked faces serving as a reminder of the life he had chosen. Strange as it may seem, he remembered each one of them. He remembered how they had begged for mercy; watching, toying with them as they got to their knees and pleaded for their lives. Tortured spirits who continued to gaze at him from the darkness of the other place, would wait for the time when he would join them.

De Blasi had been thinking about what Michele had advised him more than he was willing to admit. At least to himself. The new life that the Sicilian had spoken of had gathered more moss; a chance to start again and put the past behind him.

Behind *them*.

They had more than enough money to live on—in fact, more than his partner would have ever known—which would give them that opportunity to move on and never have to look back.

If they stayed…? He felt a pang of guilt as he thought of Michele having to fight this war alone, yet a fight that he had already bought into before he had left the Sicilian shore. And now the sudden introduction of a hooker called Beth, whom he had come by way of murdering one of Benito's crew.

De Blasi had agreed to meet the Sicilian to discuss business in less than two hours. But the question he had been asking himself throughout the night was one that remained heavily on his mind. If he was to make the decision to turn away from the life and leave the city, would Michele be able to win this war without him?

He looked up at Vincenzo and smiled. And that was when he determined that Michele had been right all along.

The war was about to begin, and one that Vincenzo had no business being involved in.

'Pack up, Vincenzo. We're leaving.'

Michele hadn't planned on taking any additional time out to go on a shopping spree through the streets of New York City but agreed with Beth that they were both in need of a change of clothing. Especially Beth, whose only available attire was a pair of high-heeled boots and a short white dress, was in need of something less provocative to wear. While her dress code was intent on luring sex-starved males at night, it was by no means an appropriate outfit throughout the day.

Even for an experienced streetwise prostitute like Beth, there was a time to dress up for business, and a time for less formal wear. And given the looks of disdain that she had experienced since she had stepped in the hotel foyer, thoughts of slipping into something more comfortable aroused her sensual needs. Michele, on the other hand, just wanted to change into something more seasonal that would allow him to feel more comfortable against the heat and humidity of the day.

Still, this was a dangerous move. So Michele made Beth aware that they would need to grab a cab outside the hotel and go straight to their destination without being exposed to any preying eyes. In addition, he had to meet up with Franco De Blasi later that afternoon, so informed Beth that their shopping tour would have to be a swift one.

After taking a quick shower and getting dressed, the couple skipped breakfast and headed down to the foyer and then stepped outside of the hotel and onto 50th Street. After pulling over a cab, they climbed in the back of the vehicle and Beth instructed the driver to take them to Macy's on 34th Street, between Broadway and Seventh Avenue.

'Sounds expensive,' Michele said curiously.

'How can a shop sound expensive?'

'Is it?'

Beth caught the cab driver's inquisitive eyes glancing through the rear-view mirror. He remained silent, though. Which allowed Beth to finish what she had started.

'Not at all… it's one of New York's most famous and largest stores, but it has everything and anything that you and I will need. Isn't that what you insisted on?'

'No. I remember saying that we needed to hurry.'

'Same thing,' Beth said smiling.

'Partners, eh,' Michele muttered under his breath.

'Did you say something?' Beth said.

'Not a word,' Michele said.

Beth smiled and met the eyes of a man whom she had warmed to like no other man she had ever met before.

The journey to their destination was a brief one, but all the while Michele kept a lookout in case they were being followed. Complacency could be unforgiving, and in this life, there were no second chances. Gianluca, even after so many years of experience, had let his guard down at the most inopportune moment, and as a result, had paid the price with his life.

One way or another—by malicious intent or sheer ignorance—each of his family members had become careless, even the soldiers who had been loyal servants to his uncle, had been mercilessly slain by way of their obliviousness to danger. And all the while Beth voiced her excitement over what she was going to wear, Michele remained aware that they could be gunned down the very moment they climbed out of the cab and stepped foot onto the sidewalk.

As they arrived at their destination, the driver pulled over and then called out his fare.

'That will be eight dollars and forty cents,' he said.

'Here,' Michele said, passing him a twenty-dollar note. 'Keep the change, but I want you to pick us up outside here in thirty minutes. Do you understand?'

'Understood,' said the driver, who was appreciative of the tip for the brevity of the journey, and an understanding that he could earn further cash when he returned to pick them back up a short time later.

'Thirty minutes?' Beth asked, grabbing Michele by the arm to signify her bewilderment. 'A girl can't go shopping in thirty minutes.'

'Would you prefer to let me pick your clothes?' Michele asked.

'Okay, thirty minutes,' which caused Michele to smile. 'Are you always this generous?' she asked.

'No,' he said. 'Never.'

Beth followed Michele out of the cab and carrying less enthusiasm than she had held only moments previously, she led the way into the huge shopping store, with Michele feeling like a fish out of water.

Having entered Macy's store on 34th Street, Michele and Beth stepped outside less than a half-hour later looking more casually dressed, and in Beth's case, less eye-catching. Beth, now wearing navy slip-on shoes, had changed her short white dress for a pair of denim jeans, a white blouse and a short blue summer jacket.

In addition, she had picked up a handbag and several pairs of knickers, which she insisted were a necessity over the coming days, and given their size, would fit conveniently in her handbag, much to Michele's disinterest. Michele held on to the comfort of his short black leather zip-up boots and exchanged his denim jeans for a new pair, a black T-shirt, a black summer jacket and a pair of black shades.

'Well? What do you think?' Beth asked.

'I'm hungry,' Michele said.

'Men,' she whispered. 'Either thinking with their stomachs or their dicks…'

'You said something?'

'Yes, I was just saying there's a hotdog stand across the road.'

'A what?'

Beth smiled. 'You've never had a hotdog?'

'What the hell is a hotdog?'

'Come on,' she said excitedly, 'I'm buying,' and carrying their bags of old clothing, she ushered Michele across the busy road.

'Two hotdogs,' she said.

Beth paid the guy and then added mustard and tomato sauce to each dog before handing one to Michele.

'You eat this?' he said.

'Yeah. Which planet are you from?'

Michele waited for her to take a bite first before trying his luck.

'Go ahead,' she said enthusiastically.

Michele took a bite, chewed a little cautiously, and then smiled.

'You approve?' Beth asked.

Michele nodded and then continued eating. Beth had seen another side to Michele that she had failed to witness in the short time that they had been in each other's company.

His smile.

Michele wiped his mouth with the napkin and then informed Beth that their cab had returned to pick them up.

'Central Park,' Michele said as they climbed into the cab.

'Certainly,' the cab driver said, and pulled away.

Michele turned to Beth. 'Listen to me, Beth. I want you to return to the hotel. It's important that you go straight to the room and speak to no one. Do you understand?'

Beth understood perfectly. 'Okay,' she said.

When the cab driver pulled over to Central Park, Beth got out and pointed Michele in the direction that would lead him to the Dairy Visitor Center and Gift Shop, where he was due to meet Franco De Blasi.

'Hey,' she said, just as Michele started to walk away. 'You never said whether you liked my new clothes.'

Michele looked into her puppy dog eyes and a forlorn expression that was just waiting for some confirmation. For the second time since Beth had been in his company he smiled.

'You look great, Beth,' he said.

Chapter Seventeen

Franco De Blasi left their apartment on Queens and took a cab that would take him directly to Central Park. From the instant he had left the apartment he had a feeling that he was being watched. Paranoia had kicked in for sure, and despite seeing nothing that would be determined as being suspicious, he remained unsettled nevertheless.

He met the driver's eyes for an instant, gazing back at him with a look that told him to mind his own business, and then looked behind him once again to see if someone was on their trail. They were in the clear, which meant that he could breathe for a moment, at least long enough for him to concentrate on his meeting with the Sicilian.

A second wave of nervousness crept over him as he thought of the conversation that would take place. As far as Michele was aware, De Blasi was in. At his side, as he promised he would be. De Blasi thought of that for a moment and wondered (on the off-chance that they could beat the odds that were firmly stacked against them) what levels their friendship could develop to, in terms of forming a greater partnership. It was a vision that had, albeit for a brief moment, taken De Blasi to a place that held position and power.

As the cab pulled over at the Grand Army Plaza at the intersection of Central Park South and Fifth Avenue, De Blasi returned to the present, and any thoughts of forming an alliance with Michele La Barbara were already gone. De Blasi leaned over and paid the driver, handing him forty dollars and telling him to keep the change. He pulled over the hood of his sweater and got out of the vehicle, glancing surreptitiously from side to side, he walked casually into Central Park.

De Blasi took a deep breath as he caught sight of Michele sitting on a park bench and smoking a cigarette. Michele met him with a nod and stood up to greet him. He sensed a nervousness in him, whereas only a day before had displayed so much bravado. A man who now looked more troubled than he would care to admit, at least on the outside.

'Let's walk,' Michele said.

Michele handed him a cigarette and held out his lighter until he had achieved his first drag.

'I see you've had a change of clothing,' De Blasi said as a means of small talk.

'I thought I'd make an effort to blend in with the locals,' Michele said.

Michele watched as he took successive deep drags from the cigarette, left holding only the butt in his fingers in a matter of seconds.

'Are you okay?'

De Blasi turned to look at him and smiled nervously. 'Yeah. Sure.'

'Then you're still in?'

Both men stopped on the pathway and De Blasi took out a small black notebook from his trouser pocket and then handed it to Michele.

'What's this?'

'Names and contact details.'

Michele looked deep into his eyes.

'You're not coming with me?'

'Mi dispiace,' De Blasi said. 'Our brief time together has come to an end, my friend.'

Michele nodded. He put a hand on De Blasi's shoulder and then both men continued to walk along the pathway.

'You decided to take my advice after all,' Michele said, which was intended to break the ice more than confirm what he already knew.

'Yeah,' he said, and felt his throat go dry before adding nervously, 'I thought it best in the long run. If anything were to happen to Vincenzo because I had not acted soon enough…'

Michele withdrew his hand from his shoulder and took out two cigarettes from the packet, and both men stopped and lit up before moving on.

'So this doesn't have anything to do with Beth?' Michele asked.

De Blasi shook his head as he exhaled the smoke from his lungs.

'No.' He may have lied a little, but for the most part, he was telling the truth. 'It's more about the time you bought me… you know, time to get out of the city before they finally discover I'm alive.'

'Well, you have made the correct decision, Franco.'

'You're not disappointed in me?' he asked like an insecure child would ask their berating parent.

'Not disappointed enough not to thank you for your help.' Michele smiled.

'Thank you, Michele. I wish we could have become better acquainted.'

'Likewise. And who knows where life may take us, my friend.'

Franco De Blasi felt an emotion he had seldom experienced over a man who only a day ago had held a gun to his head.

'Good luck, Don Michele.'

'Hey,' Michele said. 'Vincenzo.'

'What about him.'

'I like him. So long, brother.'

Michele stuck out his hand and Blasi went to reach for it. That was when his cell phone rang. He took it from his trouser pocket and looked nervously at the screen.

It was Benito Calabrese.

Chapter Eighteen

Vincenzo had been taking a shower that afternoon when Benito's crew had surreptitiously entered his apartment. He hadn't heard the Mancini brothers come in. And they were eager not to disturb him. So, having checked each room for De Blasi, Leonardo went into the kitchen to make some coffee, while Gianni took a seat on the sofa, waiting patiently for De Blasi's lover to grace them with his presence.

Since discovering the photograph of De Blasi and his lover at his home in Brooklyn, a sequence of events had led them to the apartment on Queens. When Benito and his crew were out for blood, even a city as large as New York and with a population in excess of over eight million people could leave one with nowhere to hide. The Mancini brothers had wasted little time spreading the word to their most trusted informants, and it would only be a matter of time before they had their lead.

In addition, it had come to their attention that a pimp known as Marv, who had been a close associate of theirs, had had his neck broken on 46th Street on Broadway. His right-hand man had reported the incident and claimed that this had been the result of some guy getting involved over a hooker. The description he gave was enough to suggest that he was indeed their man.

So, with Benito on Michele's trail, the Mancini brothers were taking care of business in Queens. De Blasi had left the apartment only minutes before they had arrived, and while he had managed to evade his former crew and associates once again, his worst fears were about to be answered. Instead of being the *hunter*, De Blasi had now become the *hunted*. He had left the apartment via the back route taking the steps down into the alleyway and had made his way out onto the street. Had he have stepped out of the front door, he would have come face-to-face with the Mancini brothers.

Leonardo stood in the doorway to the kitchen holding a mug of coffee. Gianni was seated on the sofa with his right leg crossed over his left knee, holding his .38 caliber gun with silencer attached pointed in the direction of the bathroom. There would be no kill here in the apartment. Instead, they would claim their prize and take him back to their boss as he had instructed.

When the sound of running water from the bathroom ceased, Leonardo smiled at his brother, who was sitting waiting for Vincenzo to enter the room. They could hear him singing in the bathroom as he dried himself, his voice almost feminine in tone, he was clearly in need of some practice. He had only a towel wrapped around his waist when he opened the bathroom door, and albeit for just a single moment thereafter, he sang as he made his way to the living room, and then urinated slightly when he caught sight of the stranger sitting on his sofa with a gun pointed straight at him.

Gianni watched intently as the urine ran down the inside of Vincenzo's left leg but refrained from expressing any sign of amusement. Leonardo, nevertheless, thought the incident humorous and did nothing to hide the fact that he found it entertaining.

With a wave of his gun, Gianni ordered a quivering Vincenzo to sit down on the sofa facing opposite him. Slowly, Vincenzo did as he was instructed, and once sat, he kept his legs and knees locked together and then he glanced nervously at the man who was standing in the doorway of the kitchen, holding a mug of coffee and carrying an expression of superiority.

'Sorry we startled you,' Gianni said softly.

Vincenzo sat trembling, yet remained silent.

'Nice place you have here,' Gianni said as he looked around the room. 'Very nice indeed. Better than that slum of an apartment back in Brooklyn, wouldn't you say?'

For a split second, Vincenzo made eye contact and then withdrew.

'What is your name?' Gianni asked.

Vincenzo's mouth and throat had gone dry, and for a brief moment, he was unable to speak. After composing himself the best he could under the circumstances, he spoke quietly: 'Vincenzo.'

'Well, pleased to meet you, Vincenzo. My name is Gianni and this is my brother Leonardo. We've been looking for Franco. Would you like to tell me where he is?'

Vincenzo lowered his head slightly and then shook it slowly from side to side.

'I didn't quite hear you, Vincenzo. Would you like to speak up?'

'I don't know where he is,' he said. 'He said he had to go out for a while.'

'And he didn't tell you where he was going?'

'No,' he said shaking his head. 'And I didn't think to ask.'

'Hmm, you didn't think to ask.'

Gianni sat forward on the sofa, and toying with the gun in his hand, he looked deep into Vincenzo's eyes. 'Vincenzo. I know you are innocent in all this, so I'm going to cut you a deal. Franco is not the man you think he is. He's a murderer and a swine, a liar and a cheat.' Gianni could see the look of hurt on the man's face, which depicted only an expression of denial. 'He's betrayed you, Vincenzo… not only has he been disloyal to his own family, but he has been disloyal to you. All to protect a traitor and a murderer by the name of Michele La Barbara.

'Does that name mean anything to you?'

Vincenzo remained silent and shook his head.

Feeling irritated by Vincenzo's unwillingness to cooperate, he smiled smugly and then looked over at his brother.

Leonardo acknowledged his brother's need for assistance, so placed the mug down on the kitchen table, and then walked into the living room and stood in front of Vincenzo, whose legs were trembling with fear. The force of the right hook that made contact with the left side of Vincenzo's temple, rendered him unconscious for almost five minutes. When he eventually came round, Leonardo raised his chin, looked him square in the eyes and smiled, before hitting him again, this time, square on the bridge of his nose, which made his brain shake and his eyes water.

When Vincenzo came to his senses, he saw Gianni leaning over in front of him. 'Now,' Gianni said, 'where were we. Yes. I want you to tell me where Franco is, and all you know about the Sicilian called Michele La Barbara.'

Part of Vincenzo wanted his lover to walk in and save him from the evil that had forced its way into their home. But there was a bigger part of him that didn't want him to return… at least not as long as the threat in their home existed. The life that Franco De Blasi had held secret for so long to protect Vincenzo, had now reared its ugly head and now there was nowhere to run. De Blasi had been part of a criminal organisation that had a code of honour. He had sworn his allegiance to the family and now he had betrayed them. For Vincenzo, his innocence had allowed only for him to see the beauty in people, but now all that was about to change.

'Vincenzo, look at me,' Gianni said. 'It doesn't have to end here for you. Franco made his decision to betray us, but for you, you have a choice. Tell us what you know and you will be allowed to get on with the rest of your life. It's really that simple.'

'He…'

'Go on,' Gianni said.

'Franco left me. He wouldn't give me an explanation, only that it was better for both of us if he left.'

'Is that the truth, Vincenzo?'

Vincenzo nodded. But as far as Gianni was concerned, with a lack of conviction.

Gianni smiled. 'You're not a very good liar, are you? Well, Vincenzo, this is difficult, so let me tell you where we stand right now. Our boss would like to talk to Franco, and you as it happens, and has told us not to return without either one of you. So, just in case you are still dazed, I will allow you one more opportunity to tell me what you know.'

'Please, I've just told you,' Vincenzo said. 'He left…'

'And you were so upset you were singing in the shower. Or were you in there jerking off over somebody else.'

Gianni stood up straight and took out a handkerchief from his jacket pocket. He rolled it into a ball and then nodded to his brother, who grabbed Vincenzo firmly by his shoulders to restrain him from any movement. Vincenzo's attempts to scream out loud were muffled by the handkerchief, which was now firmly tucked inside his mouth. The more he tried to call out, the more he began to choke.

While Leonardo held on firmly to Vincenzo's shoulders, Gianni grabbed the wrist of his right arm and then pressed the silencer into the centre of his palm. Vincenzo braced himself as the bullet went through the palm of his hand and into the sofa, and let out a stifled screech to signify the pain he was enduring.

'Are you still having trouble remembering?' Gianni asked.

Vincenzo's eyes widened in terror as Gianni placed the end of the silencer against his kneecap.

'Hey, Gianni,' Leonardo said. 'You blow a hole in his kneecap and we're going to have to carry him down the stairs.'

Gianni looked at his brother and then withdrew the gun away from its target.

'Good point,' he said casually. 'Now, Vincenzo. I want you to get dressed. You're coming with us.'

The two brothers ushered their man down through the apartment block and out onto the street without an ounce of resistance. The opportunity to call out to someone—anyone—in his neighbourhood was something he had considered, even for just a fleeting moment, but he was too afraid. Having already had a taste of the two men's savagery, Vincenzo was under no illusion that they would not hesitate to gun him down in the street if he made one wrong move.

His right hand trembled uncontrollably inside his jacket pocket. Gianni had wrapped a handkerchief around the wound as a dressing (the same handkerchief that had been rolled up and stuffed inside his mouth not too long ago), and while it did little to stop the pain or the flow of blood, it ensured they would attract no attention from outsiders on their short journey to the car.

From that point on, he could bleed all he liked, as long as he hung on to life for as long as they needed him to. The handkerchief ploy was something that the brothers had been accustomed to. First, they would render their victim powerless to speak, and from there they would inflict a certain degree of punishment, before applying the same handkerchief to aid the wound. It had become part of their method of interrogation.

Gianni took the wheel while his brother sat in the back of the car with Vincenzo, who was now looking less likely to talk than he was prior to the bullet that had been blown through his right hand.

'Hey, Gianni, he's not lookin' too good.'

Gianni looked through the rear-view mirror. 'Well, where we're going he needs to start talkin' or he's going to look a damn sight worse.'

Leonardo laughed. 'Do you think De Blasi will show up now that we have his boyfriend?'

'Can't say,' Gianni shrugged. 'The man's a rat. Still, he can only slip the net for so long. Unless he's fallen for the Sicilian? Hey, Vincenzo.'

Leonardo laughed again.

Vincenzo shivered with the pain. His entire body had gone numb and had heard little of what the two men were saying.

'Who would have thought it,' Leonardo said. 'De Blasi. He sure didn't look the type.'

'They never do,' Gianni said.

'Well, this one sure does.'
It was Gianni's turn to laugh.

Chapter Nineteen

Michele had witnessed another side to Franco De Blasi that day. The almost cool demeanour from the previous day had been replaced by a man who was ready to high tail it away from the city at the earliest opportunity. Time had given him the opportunity to think things through, and the more he had considered Michele's words of advice, the more he feared for Vincenzo, and was regretful that he had put his life in danger. He had slept that night with one eye open and a gun under his pillow. A once-trusted member of La Cosa Nostra, and the same people who he had trusted with his life, had now become strangers overnight.

There was no going back.

Even a man such as Michele La Barbara had been unable to prevent the loss of life that had been cast upon his family and loved ones, and with that in mind, De Blasi feared what might become of Vincenzo. Having left him alone in the apartment for less than an hour, he could only pray that he was safe. As much as he valued his own life, any thought of losing his lover and best friend was worse than any nightmare come true.

Having met Michele that afternoon, he had regained a little of the composure he had left, however, any self-control that he had managed to retrieve, had been withdrawn the instant he saw the underboss's name flashing on the screen of his cell phone. As he gazed at the screen, countless thoughts flashed through his mind as to why Benito had chosen to call him.

Both men looked at each other, understanding what the other was thinking. The game of death that De Blasi had played out since they had left his apartment in Brooklyn, was now over.

'You want me to answer that?' Michele offered.

De Blasi shook his head. 'No,' he said. 'I guess this one's for me.'

'Yes,' De Blasi said almost too cautiously.

After a brief pause—'Back from the dead, Franco'—came as a clear statement as opposed to a question.

'You catch on fast,' De Blasi said, this time with more purpose.

His insult to his former boss was met with another pause on the line.

'I do. And far quicker than you could ever believe.'

'What do you want, Benito?'

Benito started to laugh.

'What's so funny?'

'What's funny? Well,' Benito said, toying with him. 'It's funny that you thought you were going to betray the family and then come up with some cock-and-bull-story with your newly acquainted friend. But you know what's even funnier?'

'What?'

'The years that you've been hiding in the closet.'

Benito broke off the conversation and started to laugh again.

This time, uncontrollably.

De Blasi put his hand over the receiver and looked at Michele. 'They've got Vincenzo.'

'Yes,' Benito said. 'He's pretty. Far prettier than you, Franco. What attracted him to you, I just don't know?'

'Please,' De Blasi said. 'Let him go, Benito.'

'In exchange for what, Franco?'

'For me,' he said decisively.

'And your friend?'

De Blasi met Michele's eyes before returning to the conversation.

'I don't know where he is, Benito.'

'You don't know, or you can't remember? Well, allow me to refresh your memory, Franco.' Benito signalled to Gianni, who, having placed another rolled up handkerchief into Vincenzo's mouth, pulled it out, which caused him to cough violently as he was sat tied to a chair.

'Vincenzo,' De Blasi whispered.

Vincenzo called out to him. 'Franco!' And as Gianni pumped a bullet through his left knee, his screams echoed as far as Michele, before the handkerchief was stuffed back into his mouth.

'Yes,' Benito said. 'He's pretty, but for how long, Franco?'

'Please,' De Blasi said. 'Let him go…'

155

'The Sicilian!' Benito demanded. 'I won't ask you again. Where is he?'

'I swear to you, Benito. I don't know where he is.'

De Blasi met Michele's eyes; both men knowing full well that nothing could be done to save him.

'Have it your way,' Benito said.

Gianni pulled the handkerchief out of Vincenzo's mouth once again, this time blowing a hole into his right knee, he let out harrowing screams of torture. With a further signal from the underboss, Leonardo pulled back on the chair and dragged it back on two legs and into the next room. Gianni followed his brother, and after allowing De Blasi to hear his lover's pitiful screams for a final time, they closed the door behind them.

'See you around, Franco.'

Benito ended the call.

And as far as Franco De Blasi was concerned.

This had been the day that his heart had stopped beating too.

Michele looked deep within him and saw only the shadow of the man he had once been. Once a brutal assassin, he was now as helpless as a new-born baby and confined to a world of loneliness.

'Vincenzo,' he said aimlessly as he lowered his cell phone to his side.

'I'm sorry,' Michele said. But De Blasi never heard him.

He had drifted off to a place that he would never return from.

The former *life* that he had chosen to live by had rules, which simply had to be followed. He had broken the oath and had paid the consequences for his treachery.

The torture and murder of Vincenzo was something he would neither come to terms with nor be able to live with. No matter what rules had been broken. The sound of Vincenzo screaming as he was dragged to his death would follow him to his grave.

He looked at Michele as if he had been suddenly woken from a hypnotic episode.

'I have to go,' he said.

'Go where?'

'Back to the apartment. I have to know for sure.'

'Franco,' Michele said firmly.

De Blasi closed his eyes. 'Don't, Michele. Please don't go there.'

He refused to hear what he already knew. There was nothing for him to go back to. But nevertheless, he had to go back. And nothing and nobody would prevent him from doing so. Not even the man at his side.

Michele understood that there was no reaching him. De Blasi wasn't interested in revenge. There was no love or hate left in the man. If Benito Calabrese had been stood in front of him, it would have been unlikely that De Blasi would have pulled out his gun and killed him. The only realm that Franco De Blasi was living in now, was one that depicted Vincenzo waiting for him when he arrived back at their apartment. He wondered at the possibility, and to Michele's surprise, he smiled before returning to the present.

'I guess this is where we part company, my friend,' De Blasi said and held out his hand. 'I wish you well.'

Unable to offer any further words that might change his mind, Michele slowly accepted his hand, which was far limper than it had been when they had shaken hands only a short time ago.

Michele watched as the forlorn figure of Franco De Blasi turned and then went on his way.

They would never see each other again.

Chapter Twenty

Benito Calabrese had received word to meet his father at one of his most frequented restaurants on 45 E Street, between Broadway and Park Avenue South: the Old Town Bar & Grill. Lorenzo Esposito was also present, which unsettled the son of the Capo more than enthused him. His father was growing restless and had heard gossip about his son's recent, albeit reckless crusade. Benito was a good earner for sure, but he took too many risks, and the way Alberto saw it, perhaps one risk too many.

Benito took his place at the table and looked at the consigliere with more curiosity than respect. Curious as to why he was always at his father's side when he wanted to discuss matters of business with the Capo in private, he was becoming increasingly irritated. The consigliere sensed Benito's loathing for him, and underneath that poker-faced expression, he was laughing uncontrollably. The fact that he had evaded law enforcement for so long was a mystery to him. He was a liability, and a danger to anyone who crossed him, even for those who just happened to look at him the wrong way.

But the one thing that Lorenzo could not deny was that the ageing Capo would not live forever, and once his reign as boss of the Calabrese family came to an end, not only would his position as consigliere come into question, but so would his life. He was second in command right now, but the men beneath him were loyal to the wishes and demands of their boss, and underboss. Benito would take him out now if he could, he knew that.

Still, if there was one thing that he had learnt in all the years of his involvement in organised crime were that things changed from one day to the next. Franco De Blasi had been an esteemed member of the family, a high ranking soldier, who had displayed all the attributes that, perhaps, would have made him a captain of his own crew. But he had become a wanted man. A criminal in a lot of respects. And a man who was now living on borrowed time.

In this life, very few men lived out their time: either they died in prison or were murdered on the streets. In all the years that Lorenzo had served Alberto Calabrese, this was the most precarious of times that he had ever known. A lone man from Sicily had travelled over four thousand miles to take on the might of the most notorious family in New York City when most would have travelled further afar and went into hiding.

This man was either out of his mind or a force to be reckoned with.

Perhaps both, the consigliere considered. But kept such thoughts to himself.

Alberto Calabrese was perusing through the menu with more interest than he afforded his son, who called the waiter over to the table and ordered a bottle of lager. Unlike his father and consigliere, he had little appetite, and the thought of being in their company any longer than he needed to be, irritated him further.

When the waiter returned to the table, he placed a bottle of Budweiser in front of Benito, opened a bottle of red wine for the two men, and then began to pour. Benito waited patiently for them to place their order, and after the two men decided on their meal, the waiter left the three of them alone to discuss business.

'Well?' Alberto Calabrese said.

Benito looked at his father over the neck of the bottle as he took a drink of the cool lager. 'You were right about De Blasi. He is still alive.'

Alberto looked at his son as if the news hadn't come of any surprise.

'He won't be for much longer, though.' He smirked.

'You think this some kind of joke?' Lorenzo said. 'At this rate, the Sicilian is going to find us before we locate him.'

'Hardly,' Benito said.

'That's if law enforcement hasn't come knocking on our door beforehand,' Lorenzo added.

'You have any better suggestions, Consigliere?'

'You're a liability, Benito.'

'Yeah, and who put you in charge of the family.'

Alberto raised his hand to signify that he'd heard enough.

'Did you get any information from him?'

Benito looked at the Don puzzled. 'Whom?'

Alberto let out an exasperated sigh to show that his patience had finally worn out. 'Don't insult my intelligence, Benito. We heard about your latest exploit. Do you think that that was necessary?'

'I wanted to make sure De Blasi got the message loud and clear.'

'Oh, you made certain of that,' Lorenzo intervened. 'You're in danger of raising unwanted attention to this family. This is the twenty-first century, not the nineteen thirties.'

'You said something…'

'Did it enter your mind that by taking the action you've taken, De Blasi might have turned informer? And what if he's given the Sicilian information about us?' Lorenzo sat back in his chair holding an expression of contempt. 'Yes, good move, Benito. We now have a lone gunman on our trail who knows more about us than we do about him.'

Benito put his hands together in a prayer-like fashion and looked at both men before continuing. 'What was I supposed to do? Hmm? If De Blasi hadn't betrayed the family at the first time of trouble, then we wouldn't be in this mess. I've got my men and informers tracing his steps throughout the city. He was last seen on 46th Street helping out some hooker. We believe she's still with him.'

Alberto looked at him quizzically.

'Tell me more?' Alberto said. He was calm for now, at least.

'Apparently, one of our associates ran into him on 46th Street and ended up with his neck broken.'

'Dead?' the consigliere said.

'Quite dead,' Benito returned.

'Funny, I hadn't heard anything about it,' Lorenzo returned.

'Then you should try watching the news. It might be the twenty-first century, but there is still murder on the streets of New York.'

'But no leads yet?' Alberto said.

Benito shook his head. 'Not yet. We don't know where they are right now, but with our associates on the lookout for the girl, I'm pretty sure we'll have our man soon enough.'

'Very well. Call me when you have something.'

'Bene. What do you want me to do with De Blasi and the whore?'

'Do what you will with them, but do it quietly. Do you understand?'

Benito nodded. 'Is there anything else?'

'Yes, bring me the Sicilian.'

The two men remained silent as they watched Benito make his way out of the restaurant. Moments later, the waiter returned to the table with two plates of food, and after serving the two men and pouring more wine, he left them to talk in private.

'He's out of control,' Lorenzo said, shaking his head as he cut into his medium cooked steak. 'And he's in danger of bringing the family down. You know that.'

'I won't allow that to happen,' Alberto said and then glanced at his advisor. 'I had hoped that one day he would take over from me and run the family business. Amadeo was smarter'—he smiled—'Much smarter.'

And how Lorenzo wished that his youngest son had been around to take over the family business when that time came.

The consigliere picked up his napkin from his lap and then patted his mouth delicately. 'He worries me. He's intent on making his mark on the Sicilian and making this his own private war.'

'Are you saying that from an advisory point of view, or by way of your animosity between you?'

Lorenzo could feel his boss's eyes gazing through him as he waited for an answer. 'Both,' he said finally. 'But there's something about his behaviour right now that unnerves me.'

'Like what?'

'It's as if he'll do whatever it takes to get to him before you do.'

'He's out for revenge. And who can blame him.' The Capo wiped his mouth with his napkin as he chewed his food and then turned to face his advisor. 'Look, Lorenzo. Benito's my son. He's a live wire, in fact, he's more than that, he's a maniac. But he's loyal to the family and has always been a good earner. He just needs putting in his place now and again,' he said, and then continued to eat his meal.

'I get that,' Lorenzo said, 'but as an advisor to the family I am concerned that his unpredictability and his quest for control could bring us all down.'

'Agreed,' the Capo said. 'But right now we need him.'

'Agreed,' Lorenzo said, but with less conviction.

Tony Biágio observed Benito as he left the restaurant, barging into an innocent bystander who just happened to get in his way. As he got closer, Tony could see the expression of fury written all over his face, and that meant trouble for whoever was in the firing line. Whatever was bothering Benito right now, he would either take it out on him, or he would give Tony a rundown of his meeting in the restaurant. Either way, he would be forced to listen.

161

Tony Biágio was thirty-two years old and had known Benito since they were kids—but he still didn't know him the way good friends know one another. They had grown up on the streets together, and Alberto Calabrese was his Godfather. At five-foot-eight and under one hundred and fifty pounds, he looked younger than his years, which had earned him the nickname as the "baby-faced assassin".

His black hair was swept back with meticulous detail, and more often than not he wore dark sunglasses, despite having the bluest of eyes that could easily arouse most females. Down the side of his left cheek, there was a three-inch scar, which had been with him since he was eighteen years old. Not that the scar did anything to prevent him from attracting the women… on the contrary. To them, it made him more desirable.

The knife attack had been a turning point in his life. He had been in the wrong place at the wrong time, at least that's how he had determined the situation at that time. Tony had called into the local food store for his mother while there was a hold-up. The guy who owned the shop was busy emptying his cash register when Tony had walked in.

When Tony tried to intervene, the man wearing a balaclava and holding a sawn-off shotgun, turned round to face him. He yelled at Tony to get down on the floor, but he wouldn't listen. Even at such a young age, the thought of taking orders from some lowlife bothered him more than the risk of being gunned down from point-blank range.

The man ordered the shopkeeper to fill his bag with the money from the register and then called out to Tony once more to get down on the floor. When he failed to follow his orders, the man charged toward him with the shotgun pointed at him, but with a six-inch knife in his right hand, he lashed out, slashing the left side of Tony's cheek.

At first, Tony had failed to acknowledge the severity of the attack, but at the sight of the blood, he charged at the assailant and wrestling the shotgun from his hand, he pulled it away from him and pointed it at him.

The man held his hands up in the air and called out for Tony not to shoot. Tony glanced at the knife that was now lying on the floor, along with a trail of blood that had been the result of an unprovoked attack.

'Remove the balaclava,' Tony ordered. 'Now.'

The man held his hands up in front of him, and then slowly began to remove the balaclava. The man appeared to be in his mid-twenties, medium build and height, and of Mexican origin. Gathering his composure, he looked at Tony and considered whether he had the mettle to pull the trigger. *No*, he guessed he couldn't do it… to point a gun at a person was one thing, however, to murder someone in cold blood, was another.

But Tony was no longer the naïve eighteen-year-old kid who had walked into the store only moments before. As the blood continued to pour down the left side of his face, he ordered the assailant to get on his knees. The man did as instructed, and without further hesitation, Tony walked toward him with shotgun in hand, pushed the barrel against the man's forehead, and then pulled the trigger.

The victim's head was blown away from his shoulders, which left the shop looking more like an abattoir than a general food store. Benito Calabrese was called and arrived at the store within five minutes of the shooting. The store was closed for the rest of the day in order to allow the young man who had saved the owner to dispose of the body and to make his escape without any police intervention. Grateful for the young man's interference when it could have cost him his life, the old man praised him for his bravery, and then returned the cash to the register.

Nobody ever made an attempt to rob the store again.

Benito sat for a moment looking out of the car window at nothing in particular, and then took out a packet of Marlboro from the inside of his jacket pocket and then lit up a cigarette without offering one to Tony.

'Is everything okay?' Tony asked.

Benito turned to face him with an expression that said everything was far from okay, and then told him to drive.

'If he wasn't my father I'd kill him,' Benito said.

Tony glanced at him in astonishment and then returned his sights to the road ahead.

'And as for the consigliere… he can only hide behind the Capo for so long. He's an advisor to the family who does everything but advise.'

Tony smiled.

'What's so funny?' Benito asked.

'Nothing,' he said, still smiling. 'Just I've known you all my life, Benito. You're such a hot head that it clouds your judgement.'

'What the fuck are you talking about?'

'You've always been the same. Act first and then think later… that's your style, but you should know by now that it's not your father's way.'

Benito took a deep draw in the cigarette and then exhaled smoke from the open window.

'Are you saying I'm out of control?' he asked, looking over at the driver with an inquisitive eye.

'No,' Tony said. 'I just think that from time to time it would do you good to actually listen to someone other than yourself.'

'Do you know what I think?' Benito said. 'I'm beginning to wish I'd stayed at the restaurant.'

Tony laughed. 'For what it's worth, I think your father cares about you more than you realise. And perhaps it wouldn't harm you to listen to him now and again without feeling offended.'

'Interesting,' Benito said.

'You agree with what I said?'

'No. But I might just have discovered the family's next consigliere.'

Franco De Blasi stood outside the apartment block in Queens at dusk and observed his surroundings with almost a casualness about him. Everything appeared to be normal; nothing out of the ordinary. His black Chevrolet was parked on the same side of the road as their apartment block, bumper to bumper with other cars from the same neighbourhood—nothing appeared to be out of place.

He looked up at their apartment and wondered whether Vincenzo was at home. And then a dark realisation came over him to remind him that that would not be the case. De Blasi continued to gaze up at their home and envisioned a life that they had shared together; a beautiful life that had been destroyed by his immoral dealings. Part of him hoped against hope that this was all some kind of depraved joke, and he would go upstairs to find Vincenzo at home waiting for him; the other, a resignation that he would never see or hear from his best friend again.

He speculated how Benito Calabrese could have known about his relationship with Vincenzo, and how they had discovered their whereabouts. *How? I didn't leave any tracks for them to follow*, he thought. They'd been to his apartment in Brooklyn for sure, but…

Blasi pulled out his wallet from his back trouser pocket and searched frantically for the picture. *No, I thought I had it. I wouldn't have left it behind.* He searched again, but inside, he knew. *Damn! How could I have been so stupid,* he thought. *They must have ransacked the place in order to find something, anything that would give them a lead. That was what they did.* And that is exactly what he would have done. The slightest shred of evidence was enough to unravel a person's life, and from that point on, there was no hiding place.

Thoughts and images of his past life turned to sorrow as he contemplated the reality of the situation. Still, he had to return to their apartment—just to be certain. It didn't matter if they were in there waiting for him to return, he had to go back inside.

Everything seemed surreal. Blasi crossed the road and then made his way into the building. Holding the .22 caliber handgun equipped with a silencer firmly in his hand, he walked slowly up the stairs, watching and listening intently for the merest sound of something untoward.

But other than the familiar echoes of voices resounding from the walls of apartments, or the beating of music, there was nothing to cause any suspicion. A sudden rush of adrenaline had caused him to become breathless. Of all the hits that he had committed in a not-so-distant past, he felt a nervousness that he could neither explain nor control.

When he reached the third floor, he paused and waited. His hand trembled on the gun, and with his finger placed on the trigger, he made his way to the front door of the apartment. Blasi was perspiring and his hand shook as he put the key into the lock and then turned it. As he opened the door, that was the time when he expected to see a gun in his face, and in a strange kind of way that he could neither explain nor deny, he was inviting his own fate.

As he stood in the doorway of the apartment, for some strange reason he reflected on his first hit that had been many years ago. Benito Calabrese had given the order, and De Blasi had been summoned to do his bidding at a moment's notice, without question and without any excuses. But it wasn't until he had been given the address to go to that he knew who his target was. The same man who had introduced him to La Cosa Nostra.

***

Mike Toscani had been in a bar on Broadway chatting to a guy about football, unaware that he was in the company of a rookie police officer. He loved to shoot from the hip, talking about himself and boasting about his criminal activities, and after one too many drinks, he disclosed information that linked him to the Calabrese family. Medium height and build, his hair was as black as the night, and his eyes just as dark. Mike was oblivious to what was to come, and after having taken his newfound friend into his confidence, he had left the bar only to be handcuffed outside and then pushed into the back of a police car.

Time in police custody had given Mike a chance to reflect on the errors of his ways, and having told the police nothing that would implicate himself or the family any further, he was cautioned and then discharged without further questioning. Mike had made a decision not to talk to anyone about the whole affair, and it was the first and only time in his life when he had had the ability to keep his mouth firmly shut.

However, he hadn't contemplated that the family would have got to know about his exploits. And even if he had, he would never have considered for a single moment what would happen next.

Late one evening, Mike had been at his apartment in Brooklyn watching the football and drinking a bottle of beer, when there was a knock at his door. The short sharp rap had drawn him away from the action on the TV, and for an instant, he waited before calling out, hoping that whoever it was would go away. With half his attention on the game and the other focused in the direction of the hallway, he took a drink from the bottle, spilling ale down his chin and onto his T-shirt when the caller knocked again, this time with a more forceful drawn-out rap.

Mike wiped away the remnants of alcohol from his chin and got up from the sofa and made his way to the front door. 'Who is it?' he called out.

'Open up, Mike, it's me. Franco.'

Mike unlocked the door and then opened it to see the outline of his friend in the darkness of the hallway.

'Hey, come in, Franco, great to see you.'

Franco followed his friend into his apartment and then closed the door behind him.

'What brings you round here at this time of the night?'

'A favour,' Franco said.

166

'Why don't you take a seat while I get us both a beer,' Mike said. 'And then you can tell me all about it.'

'Yeah, why not. I'm driving, but what the hell, one won't do any harm.'

Mike returned from the open kitchen with two bottles of Budweiser and handed one to Franco. After clinking their bottles, Mike took a seat in the chair opposite, and with one eye on the game and the other on his friend, he finally asked him what he could do for him.

Franco took a drink from the bottle and looked at his friend, Mike Toscani, the man who had pulled him out of the gutter when he had nothing and had presented him with an opportunity that would transform his life. He had been there for him when others had not, and other than the crew who he now called his *family*, Mike was the closest person to him, in fact, far closer than he had been to any of his true family.

'I want you to leave the city, Mike.'

'What?'

'You heard me.'

Mike picked up the TV controls from the armchair and lowered the volume so that the two men could talk. 'Why?'

'So I don't have to kill you.'

Mike went silent for a moment, and then a huge grin came over his face, followed by uncontrollable laughter.

But Franco wasn't laughing. He remained straight-faced and located accessibly on the inside of his coat pocket, was a .22 caliber handgun with silencer attached, ready and loaded.

'Okay, you win,' Mike said, taking a drink from the bottle, and returning his sights to the TV.

'You talk too much, Mike, haven't I warned you about that. How many times did I take you to one side and tell you that one day your big mouth would get you into trouble.'

'Now, you just back the fuck up. Who the hell do you think you're talking to! It was me,' he said pointing to himself, 'who pulled your ass out of the gutter when you had nothing. I'm the very reason that you're sitting there in your trench coat and your expensive leather shoes.'

'That's enough, Mike. I haven't forgotten any of that, and I never will. Which is why I have disobeyed orders in the hope that you'll do what I've asked and leave the city as soon as possible, and never look back.'

Mike stared at his friend without uttering a word. After taking another drink from the bottle, he stood up. 'No,' Mike said. 'I'm not going anywhere.'

Franco turned his head to one side and sighed. 'Your mouth is only rivalled by that of your stubbornness. I'm asking you one more time, please… take my advice, get what few things you need and go. I'll take care of things back here.'

'And how will you do that?'

'I'll just say you were gone when I arrived here.' Franco frowned. 'They'll just have to take my word for it.'

Mike stood staring at his friend Franco De Blasi, and for the first time that he could remember, he was looking at a stranger.

'No,' he said firmly. 'This is the life we have chosen to live. It could have been me who was given an order to kill you, and as much as I love you, I would have followed my orders without question.

'So, you do what you have to do, Franco. And while you think about it, I'm going to get myself another beer.'

De Blasi watched as he made his way into the open kitchen and opened the fridge door. By the time he had taken the lid off the bottle and turned around, he saw the barrel of a silencer pointing straight at him.

'Mi dispiace,' De Blasi said, and then pulled the trigger.

The first bullet hit Mike in the chest, the force of the bullet hurling his body back against the fridge door as the bottle of beer fell to the floor. De Blasi stood up from the sofa and made his way into the kitchen. As their eyes met for the final time, he rounded off three more shots into his body and then stood over him for a moment longer until he exhaled his last breath.

His first hit had been his best friend.

There would be many more hits to come, but never one that would test his strength of will as much as having to kill his closest ally.

***

De Blasi stepped into the apartment and then closed the front door behind him. Holding the gun in front of him, he quickly moved from room to room to see if there was anyone waiting for him but found nothing. He was breathing more frantic now, however, he knew that if anyone had been waiting for him, then he would have been dead the instant he had stepped foot inside the apartment. That was the way it worked. But there was no sign of Vincenzo. In fact, no sign that he had ever lived here at all. It was like he had stepped inside the home of a stranger.

De Blasi walked into the living room and made his way over toward the window, and surreptitiously glanced outside to see if there was any movement or anything that looked untoward. But there was no sign of anything suspicious. No lone gunman standing on the corner of the street, no car that had no place being there, nothing. It was too quiet, and that unnerved him more so.

But the moment he turned away from the window he glanced down at the sofa and noticed a bloodstain. And before he had time to consider how it had arrived to be there, he saw it. Standing all alone as if it had no place being there.

It was a large brown, broken leather suitcase.

For a moment, everything went still. De Blasi closed his eyes and then opened them, hoping that what he had seen had been nothing other than his imagination playing some twisted tricks on him. But it was not to be. The suitcase was there in front of him. And even as he looked at it, he still wondered—in hope more than wonder—that this might all be some deranged trick, a message, to lure him into a false sense of security and in turn pull him back into their world.

There was a part of him that wanted to open the suitcase. But the other half understood the script. He knew Benito and what he was capable of. This was no trick. And the more he observed the suitcase, the bloodier it became.

De Blasi ran from the living room and into the bathroom where he fell to his knees over the toilet basin and vomited. *How could they do this?* he thought. What had Vincenzo ever done other than to bring love into the world? He had been drawn into a crossfire of interests and brutally murdered for his loyalty to another.

After slowly getting to his feet, he flushed the chain and then washed and dried his hands before making his way back into the living room, where he sat down on the sofa and, leaning forward, buried his face in his hands. *No,* the word echoed in his mind. But the harder he tried to relinquish any thoughts of Vincenzo's body inside the suitcase, the more he saw it.

What next?

Is this how he would leave him? Leave his lover's chopped-up body in a suitcase until someone reported a vile smell coming from the apartment. No, he couldn't leave him here. Thoughts of law enforcement entering their home to investigate the scene would be more than he could bear. It would be a story that would attract many readers throughout the city and reveal the hideous remains of a once beautiful, innocent human being.

He would take his body and bury his remains, no matter how hard an ordeal. He owed him that.

De Blasi took another forced glance at the suitcase and then stood up from the sofa. It was time to get away from here. He picked up the bloody case and felt the full weight of Vincenzo's remains and felt only repugnance for those who had condemned him to such a violent end. After taking a final look behind him—their home that had been full of beautiful memories—De Blasi made his way to the front door and then left their apartment for the final time.

He didn't have any idea where he was going to go, or even consider the possibility of life ahead of him. He walked down the stairs without a care of who might be looking at him, or even a threat to his life, and stepped outside the apartment block and onto the street. De Blasi put down the suitcase and took out a cigarette, lighting it hastily, he picked up the baggage containing Vincenzo, his lover, his best friend, and then stepped across the street toward his car, where he opened the boot and then hoisted the suitcase and placed it carefully inside.

Gazing through the darkness, he took another *forced* look before slamming the door of the boot closed. De Blasi flicked the remains of the cigarette away and then got into the car. For a moment he sat in the quiet, gazing ahead and into the unknown without the slightest notion of where he was going to go.

Then, he looked up at the apartment and saw images of the life they had once enjoyed. The two of them enjoying their own company, cooking together, drinking and enjoying their favourite shows on TV while they sat close together as lovers do. It was another time, but it was real and a beautiful part of his life that could never be taken away.

As the images faded, he returned to a cold reality, at which point something came to him, an awareness, an instinct of a trap that had been laid out for him. The Sicilian had implored him not to go back, but he had disregarded his plea. Now, there was a part of him that wished he had listened, whereas the other part of him was in acceptance that he had made the right decision. Either way, his life as he had known it, had come to an end.

De Blasi placed the key into the ignition and then paused for a moment.

He caught sight of himself through the rear-view mirror and smiled. He knew what was coming next—somehow, he just knew.

170

I enter alive and I will have to come out dead. Franco De Blasi smiled for the last time.

When he turned the key in the ignition the car exploded and then lifted ten feet into the air in a screaming furnace. As the burning shell of the car came down and hit the ground, it alerted the neighbourhood, who emerged cautiously from their homes in their numbers to investigate the devastation.

Part IV
War on the Streets of New York

Chapter Twenty-One

Back at the hotel, Beth was sitting next to the window overlooking the city. She had been sitting there for some time, thinking about the simplicity of life that she was experiencing right now. Her world had changed since she had met the stranger on 46th Street. In fact, it had changed in such a way that she wondered, even doubted, that she would ever return to it again.

During her years on the streets, Beth had witnessed many girls come and go, but mostly they came back. They would have to endure a beating first, followed by a reminder of what would happen to them should they ever decide to run away again. Working on the streets and sleeping on the streets were two different things. So, an occasional beating was considered necessary to keep the girls in check. Even when they had done nothing wrong, violence was compulsory and was considered to be an act of supremacy.

Of all the beatings Beth had ever received—most of which had been administered in public view—nobody had ever intervened. That was until the stranger from a foreign land had rescued her from the grips of brutality. For had it not been for his intervention, she would now be lying in a hospital rather than sitting on an expensive quilted mahogany chair in a luxurious hotel. She was in the company of a man who had probably murdered more men than she had slept with. But she felt safe—safer than she had ever felt in her life.

Beth was awoken from her reverie when she heard the front door open. She turned to see Michele, who looked at her fixedly without even the suggestion of a smile.

'Hi,' she said softly. Almost apologetically.

Michele nodded but remained silent.

'Are you okay?'

Michele closed the door and removed his shades. 'It's just you and me now, Beth.'

'Do you want to talk about it?' she asked.

Michele shook his head. 'There's nothing to talk about. Franco made the decision to walk away, and there was nothing I could have done to stop him.'

Beth could see a sadness in Michele's eyes as opposed to anger.

'I'm sorry,' Beth said. She knew the rest. She didn't have to ask.

'Don't be. You never knew him. And nor did I for that matter. I'm going to take a shower.'

Michele undressed and then opened the shower door and stepped inside. He stood under the showerhead and allowed the hot water to pour over him as his mind wandered in different directions. He was being hunted by the mob. They were responsible for the murder of his loved ones and had driven him away from his homeland to their domain.

It's time we met, Benito Calabrese, he thought.

The bathroom was shrouded in steam as Michele continued to allow the hot water to pour over his face. He was in no hurry to move and remained unperturbed when the shower door opened and Beth stepped inside to join him. He opened his eyes and looked at her without judgement, knowing she had not come to seduce him, but merely to be at his side. Michele put his arms around her naked body and held her close.

Benito Calabrese was at home with his family watching the evening news when he first heard of the car explosion in Queens. He smiled to himself without alerting his wife, Marie, who looked horrified upon hearing that a body had been inside the car when it exploded. The animated reporter then went on to say that remains of another body had been discovered, and while it was undetermined why and who was behind the crime, it was indicated that it could be mob-related.

Marie glanced over toward her husband who was sitting comfortably in his armchair and gave him a *do you know anything about this* look. Benito shrugged, 'Don't look at me,' he said nonchalantly, but his wife could see a smugness behind his denial that said he knew everything about the incident. Having lived with the man for so many years, she had become accustomed to his comings and goings and knew that behind the man who had charmed her into becoming his woman, there lay a life of a mercenary.

She had read the newspapers and had heard the stories. However, she had chosen a long time ago to ignore them, at least as best she could. And why not...

for while the life of a mobster's wife was not an easy one, it had afforded her a lucrative lifestyle.

So when her husband said, 'Don't look at me,' she turned her attention back to the screen and listened intently to the reporter in the hope that he would provide sufficient information that would allay her darkest fears. He didn't, and after giving the matter further consideration, she determined that the reporter was perhaps just stating what many people were already thinking.

'Hey,' Benito said, breaking his wife from her trance. 'It'll be drug-related. Count on it. And by tomorrow this will be yesterday's news.'

Benito smiled at his wife, who smiled back nervously.

'I guess you're right,' she said. Drug wars were common in the city, especially in the most deprived areas, and Queens was one of them. Seldom would a crime in the most run-down neighbourhoods be headline news, but the nature of this particular incident had not gone unnoticed. And with the murder of a notorious pimp on 46th Street the previous evening came the growing speculation of organised crime.

But Benito had something going on in his mind, which fascinated him more than excited him. That was the news on the remains of another body. And while he suspected that was the body parts of Benito's lover, he couldn't be certain. Besides, the Sicilian's downfall would not be by means of a simple booby trap. He was too smart. Blasi had given up the ghost long before he had put the key into the ignition, or he too would have been more vigilant in his approach.

Benito's cell phone vibrated on the arm of the chair, which startled him and made him curse out loud: it was Luca Rossi.

Benito had left the comfort of his living room to go into his office to speak privately to Luca, who was enthusiastic in giving him the good news he had been waiting to hear. Luca Rossi was as worthy as a sniffer dog and had an appetite to discover a needle in a haystack no matter what the odds were in finding it. If he had not have decided to devote his life to organised crime, then there was no doubt he would have made a great FBI agent.

With news that the hit on Franco De Blasi had been a success, he was eager to hear more good news that would exonerate him from any further abuse by his father and Capo, along with his consigliere, who was out for blood. Benito had too many scenarios playing out in his mind right now and was eager to eliminate those that he considered as being a nuisance to him. The Capo was demanding answers, and as the underboss, Benito had to deliver.

'Luca, what have you got for me?' he asked.

'Boss, you won't believe it.'

'The Sicilian?' Benito asked cautiously.

'The next best thing. I've found the whore. And given that it's unlikely she can afford to stay at luxurious hotels, I figure she's not alone.'

'Where is she?'

'The Benjamin, 50th Street at Lexington Avenue.'

Benito smiled. 'I know the place,' he said excitedly. 'You're right. I'm surprised they allowed her past the foyer. There's no mistake?'

'No, boss. It's her.'

'And no sign of the Sicilian?'

'Not yet. But it's only a matter of time before he shows up. I've got my man looking out for him as we speak.'

'Great work, Luca. Now that we have them we'll wait until they leave their lair.'

'Agreed.'

'But for fuck sake, don't lose them.'

'No way.'

'The Capo's already busting my balls for some answers that he wants to hear, and if we lose him again… I want you to inform me the moment they leave that hotel. Understood.'

'Understood.'

Benito ended the call and smiled. 'Excellent,' he said.

He needed some good news and now having found the needle in the haystack, it was merely a matter of time before the Sicilian was in his custody. As for the whore, he would have her hands tied behind her back while she was still alive and then have her thrown into the Hudson River. And just in case the pair had developed a sense of longing between them, then he would ensure that the Sicilian was close by to watch her drown in front of his very eyes.

Finally, everything was coming together.

But, as for informing his father and consigliere of his findings, he would tell them what he needed them to know when the time was right.

That evening, Michele and Beth ordered room service and sat by the window where Beth had settled with such comfort earlier that day. She had become enchanted to the sound of the nightlife from below; the noise of traffic and the humming of voices from the crowds who flocked the streets, the volume of which she had never considered before. She remained silent as she thought of the life that she had left behind her. A life that she could hope and pray she would never be lured into again.

Beth thought of her friend Kimberley, who she had been with for most of the day until she had made her approach toward the stranger on 46th Street. Not only had she been her best friend—she had been her only friend. And now she was dead. Killed by the people who were now tracking them down. They would not stop until they were found. She knew that.

It would only be a matter of time.

Beth looked at Michele and could see that he was deep in thought.

'Hey,' she said softly. 'You've hardly touched any food.'

'Sorry,' he said looking up at her as she sat sipping on a glass of red wine. 'I was just thinking.'

'About your friend?'

'Yes,' he nodded. They had watched the evening news, which confirmed the death of Franco De Blasi and sparked off an even greater conversation regarding the threat of organised crime. The news reporter appeared to be more concerned about creating speculation over what could have been behind the apparent murder itself, than the death of the unnamed person, or persons, given the fact that they had discovered a corpse and several body parts.

Michele had turned off the TV. He had seen and heard enough to acknowledge what he already knew.

'I'm sorry,' she said for the second time around.

'Forget it,' Michele said. 'He knew what he was doing.'

'So, who was the other guy... or woman, whose body parts they found?'

'Believe me, Beth, you don't want to know about that.' Michele looked deep into Beth's eyes, but she sensed no intimidation from him, just a warmth that she had felt from the moment they had come together.

Michele toyed with the unopened locket around his neck.

'I remember the day I got word to say that Mary's killer had been found. I remember it as if it was just yesterday. My brothers and I were on a mission in

178

another country at the time, and we were sitting around the table playing cards.'
Michele took a deep draw from the cigarette and then handed it back to Beth.

'Go on,' she said.

'We were playing poker when my cell phone rang. It was my Uncle Gianluca, so I got up from the table to answer the call in private. Hmm,' Michele allowed himself to smile, 'I remember playing my hand as I stood up to leave the table, leaving Giovanni and Luigi cursing me and arguing between themselves. From an outsider's point of view, they must have appeared to be sworn enemies rather than devoted brothers.

'Anyway, my uncle informed me that he had knowledge of the identity and whereabouts of Mary's assassin. I was unusually calm when he told me, can you believe that. However, we had a job to do first, so after we ended the call, I returned to the table and got on with the game.'

'Just like that?' Beth said amazed.

'Yes, I mean what else could I do... we were two thousand miles away from home, and it was important to remain focused on the mission we had been assigned to do.'

'You didn't tell your brothers?'

'No, not right away. As I said, we had to remain focused on the job at hand. I'd waited almost a year to find out who was responsible for my wife's death, so now having a positive ID, it was simply a matter of time before our paths would cross.'

'There's something else, isn't there?' she said.

Michele's facial expression remained grave as he gazed deep into Beth's blue eyes. 'I distinctly remember that day... how can I forget it. He was called Amadeo Calabrese, and it was his wedding day. Funny,' Michele said, 'it has always been customary for other families within the mob to be invited to celebrate weddings.'

'Why?'

'There's always less chance of an assassination taking place if you have your rival or enemy sitting in front of you. So I guess on this day he just didn't perceive of any threat on his life or that of his bride.'

'Ah,' Beth said. 'You guys think of everything.'

'Not everything,' he said, taking another draw from the cigarette. 'But I knew that that was the time for me to strike: first, he was a sitting duck; second, I thought by killing him at his own wedding it would not only inflict misery on his bride but would release some of the pain that I had carried with me since Mary's death.'

'And did it?' Beth asked.

'What do you think?'

'I think you're carrying more hurt around with you now than you have ever done.'

'Perhaps you're right. But it wasn't until now that I remember feeling a sense of apprehension before pulling the trigger. I couldn't explain it at the time, but something just didn't seem right. In fact, it seemed all too easy.'

'What are you saying, Michele?'

'I think there is a possibility that I was set up, Beth.'

Beth met Michele's eyes over the rim of the wine glass. 'Set up? By whom? Your uncle?'

Michele waved his hand. 'Perhaps?'

'Why?'

'That's what I intend to find out. However, that's not what's bothering me.'

'So what is it?'

'What if Mary's killer is still out there?'

Beth looked at Michele in astonishment.

Michele held his gaze and smiled.

But he wasn't laughing.

Michele had laid awake for most of the night; instead of experiencing the usual sequence of dreams that he had suffered for so many nights since Mary's death, he played over another scenario that he had never previously considered possible. Two years after the death of his wife and many questions remained unanswered. Could it have been possible that Gianluca had been behind the assassination of Mary? If so, for what purpose? What would he have gained by such treachery and the need to perform such a heinous act?

His uncle had never once shown any displeasure over his relationship with Mary; in fact, he had warmed to her the instant he had met her. She had been good for his nephew, and as he had been so fond of reminding Michele, "too good" for him. But Michele made light of such comments knowing that Gianluca was merely complementing the new woman in his life, and he was overwhelmed with joy when they finally announced that they were engaged to be married.

Never had there been a moment when his uncle had questioned him over his running of the family business. And even when Michele had announced that they were expecting their first child, Gianluca had displayed only excitement for the couple.

None of this made any sense.

But after reflecting on his uncle's warmer, more charismatic side, he returned to the present, and the moment he had come to realise that Gianluca had turned their lives upside down. While it was not uncommon for friends and associates within La Cosa Nostra to betray one another, such deception within their own family was just inconceivable.

But there was no doubt that Gianluca had betrayed the family; he was responsible for the murder of Luigi, and possibly even Giovanni and his wife Aliana, but for what cause? Had he gone this far just to save his own children? The Gianluca that he knew so well would have dealt with any threat coming his way, especially any threat aimed at his family.

The more he thought, the crazier each notion became. Uncle Gianluca, the family rock, behind the deaths of his own family... was all just too senseless to comprehend.

Michele tossed and turned that night. Normally composed in any given situation, he now found himself growing increasingly impatient. With his wife's murder now having resurfaced and his brothers and uncle dead, he needed answers. Having originally cursed himself for taking Beth under his wing, he was beginning to warm to her companionship. And despite the danger that existed, she had discovered a purpose in *her* life. Somehow or other, fate had brought them together. Michele was sure of that. Whether they would get out of this alive? Well, that was another matter.

As much as he had formed a bond with Beth, she remained a stranger to him in so many ways. It was a friendship that had yet to be put to the test. Not that he was out to test her. But he wondered as to whether she understood the magnitude of danger that existed, and more so, how loyal she would be to him when confronted by death. Nevertheless, it was the words that he had spoken to Beth that same evening that continued to echo in his mind.

What if Mary's killer is still out there?

Michele turned over and lay with his hands behind his head, gazing through the darkness at the ceiling.

Tomorrow they would make their move.

'You should have killed me when you had the chance,' he whispered.
With that final thought, Michele started to drift off to sleep.

Chapter Twenty-Two

Michele was up around dawn and sitting by the open window holding a cup of black coffee and smoking a cigarette. He was looking down at the city coming to life. From the 5th floor, Michele could see commuters rushing to their destination, the unmistakable sight of yellow cabs that were busy making their rounds, and shops and businesses that were ready to open for business.

This was a different life from the one he was accustomed to. The overpopulated streets, high rise buildings and the constant rumpus of activity was something he found disquieting in comparison to the serenity of his homeland. Sicily was his home, and he possessed a longing to return. He pondered on how things would be different now that there was such a void in his life.

The life that he had been used to since he was a child, now shattered by the man who had raised him and nurtured him into a man. Giovanni and Luigi—his brothers and closest allies—now memories of a time now past. Young men who had had their whole lives in front of them, quashed mercilessly by the one person who they thought they could trust.

And Mary, even in death, how could he consider leaving her all alone on the island. While her spirit had gone to heaven, leaving only the shell of her physical body behind, her grave was the one place he could go to and find solace. The one place he could still go to that felt safe.

Michele looked down with continued fascination at the masses of people who flocked the sidewalks and observed them as they scurried about like mice. Commuters, who were eager to get to their place of work, hurried along to the nearest subway or called out for a cab to get them to their destination. This was a portrait of chaos, and perhaps for Michele, a glimpse of the so-called and overrated "normal life".

Yes, the haste at which people moved to their destination. All but one. A man who had taken his place on the other side of the street. Standing on the sidewalk and looking over toward the hotel with an air of curiosity.

Michele reached for his bag and took out his binoculars. He remained obscured behind the thin veil of curtain that gently moved against the morning breeze, and looked down on the man who had grabbed his attention. He was of medium height and build, and appeared to be of Mediterranean origin. He was dressed in black trousers and black shoes, a white T-shirt and a black leather jacket. His hair was swept back carefully and he wore dark sunglasses.

Michele knew a stakeout when he saw one. Suddenly, a tall black man approached him excitedly, before talking to him and pointing over toward the hotel. Both men exchanged further conversation before shaking hands, and then the black guy walked away with a swagger. The same guy who had split the scene on 46th Street.

They'd been made.

Michele lowered the binoculars and then sat back in his chair. The decision to make a move was now academic. Somehow or other, they had been sought out by the mob and their whereabouts had been exposed. As the bedroom door opened, Beth walked out in her bathrobe, stretched and then yawned.

'Good morning,' she said.

'Get dressed,' Michele said. 'We need to go.'

'Why? What's up?'

'They've found us.'

'How?' she said, looking both anxious and confused.

Michele took his place at the window and watched as the man lit up a cigarette, all the while, maintaining his sights on the hotel.

'I have two theories: one, they followed me back here after meeting up with Franco; two, they followed you. And given that I've just seen the black guy who was around the night I met you, it seems likely that it's you who has been tracked down.'

'But that's just not possible.'

Michele turned to face her and noted an expression of confusion.

'Beth, did you come straight back to the hotel as I told you to?'

'Yes.'

'You didn't go anywhere or talk to anyone?'

'No.'

Michele didn't want to interrogate Beth more than he had done already. But he could see that she was agitated as if mulling over her movements since arriving back at the hotel.

'Wait,' she said. 'I went for a packet of cigarettes.'

'Where?'

'A shop across the street.'

Michele looked at her and then looked back down at his target.

'I'm sorry,' she said.

'Noted. Now get ready, we have to go.'

Michele studied the man closer, watching him with interest as he took a drag from his cigarette and then flicked it away from him onto the sidewalk.

The man shadowing them was Luca Rossi.

'I'm sorry,' Beth said as she returned to the room fully dressed.

'I heard you the first time,' Michele said as he placed his .38 weapon into his flight bag and threw it over his shoulder.

We'll see who's shadowing who, he thought.

'So, Beth. You wanted in. That time has arrived.'

'I guess I couldn't back out now even if I wanted to,' she said.

'Right,' he said. 'Come over here, Beth.' Michele handed her the binoculars and guided her to the man who had now become a target of his own.

'Recognise him?'

'You mean as a client?'

'Stop fooling around.'

Beth looked at him once again before shaking her head. 'No, never seen him before.'

'You're sure?'

'Positive.'

Beth stepped away from the window and handed Michele the binoculars. 'What next?'

'It's time for us to check out,' Michele said.

It was 7.50am when Beth stepped out of the hotel and stood on the sidewalk as she waved over a cab. She was fully aware that she had been targeted by her assailant, and she could sense that he was making his way toward her without even looking. Inside, she was nervous. Michele had come up with a plan to take the initiative, but like Beth was a testament to, the odds of something going wrong could go wrong when you least needed it to. The safety net she had become accustomed to in the time that she had been secluded inside the hotel walls, was now over.

Seconds felt like minutes as she waited for a cab to pull up alongside her, and when it did, she stepped forward and opened the passenger side door and climbed in. As she closed the door, she heard the back door open and then close, and the next thing she knew, she had a gun pointed at her head.

'Hello, princess,' the stranger said.

A nervous middle-aged cab driver of Hispanic origin glanced through the rear-view mirror and was then ordered to turn away and drive. Unable to understand his instruction, he held his gaze on the man who was sitting in the back of his cab with a gun pointed at his female passenger. 'Did I not make myself clear,' he said, turning the gun toward him. 'Drive!'

No one heard the back door of the cab open and then close. It all happened too quickly. Michele had taken the initiative with surreptitious movement, and the next thing Luca Rossi knew, he felt the barrel of a silencer pressed firmly against the right side of his temple.

'Don't you move or I'll blow your head off,' Michele said and reached over with his other hand and slowly took the gun from Luca, which he let go of without any resistance.

Michele turned his attention to the driver, who was now wide-eyed and trembling with fear. 'You heard the man, now drive.'

'No way,' he said in a state of panic, and opened the door and almost fell out onto the sidewalk as he clambered out of the cab.

'Beth,' Michele said. 'Can you…'

'I'm on it,' she said, and climbed over into the driver's seat and slammed the door shut.

'Let's go before someone calls the police,' Michele said.

Beth looked through the wing mirror and watched the cab driver as he drew attention to himself as he tripped and stumbled his way through the crowds of people. This had been his first pickup of the day—and his last.

'When you're ready,' Michele said calmly.

Beth put the car into gear and then slowly pulled away to join up with the mass of traffic on the busy streets of New York City. For now, locating them would be like attempting to find a needle in a haystack, however, once the hysterical cab driver reported his car stolen, made a statement regarding the hold-up, and gave the police his cab number, then the NYPD would be out in force searching the streets for them.

With the homicide of a renowned pimp and two as of yet unidentified men (despite the owner of the Chevrolet being identified as Franco De Blasi, forensics had yet to confirm that he had been the driver of the vehicle), the police remained vigilant. Still, for now, the Sicilian had obtained the upper hand, and it was his turn to send Benito Calabrese a message.

Samuel "The Knife" Johnson had been hired to locate Beth and then inform Luca Rossi as to her location. He was ordered not to approach her under any circumstances; instead, to ensure he reported to Luca, which would then enable the underboss to set his plans into motion. Samuel had watched the couple leave the hotel that day and had remained on a stakeout when Beth returned around an hour later. Her change in clothing had thrown him slightly, but there was no mistake that she was his girl.

Careful not to be noticed, he had remained at a safe distance, knowing that if she had spotted him, then it was game over, along with any chance of him being sworn into the Calabrese family as a valuable associate.

Samuel Johnson had a score to settle. It was because of Beth that his colleague and pimp had been murdered by the hands of the Sicilian. Furthermore, he was looking to make an impression on Benito Calabrese, which had the potential of seeing him catapulted from one form of organised crime to another. He had made a deal with Benito, that when Beth and Michele La Barbara were in his custody, the whore would be handed over to him for him to deal with personally. The craving for power gave him a new lease for life, and having displayed his loyalty to the underboss, he was ready to serve the family.

Of course, he hadn't just stumbled on their whereabouts. A friend of a friend had seen Beth standing with a guy outside of the Benjamin the same evening that his colleague had been killed on 46th Street. The guy had been sitting at the traffic lights when he spotted her but mentioned nothing about it until he heard the news of the incident and her alleged involvement.

But Samuel was happy to take the credit, and from being told where Beth had last been seen, he had taken it upon himself to confirm their location. And when he saw them come out of the hotel together the next day, he smiled to himself, knowing that his find would have its rewards. Initially enraged by the murder of his close friend, his allegiance had now moved on to a more powerful organisation, and from that point on, he mourned no more.

Having left Luca Rossi on 50th Street, Samuel was picked up by Tony Biágio on 46th Street and Broadway, who was accompanied by Tommy Byrne, the Irishman, whose huge frame sat wide in the back seat of the car. Samuel felt the Irishman's huge hand grab the right side of his shoulder, followed by a pat to confirm that all was well.

'Well done,' he said. Samuel turned nervously to see the Irishman smiling at him. 'The boss is one happy man.'

Samuel smiled, but for some reason, he could not explain, he felt uneasy.

'Where are we going?' he asked.

'To see the boss,' Tony said. 'Relax… everything's good.'

Samuel sighed a breath of relief. 'You got a cigarette?' he said to the driver.

'Sure,' Tony said, and reached inside his jacket pocket and handed Samuel the packet of cigarettes and lighter.

'Thanks,' he said.

'Prego,' Tony said.

Few words were spoken between the three men as they drove through the streets of New York in the early rush hour traffic. By the time they had arrived downtown, the driver pulled over at the back of a local butcher shop on Mulberry Street, and at which point a transparent bag was pulled over Samuel's head. As he fought and kicked out against the grip of the Irishman's hold, it was only a matter of time before he began to weaken, and finally, his weak, lanky frame gave up the fight for life.

Tony Biágio watched curiously as Samuel's body released a final gasp of breath, and then observed his head as it turned to face him, his eyes gazing at him, even in death.

'Come on,' the Irishman said. 'Let's get him inside and get this over with.'

'You choppin' or baggin'?' Tony asked casually.

'Hey, I want to be in and out of here real soon,' the Irishman said.

'Then I guess you're choppin'.'

Michele turned his attention to the man who had been on a stakeout that morning, Luca Rossi, and withdrew the sunglasses from his head.

'Sit back and relax,' Michele ordered, and then withdrew the barrel of the gun from his temple.

Luca's dark eyes gazed back at Michele as he sat back against the chair. First De Blasi and now him... he had felt the wind almost blown out of his sails. Franco De Blasi had certainly played ball with the Sicilian or he would have been dead a lot sooner. Even face-to-face with death, for Luca, to consider betraying the Calabrese family was unthinkable. Michele would have to kill him. You lived by the sword—you died by the sword, and that was where Luca came out.

There would be no compromise.

'Beth,' Michele said, 'drive carefully and keep an eye out for anybody who might be on our tail.'

'I hear you,' she said.

Michele turned to face Luca Rossi, who held his gaze with unflinching determination.

'You've been watching us,' Michele said.

Luca remained silent.

'I've been watching you,' Michele said mockingly.

'You don't know what you're involved in,' Luca said.

'Then this is your opportunity to enlighten me,' Michele said, pointing the gun at Luca. 'But you can start by telling me who you are?'

'My name is Luca Rossi,' he said proudly.

'Please to meet you, Luca.'

'Fuck you,' Luca said, and then looked straight ahead to avoid any further eye contact.

Beth glanced through the rear-view mirror and met Luca Rossi's eyes for a moment before returning her sights to the road ahead.

Michele sat forward in the seat as if he was contemplating what to say or do next, when suddenly, he sprung his elbow back, which caught Luca on the nose, and knocked him unconscious. Beth jumped, causing the cab to move erratically for a moment, before steadying the vehicle back on the road.

'Well, that's one sure way of getting him to talk,' she said sarcastically.

'Give him time,' Michele said, 'he'll talk.'

Chapter Twenty-Three

Beth made her way through the streets of New York City driving a stolen cab, holding a calmness that she had only just discovered. In the back seat were two Mafiosi, who were both out for blood. With few options of a safe haven coming to mind, Beth headed toward Riverside Park, where the riverbank stretched for a distance between 59th Street to 155th Street. This was risky, but right now, under the circumstances, it was the best she could offer and so followed her gut instinct to locate the most secluded spot where they could go undetected.

Trusting her intuition, Michele made no comment as to their whereabouts, instead, he observed the man at his side, who was slumped back against the back seat of the car like a rag doll. Luca Rossi had begun to show the odd sign of consciousness, so Michele pointed his gun in front of Luca's face, to ensure he had his undivided attention the instant he came round.

'Luca,' Michele called out to him.

Luca moaned slightly and his eyelids flickered to signify that he was finally coming round. Michele was fully aware that his captive might wake up without the slightest notion of where he was and why, which could result in him instinctively lashing out violently towards him. Of course, with a gun pointed at his head, Michele hoped that he would see otherwise, which might then force him to relax a little before being questioned.

Michele watched as Beth took out a small bottle of water from her bag to take a drink, and then called out to her to hand him the bottle. She did as requested, and watched curiously as Michele held the bottle over Luca's head and allowed the water to slowly trickle over his face, at least enough to encourage him to wake up. It had the desired effect; Luca squinted and grimaced as he turned his head from side to side, he was finally regaining consciousness.

Luca opened his eyes and then took a moment until he became aware of his surroundings. He looked at Michele, at first with a puzzled expression, however, memories of the foiled hijack came flooding back when he acknowledged the gun that was pointed only a short distance from his face.

'Here,' Michele said, 'take a drink,' and held the lip of the bottle at Luca's lips. Luca opened his mouth enough to take a drink, spilling some of the water down his chin as he did so. Slowly, Luca raised his hand and touched the bridge of his nose, grimacing with the pain, he returned his attention to the man at his side.

'Hurts?' Michele said.

'What do you want from me?' Luca asked.

'I'm glad you asked. Who sent you, Luca? And what were your orders?'

'I guess you didn't hear me the first time around,' he said defiantly. 'Fuck you.'

Michele met his gaze and nodded. He leaned forward yet again and then launched himself back against Luca, his elbow connecting with the bridge of his nose a second time around, which caused it to break with immediate impact. Beth cringed from the sound of the fracture and covered her hands over her face. When she finally released her hands from her face, she looked up once again to see Luca's body laid back against the seat, and he was snoring loudly as if in deep slumber. Holding her gaze through the mirror, she looked at Michele.

'What?' he said.

'I said he wouldn't talk,' she said sarcastically.

'Trust me, he'll talk.'

'Well, perhaps it would be a good idea to get him talkin' before you kill him, or more importantly before the cops arrive.'

Ten minutes later and Luca Rossi started to show the first signs of consciousness. He was dazed and his nose was now broken and bleeding freely. Michele handed him a handkerchief that he had discovered (among other things) when he searched his jacket pockets, which he took willingly and then held it carefully against his nose to prevent him bleeding any further.

Since his plan had been foiled, he had had little time to think about anything in particular, other than a feeling of embarrassment that he had allowed himself to be hoodwinked. His pride was hurting more than the beating he had taken, and if he managed to survive his current predicament, such negligence would not go unpunished. Despite having proved himself a valuable asset to the family, this one mistake would be enough to have him killed.

Still, he would remain loyal, nevertheless. He had been duped and his ego bruised, but he would never sell himself or the family out to anyone.

'Shoot me and get it over with,' Luca said. 'I ain't telling you shit.'

'In time, Luca,' Michele said. 'But I suggest you start talking before things get a hell of a lot worse.'

Still holding the handkerchief at his nose, Luca said, 'You're a dead man. They'll find you eventually, and that goes for the whore too.'

Michele nodded and then reached inside his jacket pocket and took out Luca's wallet. Luca looked nervously at Michele, who smiled before opening the black leather wallet to reveal a picture of his wife and two young children.

'You have a beautiful family, Luca Rossi. You're a lucky man. You must be very proud.'

'Leave them out of this,' Luca said.

'Just like you left my brother and his wife out of all this…? Start talking, Luca, or I swear you'll have their blood on your hands.'

Beth listened intently and felt a cold shiver run down her spine as she envisaged such a violent assault on an innocent family. The man she thought she knew: could he be capable of performing such a heinous act? Surely not. She prayed it wouldn't come to that, but she knew that Luca Rossi would have to start talking, which would mean betraying his so-called *family* in order to protect the ones he loved.

'You wouldn't,' Luca said, gazing at the photograph of his wife and two girls.

'Believe me, I will unless you tell me what I need to know. I have no conscience, Luca. I lost my faith in God a long time ago. You might love your family, but they are strangers to me. They have but one purpose for me, and that is to get what I want from you.

'Now, take a good look at that picture, because if you don't start talking, the next time you will see their faces will be on the other side… that is of course if there is a place for you there.'

Luca stared hard at Michele.

'I need a cigarette,' he said.

Michele took out two cigarettes from the packet and handed one to Luca, who took it eagerly with a shaking hand and placed it in his mouth. Michele held up his lighter and Luca inhaled deeply on the cigarette, holding the smoke in his lungs, before releasing it out through his mouth. Michele lit up a cigarette, took a deep draw and then handed it upfront to Beth, who lowered the driver's side window ever so slightly to gain some air.

Still dazed from the assault, Luca now faced the ominous task of interrogation, at the hands of the Sicilian. Since swearing his allegiance to the Calabrese family many years ago, this was the one and only time when his loyalty had been tested. His devotion to the family was unbounded. But his love toward his family was unconditional. Now, with the barrel of Michele's revolver only a matter of inches away from his face, time was running out for him in which to make a decision as to whether to talk to protect the ones he loved.

As for his own life—it was already over.

'So,' Michele said, 'are you ready to talk?'

Luca stared hard at Michele, with a look of defiance that said *fuck you*, but with eyes that said *anything, just don't harm my family*.

Sat in the driver's seat, Beth closed her eyes and winced, fearful of what was coming next. Having already suffered two brutal assaults, she considered that any further violence inflicted upon him would result in his death. As for the threat that Michele had made to Luca, Beth considered that he may have been bluffing. But the very notion that he had even suggested such a monstrous act, unnerved her.

Beth thought back to when they had left the hotel and the comedy of events that had led to the cab driver falling out of his vehicle and running away from the scene in a state of frenzy. It was obvious—at least to her—that he had gone straight to the police and had given them a full report of the hijacking incident, along with a description of the two men and woman involved. In addition, and more significantly, he would have given them his cab number, which would have elevated an immediate search for the vehicle.

It was only a matter of time before the NYPD would be hot on their trail.

Suddenly, the silence was interrupted when Luca's cell phone vibrated loudly from his inside jacket pocket. Beth observed both men through the rear-view mirror as they met each other's gaze.

'Answer it,' Michele said.

Luca reached inside his jacket pocket and pulled out his cell phone.

It was Benito Calabrese.

'Hey, Luca. Any news?'

Luca was looking down the barrel of a gun and simply at a loss for words.

'Can you hear me?'

'I hear you, boss.'

Michele held his hand out for Luca to pass him the phone. Luca did as he asked, and could hear his boss's voice becoming more animated.

'Luca's not speaking right now.'

Benito remained silent.

'I know you're there, Benito. But just so I know that I have your complete attention…'

Beth closed her eyes and turned away, holding her hands up to her ears. The gunshot from such a close distance had spread the top half of Luca's head against the rear window, where a shower of blood, remnants of skull and brain tissue blocked any possible view of looking inside or out.

'Now,' Michele said. 'Where were we?'

Benito held off from any immediate response as he considered what had just occurred. Luca was not the kind of guy to get caught out that way. He was an experienced assassin, with a methodical approach to any mission, he was one of Benito's most trusted and organised men.

Benito took a deep breath: 'You killed Luca?'

'Yes, but not before he talked.'

'Luca wouldn't tell you shit.'

'When a man is staring down the barrel of his gun while being shown a photograph of his wife and children, it doesn't take long to discover where their true loyalty lies.'

'You're bluffing,' Benito said.

'I gave him my word I wouldn't harm his family if he talked. He talked.'

'You mean he took the easy way out?'

'Depends,' Michele said.

'On what?'

'Whether I'm a man of my word.'

Michele ended the call leaving the Calabrese underboss to figure out his next move.

Having almost forgotten about his female companion, Michele caught sight of Beth, sitting forward with her hands up to her face. The sight of their dead passenger and the blood- and skull-stained rear window, had made her want to vomit.

'Time to go,' Michele said, as he put Luca's gun and cell phone into his jacket pocket.

'Sooner the better if you ask me,' she said. She grabbed her bag and then stepped out of the car.

Michele got out just as Beth was lighting up a cigarette.

'Let me know if this is getting too much for you, Beth.' He smiled.

Beth was leaning against the driver's side door and responded with only a look of contempt.

'Where are we going?' she asked. 'Assuming that is we're not arrested or killed in the meantime.'

Michele held up the picture of Luca's family and his driver's license that he had pulled out of his wallet. Providing the license wasn't a phoney, it would give him the address he was looking for.

'You're shitting me,' she said.

'No, I'm not shitting you. And the sooner we get to them, the better.'

'Why?'

'Because this will be Benito's next call.'

Michele tore the material from Luca's shirt and then twisted it to form a rag. Beth stood watching curiously as he made his way to the rear of the car. *That guy is strange*, she thought and shook her head, wondering how they had so far managed to evade the eyes of even one passer-by since they had parked up on the riverbank. The police would be hot on their trail by now, and given the nature of the crimes that had taken place in the last forty-eight hours, it was likely the FBI would now be heavily involved.

Michele slammed the boot closed and appeared holding a gasoline can. He handed Beth his bag and then she watched as he doused the back of the interior of the cab in gasoline and then slammed the door closed. He opened the fuel cap and then stuffed the rag inside and then pulled out his lighter.

Realising what was now taking place, Beth went into a state of panic. Holding both hands up against her ears, she ran away from the cab with no sense of direction as to where she was heading, screaming frantically as she waited for the explosion to take place.

Michele watched as his companion dropped his bag and then ran for cover screaming, and wondered with genuine curiosity, what had gotten into her. Returning his attention back to the job in hand, he flicked the wheel of the lighter and then carefully lit the end of the rag, before picking up his bag and then casually walking away from the vehicle.

When the explosion came, Beth immediately hit the ground covering her head, screaming and calling out names that Michele could neither make out nor understand. Warily, she looked up at the burning wreckage, and when a second explosion came throwing bits of debris into the air, she screamed out once again, while covering her ears and lying face down on the ground. When she finally decided it was safe enough for her to release her hands away from her ears, she looked up only to see Michele standing over her.

'Are you crazy!' she yelled out to him.

Michele looked down at her and then afforded himself a smile.

'What,' he said casually, 'you think we should have taken him with us?'

'You've got a warped sense of humour, Michele. Was blowing his brains out not enough for you?'

Michele waved his hand at her as if to dismiss her claim, and then took a look around to observe their surroundings. That was the first time that morning he had considered police intervention, and with an understanding that he was on foreign soil, he returned his attention to Beth and offered her his hand to help her to her feet.

'Come on, Beth,' he said calmly. 'It's time to go.'

Chapter Twenty-Four

Michele and Beth left behind the burning wreckage on Riverside Park and made their way toward their next destination, which given the address on Luca Rossi's driving license, was downtown in the West Village. Once a working-class Italian neighbourhood, West Village had become a more lucrative area, even home to many celebrities.

This was a risky move—and Michele knew it. Playing a game of bluff with the underboss of the Calabrese family had perhaps created another problem that had not previously existed. And while he had given Benito something to think about, he had opened another door that perhaps need not have been opened. The lives of Luca Rossi's wife and children.

But as far as Michele was concerned this was an opportunity to get to Benito Calabrese, and when one choice was all you had, then it was a risk worth taking. Benito was desperate to get to Michele, so much so, he had had his men scour every inch of the city while committing a number of vile atrocities.

Some of his victims had paid the price for their betrayal, while for others, like Samuel "The Knife" Johnson, they had served a purpose and had subsequently become an inconvenience. However, the death of Luca Rossi had only added to his deranged mental state, not because he had lost a valued member of his crew, but that Luca had fallen foul of the Sicilian, just as Franco De Blasi had before him.

The time had come for the underboss of the Calabrese family to send the Sicilian another message, and just like the last, it would involve the murder of innocent people. It was just a case of who would get there first.

As Michele and Beth made their way along West End Avenue, it was ironic that their next move would be to call a yellow cab over to take them to their next destination.

'Knowing our luck, we'll probably get the same driver,' she said.

'Very funny,' Michele said.

'Hardly. But if we should live through this, you owe me dinner, right?'

'Right,' Michele said, who was too busy looking around him to pay attention to Beth's needs.

'And let's allow the cab driver to do the drivin' this time around,' she said.

'Right,' Michele said.

Beth signalled over a yellow cab on 70th Street and Broadway, and the couple got into the back of the car ready to embark on yet another precarious part of their mission. Fortunately, there was a casualness about the driver that suggested he had heard nothing about the incident on 50th Street earlier that day, and if he had, then he wasn't showing it.

Still, Beth kept a watchful eye on the driver, just in case he did anything suspicious. Her experience at the hotel had made her more vigilant, and other than the man sitting at her side, she trusted no one.

Michele had been quiet since speaking to Benito Calabrese, and he remained deep in thought as the taxi began its journey through the busy streets of New York. He was making it up as he went along, but as he had discovered so often in the past with any given no-win scenario, there was always a way out. And in all cases, a way to exploit the situation.

'Why?' Beth asked.

'Why what?' Michele said.

'You said that we were going to Luca Rossi's home to save his family.'

'That's correct.'

'I don't understand.'

Michele looked at the cab driver—who was too busy listening to his favourite radio programme to be interested in the conversation of his passengers—before returning his attention to Beth. 'You will remember I told Benito that Luca had spoken up to avoid any vengeance on his family,' he said loud enough for her to hear.

'What about it,' she said.

'I have a strong feeling that Benito will now order his men to go to Luca Rossi's home and murder his family.'

'A feeling? You want to go to Luca Rossi's family home based on a hunch. And then what? Just ring the doorbell and introduce ourselves as the couple who murdered her husband and left their children fatherless.'

Michele remained silent as he continued to gaze out of the window, leaving Beth with a sense of guilt that she had been too outspoken on this occasion.

'I'm sorry,' Beth said. 'I shouldn't have said that.'

'Forget it. I've seen enough from Benito Calabrese to understand his depraved mentality. Even if he thinks I'm bluffing, he won't take the risk of allowing Luca's family to live just in case his wife talks to the police. It's only a matter of time before the police will call at her home, and who knows what she knows?'

'Okay,' Beth said, 'I get that. So why put that idea into Benito's head in the first place.'

'Because if I'm correct in what I have said so far, he will have already made the order for someone to go to the house to take care of Luca's wife and children.'

'Care being the operative word,' Beth said. 'You mean you actually want him to send somebody round to their home?'

'Indeed. This is an opportunity for us to turn things around in our favour, Beth.'

'How do you intend to do that?' she asked.

Michele turned to face her and just gazed into her eyes without saying another word.

'Oh shit,' Beth said. And not for the first time.

Alberto Calabrese was at his home, sitting and pondering over the words that his consigliere, Lorenzo Esposito, had spoken to him when they were dining at the Old Town Bar & Grill. Lorenzo had chosen his moment well before discussing his thoughts about the Capo's son, the underboss of the family.

There's something about his behaviour right now that unnerves me.

It's as if he'll do whatever it takes to get to him before you do.

As an advisor to the family, I am concerned that his unpredictability and his quest for control could bring us all down.

He had been reflecting on his advisor's comments since he had arrived home, which had afforded him the space to think things over without the intervention or thoughts of others. The more he considered Lorenzo's words, the more he acknowledged that he had been living in denial. Benito was indeed making this his own private war with the Sicilian—*but for what purpose?* he wondered.

Matters had spiralled out of control since Franco De Blasi had failed in his mission to bring the Sicilian directly to him from the airport. And now, despite his authority as the overall family boss, he wondered just how much of his son's dealings that he was unaware of? Murder was simply part of the *life*, and for the most part, it was accepted. But the lengths that Benito was willing to go to in order to obtain his objectives, were very different from his own.

He had become more arrogant and disrespectful of late—more so since the death of his brother, Amadeo. And as Alberto sat in his armchair, holding a glass of whisky, he considered how unpredictable he had become, but more so, *his quest for control* as Lorenzo had put it. That could ultimately bring the family down.

Alberto drank back the whisky and then picked up his cell phone. He then called his advisor, who answered the call almost immediately.

'Lorenzo. We need to talk.'

'Do you want me to call at your home?'

'Yes,' Alberto said. 'Immediately.'

'On my way.'

Alberto ended the call as sharply as he would any other. Conversations were for get-togethers, not for phone calls. He stood up and poured himself another whisky and looked up at the family portrait that hung proudly above the antique Italian white Carrara and grey marble fireplace. His grey-haired wife gazed back at him with those wide brown eyes that had captured his heart many, many years ago. She was smiling, as she always did when her family was around her.

A time when she knew they were all safe. Benito and Amadeo were sat in front of them, their eyes and smiles telling a different story. Alberto studied Benito's facial expression more now than he had ever done before. He had a look of a man that had other things on his mind.

Amadeo, on the other hand, held a smile that was genuine. Unlike his brother, Amadeo was able to step away from the *life* in order to embrace his family life when he needed to. That, among other things, was what made Amadeo so special and trustworthy in his father's eyes. And the more he looked at Benito, the more he saw a man with little compassion or love for his family.

Benito had been on the road to chaos for some time.

The time had now come to find out just how far he had gone.

Chapter Twenty-Five

Benito Calabrese had already considered his next move before the Sicilian had abruptly ended their telephone conversation. He had made an immediate judgement that Michele wasn't bluffing and that Luca, his most trusted associate, had put his family before his *own family* and had folded under interrogation. Just like Franco De Blasi, Luca Rossi had taken the oath never to betray the family. Therefore, everything in Luca's *other life*—his wife and children—came second.

More importantly, Benito was fully aware that the ageing Don would be less than humoured by this latest episode, and so decided that for now at least, it was something that was best swept under the carpet. Luca Rossi would have soon become a made man, which meant him having his own caporegime. This had already been agreed by the boss, who respected Luca for many reasons, but most of all because of his ability to earn money.

For now, Benito shrugged off any possible tirade from his father, knowing that he had more important business to attend to. Again, this was something that his father and consigliere did not need to be aware of. He called the Mancini brothers to inform them of their mission and arranged to meet them in a more unfamiliar location downtown in a bar called Gottino on Greenwich Avenue. The bar itself had only five tables and a long marble bar, but given its location, it was an ideal venue for the three men to discuss business.

Benito was already sitting at a table with a glass of beer when the Mancini brothers entered the bar. They looked nervous, probably because Gianni had sensed an anxiousness in his boss's voice when they had spoken on the phone less than a half-hour ago. He didn't ask if anything was wrong, but he knew all the same, and when they looked over at him sitting at the table, he looked more troubled than either one of them had ever seen him before.

'What you havin'?' Gianni asked his brother.

'Get me a bottle of cold beer,' Leonardo said. 'And make sure it's cold, bro,' and then he made his way over to the table to see his boss—the underboss of the Calabrese family—who had already stood up to greet him.

Leonardo could sense that his boss was anxious, irritable almost. The events that had unfolded since the Sicilian's arrival had now taken the family on an all-out war against one man on the streets of New York. While Alberto Calabrese had made every attempt to tighten his grip on his out-of-control son Benito, the underboss was damned if he was going to allow this one man to take the family down. Even in death, he cursed Franco De Blasi for having taken the family on a downward course that was now spiralling out of control.

The recent spate of murders had alerted law enforcement, who had already determined that the nature of the crimes were mob-related. The death of Luca Rossi would no doubt lead to further police involvement in the coming hours, which would inevitably create enough headlines to alert his father. The way he saw it, the only way he could escape Don's wrath would be to bring Michele La Barbara in and make him stand before him. All else would be forgiven.

Of that much he was certain. The ageing Capo had no intention of spending his final years—perhaps days—behind bars. It was his intention that when his time as the boss of the family came to an end, he would leave behind a legacy so strong, that the family would go on to succeed for many years to come.

Benito waited until Gianni joined them at the table, and after greeting him with a firm embrace, they sat down ready to begin the meeting.

'Luca Rossi's dead,' Benito said and looked at two faces of bewilderment.

The brothers then looked at one another, puzzled by what their boss had just said, and then turned back to face him, hoping against hope, that this was all just some sort of twisted joke. But the expression on their captain's face told them all they needed to know.

'Luca... dead?' Leonardo said disbelievingly.

Benito nodded solemnly, switching his gaze from brother to brother.

'What happened?' Gianni asked calmly.

Benito took a drink from the bottle and then shrugged, almost too casually for the brothers' liking. 'He got careless and paid the price.'

'The Sicilian?' Gianni said.

'Yes, the Sicilian,' Benito said with a hiss of contempt and then winced as if the name had left a bad taste in his mouth.

'How do you know?' Leonardo dared to ask.

'Luca had called me when he was outside of the hotel on 50th Street, just before he picked up the whore. I can only assume that his plans to capture them backfired and he ended up looking down the barrel of a gun rather than holding one.

'About an hour or so after I'd first called him, I made contact with him again for an update. This time the Sicilian answered the call and then the next thing I heard was gunfire.'

'Fuck,' Gianni said and slammed his bottle down on the table.

'It gets worse,' Benito said gravely.

'How can it get any fucking worse,' Gianni said bravely. He was animated, and Benito was quick to motion his hand as a sign to calm down.

'Luca coughed up about our operation…'

'Luca—no way,' Leonardo said, cutting off his boss.

'Believe it. Barbara had a gun at his head with one hand and a picture of his wife and family in the other. Face up to it, men, he broke the oath to save his family and now the Sicilian knows everything.'

Gianni sat back in his chair and took a drink from the bottle. 'So now what?' he said.

Benito stared firmly at both men. 'I'm glad you asked.'

'What,' Gianni said.

'You heard me,' Benito said.

'But why make the hit on his family,' Gianni whispered as he leaned over the table. 'What purpose will it serve?'

Benito looked at Gianni. 'First, we do it because I say so. Besides,' he said sitting back, 'there's no knowing how much information he's told his wife, and once she discovers her husband isn't coming back home ever again, she might think that we have betrayed him and then rat us all in. Are you getting the picture?'

'Luca wouldn't have told his wife shit,' Leonardo said.

'Perhaps,' Benito said. 'But I'm not going to take any chances.'

'There has to be another way,' Gianni said.

Benito shook his head. This was becoming tiresome. Having already given the order, he was now being questioned by his men over his reasoning for such a heinous crime. 'There is no other way. If there was, then I would have thought of it already.'

'But…' Leonardo said, pushing the boundaries of insult so much further than either one of the brothers had ever done before.

'No buts,' Benito said.

As he looked across the table at the two brothers, he waited patiently before proceeding any further, urging them, daring them to speak against him one more time.

'Now,' he said finally. 'I need you both to carry out this hit. Are you up to the task, or do you want me to find somebody who is?'

Nobody was given the option of turning down a hit. If you did, then someone would be putting a hit out on you. There simply wasn't an option. Gianni and Leonardo were feared mafia hitmen, yet there were many other associates within the family who were anxious to make a name for themselves. Soldiers, who had chosen the life and would kill at a moment's notice would make the hit without an ounce of hesitation.

But this was no ordinary hit.

And for the two brothers, the cold-blooded murder of a mother and her two children was a monstrous act. More unspeakably wicked than any other crime they had ever committed previously. This was not just any family; this was the family of one of their closest friends. They had been invited to the Rossi home on many occasions, and both men were godparents to their children, which in a perverted way, was what made Benito's decision all the more easier. Two familiar faces calling at the Rossi home would ensure that Luca's wife, Beatrice, would invite them inside without any sense of suspicion.

Leonardo had been more vocal than his brother but had been reduced to silence by his boss, who laid out a veiled threat if they were unable to proceed with their directive. Benito wasn't in the mood for any bullshit. Being questioned by Il Capo and consigliere was bad enough, but to be grilled by those beneath him was just unacceptable.

Still, Leonardo was convinced that there was more to this operation than met the eye. Benito was running the family behind his father's back, disregarding and disrespecting "The Boss", Alberto Calabrese, for his own gain. *What the hell is going on?* he wondered.

Gianni was holding a similar thought to that of his brother. Benito was only telling them what he wanted them to know. That much he understood. Whether they carried out his orders or not, he was fearful of what lay ahead. For once the Capo became aware of their operation, which would no doubt provoke further involvement from law enforcement, then it was likely that both he and Leonardo would end up getting whacked. As for Benito, he would have no qualms laying the blame at somebody else's feet in order to escape the wrath of his father, to which end Gianni concluded that they were being set up for insurance purposes.

'Okay,' Leonardo said.

Benito looked at Gianni in the hope of a similar response.

Gianni nodded and then after a drawn-out sigh, he said, 'Sure. Whatever you want, boss.'

'Bravo,' Benito said. 'And not a word to this to anyone—Capisce.'

'Understood,' Leonardo said.

Gianni didn't reply.

Both men remained silent and deep in their own personal thoughts as they made the short journey to Luca Rossi's home. For the first time in their lives, Gianni and Leonardo had a conscience and were now questioning their motives. The life they had chosen now had a sour taste to it, and while murder was often carried out by someone who you had known, perhaps even loved, for most of your life, it seemed inconceivable for either one of them that they would be the ones to commit this fiendish act of violence.

Luca's wife, Beatrice, was fully aware that her husband was part of a crew, and that his business dealings were less than that of a legitimate nature. However, having provided his family with a lucrative lifestyle, Beatrice was remiss to question any of her husband's activities, and so had learnt how to block out any pessimism that had any potential of turning her world upside down. Luca would never discuss business in front of his wife—and Beatrice would never ask. That was the deal. And with that arrangement in place, his wife would remain free from any lawful or unlawful retribution.

Or so they had thought.

Leonardo held both hands on the steering wheel as he focused on the road ahead, yet he could sense his brother's eyes gazing fixedly at him. 'What?' Leonardo snapped.

'You know damn well what. You and I know this is wrong, so why the hell are we going along with it?'

'What do you suggest we do, eh? Go against Benito's orders and save them instead?'

'It wouldn't be such a bad idea…'

Taking his eyes off the road, Leonardo stared at his brother. 'Are you out of your fucking mind? And then what? Meet the same fate as De Blasi.' Leonardo returned his sights on the route ahead and sighed. 'No, brother. I guess we'll just have to see this one through and then live with the consequences. Either that or end up being buried inside a suitcase.'

'I don't know whether I'll be able to do that,' Gianni said.

'You know the rules; we get the call and we carry out our orders. And if it were the other way round, Luca would do the same.'

'Don't do that,' Gianni said, while lighting up two cigarettes, he handed one to his brother, who grabbed it from him with urgency and took a deep drawn-out drag.

'Don't do what?'

'Turn this thing around in an attempt to make it sound self-righteous.'

'I wasn't doing anything of the kind. I'm simply saying that we have been given an order and we have to carry it out.'

'And what if you were given the order to take me out?' Gianni said. 'Then what?'

Leonardo stared at his brother. 'What kind of a question is that?'

'What would you do?'

'You're serious?'

'You bet I am.'

Leonardo turned away and shook his head. 'I can't believe you're asking me that. You know damn well I wouldn't carry out such an order.'

'Me neither,' Gianni said. 'But you know what would happen.'

'Sure I do.'

Gianni took a drag from the cigarette and blew smoke out of the open window. 'Benito must have lost his mind if he thinks he can get away with this one. I can handle cutting a stranger up and then dumping his body parts in a suitcase, but putting a gun to a child's head and pulling the trigger… but you know what else is on my mind right now?'

Leonardo glanced at his brother.

'What is it that Benito is so scared of? He thinks that Luca talked, right?'

'Right.'

'About what?'

Leonardo shook his head. 'Non lo so,' he said.

'Me neither,' Gianni said.

'Okay,' Leonardo said, cutting his brother off. 'Here's the plan. We'll ring the bell and behave as normal as possible until Beatrice invites us into her home.'

'Then what?'

'Then you tell her that you need to talk to her in private, at which point I'll offer to take the children up to their bedroom while you break the bad news. Once you've told her that her husband isn't coming home ever again, I'll wait for the screams. That's the moment when we make the hit.'

Gianni gazed at his brother in bewilderment. 'You're crazy.'

'So you keep saying.'

'God will never forgive us,' Gianni said.

Leonardo looked over at his brother. 'We lost that right many, many years ago, mio fratello.'

As the Ford Mustang came to a halt outside of the Rossi's family home, Leonardo turned off the engine and then looked at his brother, who was already busy screwing on the silencer to his revolver.

'Let's get this over with,' Leonardo said.

'Sure,' he said calmly. 'So we'll stick to your plan.'

'Thanks for reminding me.'

'I still don't like this,' Gianni said.

Leonardo made the sign of the cross and then opened the driver side door. 'Me neither,' he said.

Chapter Twenty-Six

Beatrice Rossi was in the kitchen of her suburban home, preparing dinner when the doorbell rang. She had called her husband three times that day; all three calls coming after his demise, and Michele had been forward-thinking enough not to answer any of them. Not that her husband's failure to answer either call troubled her in any way. She had called merely to check in with him, just to hear his voice and ask him what time he thought he might be home for dinner.

Nothing she hadn't done before, just as it wasn't unusual for Luca to call his wife from time to time, to check up on how the kids were doing, and to tell his wife how much he loved her. 'If I'm busy I won't answer,' he told her. And 'likewise,' she told him and then laughed. Beatrice had become accustomed to portraying the suburban housewife—and she loved it.

At a slender five feet five inches tall, brown shoulder-length hair, dark seductive brown eyes and a smooth dark complexion, Beatrice looked after her appearance at all times, even if she remained at home, dressing in her usual materialistic fashion. Dressed in a short white flowery dress and blue high-heeled shoes, she looked more like a woman who was ready to go out and spend a night on the town than one who was portraying a domesticated housewife. But that was the way she was and this was the life that she had become accustomed to.

It was 3.30 in the afternoon when the doorbell chimed for the second time that day. The children were upstairs playing, and when the doorbell rang again with two successive chimes, Beatrice put down the kitchen knife, took another drink of Rosé from the wine glass, and then made her way to the front door.

Her husband had reminded her to remain vigilant just in case they were ever visited by the Feds, who were poking around in the hope of finding something that would back up any of their suspicions. Rarely would they call around, and when they did, Luca was always out, leaving Beatrice to play the accommodating wife, who would welcome them into their home with a smile and allow them to search for whatever it was they hoped to find. Luca would laugh at the tales his wife would tell him. He was smart—and too smart for them, and much to their frustration, they knew it.

Beatrice opened the front door to the familiar, friendly faces of the Mancini brothers. She smiled and then greeted them, before welcoming them into her home, stating that their visit was unexpected yet welcome one. On the surface, everything seemed to be normal; their smiles and amiable small talk, designed to keep their *victim* calm until that fateful moment arrived. Now that the time had come for them to carry out their orders, they had forgotten the hysteria of the conversation they had endured for most of the journey to the Rossi home.

The fact that this was no courtesy call, or a family get together, had rendered both men sick to the core. But now that the moment had arrived and they had to step up and make the hit, they were as composed as always. Other than having the murder of a young family on their conscience for the remainder of their lives, this was a routine hit, and nothing could possibly go wrong.

The husband and father of two would not be coming home to save his family.

As Leonardo turned to close the front door behind him, he heard the distinct sound of a "thud", from a gunshot with a silencer attached, and then turned to see his brother's lifeless body slump to the floor.

Gianni had been murdered by Luca Rossi's gun, which was now in the hands of the most feared man in Sicily. It hadn't dawned on either man or their boss that their foe would have taken the same steps as they had, but with a much different motive.

To save the lives of the Rossi family.

Fortunately, he and Beth had arrived at the Rossi home first.

'Take your gun out of your pocket and then let it drop to the floor,' Michele said calmly.

Leonardo looked into Michele's piercing blue eyes and followed his instruction without displaying any form of resistance. He looked down at his brother's body and met his eyes, which glared back at him in an accusatory fashion.

'Good,' Michele said. 'Now, take a seat.'

Beth was upstairs with the two children and found herself entertained by a childhood she had never been fortunate enough to experience. Both children had warmed to her immediately. It was their mother's trust in a person that made it okay with them to allow them into their own space. Unaware that their future was determined by events that were unfolding beneath them, they were eager to show Beth their most treasured possessions.

At nine years old, Sofia Rossi was a replica of her mother in more ways than one. She had the same brown eyes and dark skin tone and was dressed in a similar aesthetically pleasing fashion. Her brother, Francesco, was a year younger and carried the look of his father.

Of course, those young innocent faces that looked at her with such glee were not yet aware that they would never set eyes upon their father ever again. She felt a pang of guilt knowing that she was responsible, to some degree, for the death of their father Luca Rossi but reminded herself very quickly that had they not foiled Luca's plans, then they would now be at the behest of the Calabrese family. As she continued to converse with the children and hang on to their every word, she accepted that her role and that of the man downstairs was to protect this family from certain death and then set them on the road to freedom.

Downstairs, Leonardo took his place on an armchair, maintaining eye contact with Michele as he did so. Michele turned to Beatrice and whispered something to her, and after responding with a whisper— 'Leonardo'—she made her way out of the living room ready to join her children upstairs in their bedroom.

Michele sat down on the arm of the sofa facing Leonardo, allowing his gun to lie across his lap in a non-threatening manner. He looked at Leonardo, who gazed back at him with an expression that neither spelt hate nor anger.

'Your brother,' Michele said. 'I can see the resemblance.'

Leonardo held his gaze at Michele, before turning to look at his brother's lifeless body that lay slumped across the living room floor only a few feet away from where he was sat. Gianni was still staring blankly at his brother, his eyes open wide and his facial expression was one of surprise, he had a bullet hole in the centre of his forehead. Blood had showered a portion of the living room wall, the beautifully ornate showroom coated in antique white, now dressed in crimson red. Blood seeped from the back of Gianni's head, slowly spreading across the solid wood flooring.

Leonardo forced himself away from his brother's gaze and turned to face his adversary.

'You'll get as much from me as you did from my brother,' he said. 'So, why don't you stop wasting our time and just get this over with.'

'Who are you protecting, Leonardo? Your boss, or your allegiance to the oath?'

'Is that the same shit you pulled with Franco De Blasi? Well, fuck you. I ain't no rat and I ain't telling you shit.' Having resigned himself to meet the same fate as his brother, Leonardo managed to smile smugly at Michele as if to indicate that he had reached a stalemate.

Michele sighed and then stood up from the arm of the sofa.

'Fine,' he said, 'have it your way,' and making his way swiftly toward Leonardo, he pressed the end of the silencer firmly against his forehead and then pulled the trigger. As a shower of blood and fragments of skull sprayed the wall behind him, his body slumped back against the armchair in a brutally rapid fashion.

Michele withdrew his sights from Leonardo's body and observed his surroundings that now resembled that of a slaughterhouse, after which he walked to the bottom of the stairs and then called out to Beth.

Having heard him call out to her, Beth left mother and children, yet promised to return soon enough. Beatrice nodded, while her children, who were oblivious to any danger within the safety of their home, continued to play together in their customary cheerful manner. For Beatrice, the news of her husband's death had not had time to sink in.

From the instant she had been informed of his demise she had had to continue to play the charming housewife and mother, to ensure that no harm came to her and her children. As she sat and watched them play without a care in the world, she only wished that they could be spared the horror of such news that would inevitably tear their world apart.

When Beth entered the living room, she looked around wide-eyed and aghast at what she saw. 'Shit,' she said. 'Michele, this isn't Sicily. You know it's only going to be a matter of time before the police find their way here, and then find themselves another step closer to finding us.'

'Wrong,' Michele said calmly. 'The police will only find themselves another step closer to bringing down the Calabrese family. It's up to us to make sure we get there first.'

Beth looked curiously at Michele.

'And how do we intend to do that?'

Beth did as Michele requested, and having rummaged through Leonardo's jacket pocket for his car keys, she drove his car from outside of the Rossi family home, and into the garage that was accessible from the kitchen. Once the car was parked up inside, Michele lowered the shutter to the ground to ensure any movement from within was concealed from any prying eyes.

'This is risky,' she said.

This was as anxious as Michele had seen Beth since they had met that night. Her concerns were noted, but as far as Michele was concerned, every move they made had a risk attached to it. Once the police discovered the burnt-out vehicle and the corpse of Luca Rossi, it would only be a matter of time before his body was identified, which would lead the investigation right at the Rossi family home and beyond.

Beth helped Michele to drag the Mancini brothers' bodies from the living room, through to the kitchen leading into the garage, and then into the back seat of the Ford Mustang. It proved to be hefty work for Beth, who had held their legs while her companion carried them by wrapping his arms around their mid-torsos. But it was the eyes of Gianni that gazed back at her, which freaked her out and made her wonder if she would suffer a similar fate before the day was out.

Both of these men had once been renowned professional assassins. They had been a force to be reckoned with when they had been on their own, but together, they had been unstoppable. Until now. They had simply been in the wrong place, at the wrong time.

And up against a formidable foe.

Once the bodies were sat upright in the back seat, Michele strapped them in by their seat belts, and then slammed both doors closed.

'Why do I get the feeling you've done this kind of thing before,' Beth said.

Michael took in what she had said and his expression was one of deep thought. 'No,' he said, 'not that I can remember.'

'But you have a plan, right? Or do we intend to take them for a drive around town?'

Michele looked at Beth.

'Please, tell me you're not serious,' she said.

Michele continued to look at her.

'Okay, you are serious. We'll never get away with it. And what about Luca's wife and children? What will happen to them now?'

'Until this is over, they need to get as far away from here as possible. Anything else?' Michele asked.

'Yes. I'm afraid,' she said despondently.

212

Michele reached out and raised her chin softly with his fingers, and Beth looked back at him almost ashamedly. 'It's okay to be afraid, Beth. Being afraid is what keeps us alive.'

'You...' she almost laughed. 'You afraid? Of what?'

'Many things,' he said. 'But I choose to face my greatest fears head-on. As for you, Beth... you are without doubt the bravest woman I have ever met.'

For the first time since they had met, Beth remained speechless.

Chapter Twenty-Seven

'Did you kill my husband?' she asked out of the blue and in almost a whisper.

With the dead bodies of the Mancini brothers sitting upright in the back seat of the black Mustang, Michele and Beth turned their attention to Beatrice Rossi, who had returned to the living room and was staring at the walls of blood in a trance-like state. Her day had been just like any other until the strangers had called. She had opened the door with a smile, and from that moment on, everything was about to change.

Her maternal instinct had made the decision to act quickly and decisively that day. The strangers had informed her that her own life and the lives of her children were in mortal danger if she failed to do as they said. She could mourn her husband later, but for now, she needed to be strong for her children if they were going to make it out of this alive.

Beth made coffee while the children remained upstairs in the bedroom, playing together in their own cosy environment, just as they had done so before the two strangers had entered their home only an hour before. Their bedroom was their sanctuary away from the fiendish acts of violence that had occurred in the room below them. They would never know how were lucky they were to be alive, and it was only by the grace of God that the *good guys* had called at their home minutes before the *bad guys* had arrived that they had survived.

Beth looked at Michele and wondered what story he was going to cook up in order to pacify the wife of a deceased Mafiosi. A guy who she hadn't seen or heard of before knocks on her door to tell her that her life is in danger, *and oh, by the way, I murdered your husband, but not to worry, I'm here to save you.* Beth knew there was more to it than that, but from a grieving widow who had just had her world torn apart, it seemed unlikely that there was anything he could say that would pacify her.

'Your husband asked me to protect his family,' he said softly. 'I have kept my end of the bargain, and now the time has come for you to take your children and go… far away from here. Do you understand?'

It wasn't clear whether she believed the man standing in front of her had been responsible for her husband's death, or whether she simply didn't have the nerve or emotional strength to question him any further. Beatrice knew that her husband lived a very different life outside of his suburban home. A life that had its risks. She understood that. And as much as she had tried to hide it to herself, she always knew deep inside that one day he would fail to return home.

That day had arrived.

'Do your parents live nearby?' Beth asked, her words waking Beatrice from her sleepy haze.

Beatrice shook her head. 'No. My parents live in Boston.'

'Then go and tell the children that they're going to Boston to see their grandparents, but quickly,' Michele said. 'We don't have much time. Others will come. Beth, go with her.

'And, Beth…'

Beth stopped and looked at him.

'Use the passageway. Keep the children out of here.'

Approximately twenty minutes later, Beatrice and her two children were sitting in their red Jeep Cherokee that was parked up on the drive, carrying only three cases packed with clothes, and several boxes and bags carrying their most treasured possessions. The drive to Boston would take no more than four hours, which would allow them to arrive at their destination by early evening. Any hopes of making a return to their home would depend largely on a number of factors, the main problem being the very threat to their lives.

With the discovery of the wreckage of the burnt-out car and an unidentified corpse, forensics and the pathology team would be given the grim task of making an identification. Given the condition of the body, they would have to depend on dental X-rays and dentures, or DNA analysis, as a possible means of identification. However, the charred remains of the body would most probably rule out DNA analysis, leaving only dental records, surgical implants, skeletal diseases, or information regarding personal injuries. Either way, it would take some time to make any precise ID, which would keep law enforcement or federal agents from the Rossi home, at least for the time being.

But all that aside, the house that Beatrice Rossi had once called her home, no longer held the warmth of love that she had become accustomed to. Her palace had become a crime zone, and as she glanced at her home for perhaps the final time, she would leave with only a final memory of the moment when two strangers had called at her door.

Everything was surreal to her right now, and she was finding it difficult to take everything in, and as she drove the car off the driveway of her family home, she reflected on the final words that Michele La Barbara had spoken to her: *If you value your own life and the life of your children, then tell no one where you are going and why.* Beatrice Rossi would need to remember those words for some time to come.

Beth got into the car and turned to look at the two dead bodies that were strapped and sitting upright in their seats. Once professional killers, the Mancini brothers' lifeless eyes gazed through the darkness, making Beth feel more fearful of them than she did when they were alive.

Ready to leave the Rossi household, Michele raised the shutters to allow Beth to drive the vehicle forward enough to clear the garage, and then he lowered them for the final time before climbing into the passenger side to join her.

'I can't believe we're doing this,' she said. 'Do you realise what will happen to us if we get caught?'

'I imagine it won't be good,' Michele said calmly.

'You have that right. They'll probably take us straight to the nearest mental asylum, lock us up and then throw away the key.'

'Relax, Beth,' he said. 'Just keep calm and everything will be okay.'

Beth took a deep breath and then slowly pulled the black Mustang off the driveway. 'Keep calm he says. Okay, I'm calm. But please tell me you have a plan?'

Michele lit up a cigarette, took a drag, and then handed it to Beth, who snatched it from his fingertips in a state of urgency.

'Yes, I have a plan.'

'Well? Since we're partners, do you think it would be a good idea to let me in on it? Or at least tell me where we're going?'

'In time, Beth. I don't want to make you any more nervous than you are right now,' he said smiling.

'I don't think it's possible to feel more nervous than I do now. Two dead passengers sitting in the back seat and a Mafioso alongside me riding shotgun.'

Beth handed the cigarette back to Michele and then caught sight of the two dead men through the rear-view mirror. For a moment she had a glimpse into whatever hell they were gazing into and was fearful that that place was waiting for her, too. The only thing between her and an eternal abyss of darkness was the man at her side.

'Hey,' she said. 'I just want you to know that you did a good thing back there.'

'I seem to remember you being there, too.'

'What do you think will happen to them now?'

Michele shrugged. 'Who knows? We did what we had to do, Beth. And now they're safe, for the time being at least.'

'So, do you want to at least give me an idea of where we're heading?'

'To meet Benito Calabrese.'

Driving through the streets of New York in broad daylight with two dead mobsters sitting in the back of the car was, even for Michele, a risky move. But, for what he had in mind, it was a risk worth taking and if successful, would present him with an opportunity that had so far eluded him since his arrival in the city.

Benito Calabrese was pulling out all the stops to find him. He wasn't out to kill him just yet. It would be up to his father, Alberto Calabrese, to decide his fate. As far as the boss of the family was concerned, he hadn't lured him away from his homeland over four and a half thousand miles away simply just to have him killed on the streets of New York. Had he have wanted to have him assassinated, then that would have been carried out in Sicily in a move that would have rid the family of each of its members one by one.

But the boss had decided that that was too easy, and would far from relieve him of the pain that he was enduring day in day out. No. He wanted the Sicilian *murderer* in front of him, and on his knees, and then he would make him accountable for the crime he had committed. He alone would seal his fate.

Alberto Calabrese had for some time outgrown the need for violence, using a more legitimate approach to business, he had ensured the family's survival when some of the other of the New York families had fallen foul to law enforcement and were either dead or in jail. He knew his son and underboss

Benito Calabrese ran illegitimate business dealings and had a tendency to place himself in the limelight too often, but he was a good earner, and after losing his other son, Amadeo, to a cold-blooded act of murder in Sicily, Benito had been the rock that had held the family together. Because of this, his father had been more tolerant toward him, understanding that during his darkest moments of mourning, his son had ensured that any business matters were taken care of.

The execution of the young woman and newlywed husband who were sitting tied to a chair facing each other had been the only murders he had committed in many years. He had pulled the trigger without an ounce of remorse, fuelling the fire inside him for the moment when he would have his son's killer in front of him.

But that *rock of the family* had become erratic and a danger to the future of the Calabrese empire. Having seemingly been betrayed by members of his crew, Benito had been compelled to revise his father's order.

Benito had now made this his own private war with the Sicilian.

Beth listened intently to Michele as he explained his rationale for driving two dead bodies through the city in broad daylight. There was a casualness about him that both infuriated her and calmed her, but also a belief that somehow everything would work out just as he planned it. As he continued to discuss his latest plan, she glanced from wing mirror to wing mirror for any sign of a police car or any other suspicious vehicle in pursuit, waiting for any moment when a siren would wail, followed by the familiar sight of blue flashing lights.

Despite her best efforts to avoid making any eye contact, Beth felt almost compelled to look at the two decomposing, wide-eyed corpses that just stared back at her through the darkness of their dingy world. It was then that she thought that it could have been her and Michele sitting in the back seat while the Mancini brothers sat up front, boasting of their exploits and how they would dispose of their bodies. But that hadn't been the case. And for the two brothers, they had now gone to a place deserving of the crimes they had committed on earth.

'You didn't think to close their eyes,' she muttered.

'They're dead, Beth. Only the living can hurt you.'

'Now I feel better,' she said sarcastically.

But in between her gripes of displeasure and her bouts of restlessness, she heard Michele's logic—outlandish ideals—but genius, nevertheless. In her own private thoughts, Beth considered that this was what movies were made of. Far-fetched scenarios that simply could not be anything other than fictional humour. Except this wasn't funny, and the storyline, never so real.

When Beth drove along Hester Street in Little Italy, Michele instructed her to pull over at the earliest opportunity. 'Downtown,' Franco De Blasi had said, so that was where they headed, on the lookout for a location that wasn't too crowded, but not a desolate wasteland either. The dark-tinted windows on the black Mustang obscured the two dead bodies sitting upright in the back seat, but they were visible nevertheless, and if it were not for the absurdity of the idea that one could drive around town with two corpses as passengers, then the drama would have been over in no time at all.

As it was they had been driving through the city unnoticed, and while Beth's heartbeat had reached a flutter, Michele was a steady as ever, composed, and focused on the job at hand. The deaths of three mobsters had allowed Michele to obtain further ammunition, along with their cell phones and ready cash. And when the moment arrived for them to pull over, he picked up Gianni's cell phone and looked up underboss Benito Calabrese.

Turning to face Beth, he refrained from making the call to Benito for just a moment longer—long enough to ensure that she was ready alongside him, just as she had been from the time they had met.

'Are you ready,' he said.

Beth looked at him and observed his calm demeanour, a composure that he was able to hold on to, no matter what the circumstances. She wondered how the hell they had managed to get this far without having been picked up, or even killed for that matter. But they were here nonetheless. Suddenly, the calmness that Michele portrayed settled her somewhat, and her mind rekindled images of the night when they had met. Only days ago, but for what they had gone through together since that time, she felt that their kinship had been for an eternity.

'Yes,' she said. 'Let's do it.'

Chapter Twenty-Eight

Benito Calabrese was at his family home in Gramercy Park, relaxing with his wife and three children when his cell phone rang. Benito portrayed the family man very much like Tony Soprano, revered by his *close* friends and family, regularly attending his neighbourhood church, Cadillac parked up on the driveway, and a vicious murderer… all the attributes to the fictional protagonist.

The only distinguishing features that separated him from the fictional character was that he was not seeking therapy—despite his sociopathic tendencies—and that he refused to get involved with other women unlike many of his crew and associates who most, with the exclusion of his father Alberto Calabrese, had mistresses.

Benito owned five restaurants in the city, which, despite the money obtained to set up each business had by way of drug money and racketeering, they were all legitimate and popular haunts for locals and tourists. The success of each business was merely a smokescreen, which allowed him to go about his illicit dealings and murderous campaigns, without suspicion from law enforcement. Besides, where murder and racketeering were concerned, there was always somebody else further down the chain of command who could and would take the fall.

Benito's wife, Marie, knew all too well who his father was, and what the Calabrese family represented; after all, she had fallen for her future husband many years ago, and the thrill of going out with a gangster gave her life meaning, and aroused her more than dissatisfied her. She was married to a hood and he had afforded her the life she had dreamed of. Their children attended private schools and money had presented each of them with the opportunity to enhance their careers in the future.

Marie didn't ask her husband about his illegal activities; instead, she would just pray to the Lord for her husband's safe return home after leaving their house each morning. Her husband lived a double life: a devout churchgoer and a loyal family man, and that of a cruel underboss, who took great pleasure in not only ordering the death of people but actually taking out the role of murder himself when he felt the need to do so.

Having discussed business with the Mancini brothers, Benito had had his driver Tony Biágio, drive him home. He had a meeting to attend later that evening with his father and consigliere, and so far he had nothing to offer the Capo in terms of any news of the Sicilian. Clearly, his father's patience was running out, which meant that Benito's position as underboss and potential successor as the overall boss of the Calabrese family, was looking more precarious than ever.

When Benito picked up his cell phone to answer the call, he got up from the sofa and went into the drawing room to speak in private.

'Hey, Gianni,' Benito said with an air of casualness about him. 'You guys took your time getting back to me, I was beginning to think you had bailed out.'

'You're becoming too predictable, Benito Calabrese,' Michele said. 'And your men are dying as a result of your incompetence.'

At the sound of the Sicilian's voice, Benito's passive behaviour quickly turned to anger. He didn't need or want to ask of the whereabouts of the Mancini brothers, as the voice on the other end of the phone was a testament to all he needed to know—Leonardo and Gianni were dead. For a moment, he was lost for words—too irate to speak and embarrassed that he was not in control of the situation.

'Benito,' Michele said. 'I want you to listen carefully to what I have to say.'

'I'm listening,' Benito said under heavy breathing.

'Now, you need to listen and then act fast if you want to avoid any police involvement. I have your friends, Leonardo and Gianni are here with me, sitting in the back seat of their car. They're unable to speak with you right now, or in the future to be more precise, however, allow me to fill you in on some important details.

'In less than two minutes from now, I'm going to end this conversation, and then place this cell phone in Gianni's inside jacket pocket. From that point, it will only be a matter of time before someone becomes aware of the bodies in the car and then calls the police, and if they get here before you do, it's game over. Once they discover the cell phone and the time and location of the last number called, I guess they'll have little trouble in connecting you to all the murders that have occurred recently around the city. And, probably, not to mention a few others, which will see you going to jail for a long time.

'So, it's your choice, Benito.'

'I think you underestimate me,' Benito said.

'I think you overestimate yourself,' Michele responded. 'The car is parked opposite a jewellery shop on Hester Street. The key is in the ignition… I'd get going if I were you.'

As promised, Michele ended the call, and then opened the passenger side door and stepped out onto the street. He opened the back door and leaned in, placing the phone in Gianni's inside jacket pocket.

'Come on, Beth,' he said. 'It's time to go.'

That afternoon, Tony Biágio received a call on his cell phone to say that he was going to be picked up within the hour and then taken to see the boss. The pickup would take place on Bond Street, Lower Manhattan, which was approximately a ten-minute walk away from his apartment in East Village. Strange, Tony had thought, that he had been called to see the boss, after all, he had only been in his company that day and besides, Benito would just instruct him to make the journey over himself.

'It's not Benito who wants to see you. It's the boss.'

The boss—*Il Capo!*

Alberto Calabrese.

Tony Biágio's Godfather.

The fact that he was Godson to the Capo would carry little weight if he was being convicted of a crime against the family.

But what crime had he committed?

Tony was too busy trying to figure it all out when the call ended abruptly. He had never been called to see the boss. Never. Something was wrong, which made him reflect on some of the actions he had taken over a number of weeks, ranging from his relationship with the underboss, the women he had slept with, which, depending on which woman you slept with could mean an awful lot of trouble, even death, to who he had been seen talking to, and what felonies he had committed.

He couldn't remember every action or crime he had carried out over a number of days, weeks or even months, but the list had been endless, but nothing that he could think of that would constitute a crime against the family.

The order for him to attend a meeting with the boss had unsettled him. He knew how it worked; he'd been in the life long enough to know that you could walk into one room and never come back out. *Friends*, who had known *you* all your life, would welcome *you* with smiles and warm embraces, giving *you* a false sense of security until the moment came when *they* would pull the trigger.

That was the *life*. That was how it worked.

Tony checked his watch; it was 3.15 in the afternoon, and he'd been told to be stood waiting on the corner of Bond Street between Lafayette Street and The Bowery at 3.50, and from there he would be taken to see the boss—Alberto Calabrese.

The fact that he had not been instructed to make the journey himself or even that he would be picked up outside his home signalled trouble. Tony had lost count of the times when he had been given the order to pick people up—some of them associates, others, members of their crew—and he would be the one who would take them to their final destination.

He reminded himself once again how some would walk in but never walk out.

Now, he was the one who would have to take a seat in the passenger side, and with a strong possibility that there would be somebody sitting in the back. He would know the driver—possibly both men—and the journey toward their destination would be an anxious one.

Tony strode back and forth in the living room of his apartment as he thought deeply about how he could possibly have displeased the Capo. Benito was pissed when he had got into the car that day. Tony had humoured him and had gotten away with it when many others would have paid the price for such mockery, no matter how jovial he had been. He was pissed off with the world right now, particularly his father and consigliere, who were the only two people on the planet who had the right to question him, and more so, make demands.

Tony put out one cigarette and then immediately lit up another. His head was in a spin, and with a final draw on the butt end of a cigarette, he checked his watch again, and then grabbed his jacket and, perhaps for the final time, left his apartment.

Tony Biágio left his apartment in East Village and made the ten-minute walk to the pickup point on the corner of Bond Street. This was a very different Tony Biágio who, for the first time that he could remember, felt an overwhelming sense of vulnerability. As he made his way toward the pickup point, he considered calling Benito, hopeful that he would be able to shed some light on the situation and allay his worst fears.

But something inside was telling him not to. His meeting with the Calabrese boss was nobody else's business, and making it so, could prove to be detrimental in a host of different ways.

No. Any contact with the outside world would be shut out completely from this point, and provided he "lived to tell the tale", he would ensure that whatever Alberto Calabrese wanted from him, would remain between them.

Having reached his location on Bond Street with almost five minutes to spare, Tony lit up a cigarette—his seventh since he had had the call—and inhaled deeply into his burning lungs. Smoking was detrimental to his health, he was aware of that, but nothing in comparison to living the life of organised crime, where the high life could turn into the low life in the space of a heartbeat.

As Tony Biágio contemplated his own existence, a black Cadillac XTS drove up to the side of the road. Realising his lift had arrived, Tony flicked the remainder of the cigarette away and then made his approach to the vehicle, but before he managed to open the passenger side door, the back door opened and out stepped Lorenzo Esposito, the family's consigliere, onto the sidewalk.

'Hello, Tony,' Lorenzo said smiling.

'Lorenzo,' Tony said looking shell-shocked.

'Hey, take a seat in the back, Tony.'

Tony stood and stared at the consigliere for an instant, confused and unnerved as to what was coming next.

'Hey, relax,' Lorenzo said placing his hand on his shoulder. 'Everything is going to be fine. Trust me.'

The consigliere took Tony's place in the passenger seat of the car, leaving Tony feeling less than relaxed but with no option other than to follow the order he had been given. Cautiously, he made his way to the rear of the car and then climbed inside, and once the back door was closed, the vehicle drove away from the sidewalk.

Instead of a barrel of a gun pressed against his head, Tony felt the firm grip of Alberto Calabrese's handshake.

'Hello, Tony. Good to see you. And thanks for dropping by at such short notice.'

Did I have any choice? Tony thought, but managed to cover his thoughts with a smile. 'It's good to see you too, Godfather,' he said, and for an instant, wondered whether he should have said it.

'Hmm,' Alberto smiled. 'Sit back and relax, Tony. And let's talk.'

For some strange reason that Tony could not explain, he felt that this was not the day when he was destined to meet his maker. The boss clearly had other ideas, and whatever he wanted from him, it was evident that murder was the furthest thing from his mind.

At least for today.

Relief maybe. But business was business and Alberto Calabrese had a job for his Godson to perform, and one that would ultimately test his strength of character and betrayal.

'I need you to do something for me, Tony,' he said.

'Of course,' Tony said, meeting his cold dark eyes for the first time since he had taken his place in the back seat of the car. 'Anything.'

Alberto smiled. 'Good. I knew I could count on you... didn't we say so, Lorenzo?'

'We did,' Lorenzo responded from the front of the vehicle.

Tony glanced forward and for the first time noticed the driver, whose eyes he met through the rear-view mirror. It was Niccolo Bianchi, a member of their crew, suave and sophisticated and a born gambler, but a good earner for the family. Tony often wondered how he carried such luck around with him, still, decided that his luck would only last so long, and when it came to an end, he would be in a whole lot of trouble.

Upon hearing Alberto's voice once again, he withdrew his gaze from the rear-view mirror and gave his boss his full attention.

'I know you're close to Benito,' Alberto said, and then waited for confirmation.

'Yes, I'd say we're pretty close,' Tony responded firmly.

Alberto looked at him. 'Good... very good in fact. When was the last time you saw him?'

Shit, Tony thought. *Is he testing me? Is he asking me a question he already has the answer to?*

'I saw him earlier today,' Tony said. 'After your meeting with him in the Old Town Bar & Grill.'

'How did he seem to you?'

'You know Benito…'

'No, I asked you, Tony. How did he seem to you? Was he calm or was he angry at all?' Alberto turned to look at him once again, this time holding his gaze with a calm intensity that suggested he would not ask the same question a second time around.

'He wasn't in a great mood, no,' he said.

'Did he say why?' Alberto asked sitting back once again.

'Yeah. He doesn't like being told what to do.'

Alberto smiled. 'He never did. Even as a child he would resist. Okay, Tony, I want you to keep close to him, keep track of his movements, and inform me when he makes his next move. Can you do that for me, Tony?'

'Sure,' Tony said.

'Good. Pullover at the nearest sidewalk,' Alberto ordered the driver.

When the vehicle eventually came to a stop, Lorenzo Esposito got out of the car and opened the back door to allow Tony to make his exit.

'Goodbye for now,' the ageing Don said, and the two men shook hands. 'And not a word of this to anyone.'

'Capisco.'

Tony climbed out of the car and was handed a card by the consigliere. 'Here's my number if and *when* you need to get in touch,' he said.

Tony nodded.

'Thanks for calling by,' he said, and then climbed into the back seat next to his boss. As the car drove away, Tony took out the packet of cigarettes from his jacket pocket, and with trembling hands, he lit one up and then walked away without the slightest notion of where he was or where he was heading to.

Of all the thoughts that had been going around in his head since he had received the call that day, nothing could have prepared him for what had come next. He had been ordered to betray the underboss of the family, Benito Calabrese, the man who had more or less raised him, and in many ways, was his right-hand man. Benito shot from the hip in front of Tony because he trusted him. He trusted him to keep his mouth shut and to be on call whenever he required his services, which was why his father had sought Tony out as the one man who could act as an informer.

A *RAT!*

That's what he had now become, and as he walked aimlessly through the streets of New York, he wondered whether death would have been a more preferable option.

As he took a final drag from the cigarette, he felt his cell phone vibrate inside his jacket pocket, so he grabbed it hastily before the call ended.

The caller was underboss Benito Calabrese.

His friend.

Chapter Twenty-Nine

Michele had played a masterstroke in terms of luring Benito Calabrese out of his cave, however, there was still no guarantee that he or one of his crew, would arrive at the scene before the police. After all, it would only be a matter of time before a curious passer-by would make the grim discovery, which would then spark off a chain of events that would spell disaster for the Calabrese family. Michele assumed that Benito would not be the one who would turn up to retrieve the vehicle parked up on Hester Street, instead, instructing one of his crew to take the risk, including any heat that might come with it.

'Your move,' he had said out loud when he had ended the call. He was taking out the mob single-handedly, working his way up the family tree, and closing in on his main target, Alberto Calabrese, who thus far, had remained virtually anonymous. Despite learning why the boss of the notorious New York crime family had lured him over to his domain, something still didn't sit well with him. His sixth sense was working overtime, sending him signals that things were far from how they had seemed.

Alberto Calabrese's son had murdered Mary.

Michele had avenged her death.

Now, the father was out to take revenge for his son's murder.

But the question that had been burning Michele's heart and mind since his wife's death, was still very much at the forefront of his mind.

Why?

Why kill Mary? It wasn't as if he had ever posed a threat to the New York crime family.

None of this made any sense. The only thing that Michele was certain of was that he would get to the bottom of it all before the day was out.

Beth had remained at Michele's side as she promised she would, yet her nerves were crumbling. The bravado that she had displayed back in the cosy environment of their hotel room was now a distant memory, and the violence that had followed since was perhaps more than she had bargained for. She had discovered that being "streetwise" and "street crazy" were two different things. But, despite her sporadic emotional antics, she had displayed much bravery and her loyalty to her companion was never in question.

Beth's life had been one that was full of uncertainty. Being used and abused as a child and onward through her teenage years and into adulthood, nothing had changed. She had survived on a day-to-day basis, making a living on the streets, sleeping with strangers and being owned by men who didn't care for her. The story of her life, she had thought, yet one that she had become accustomed to.

Until now.

Michele had shown no feeling toward her in terms of romance, however, he had treated her like a human being—an equal, and right now, his most trusted companion. Together they had "beat the odds", where many would have perished.

But their mission was far from over, and danger, very much ahead.

For Benito Calabrese, there was so much at stake, but right now, he was hurting, his ego, shattered. The Sicilian would be watching, waiting for him or one of his men to arrive at the scene to collect the Ford Mustang carrying his two dead friends. That much he understood. He had to act quickly but precisely to ensure that the course of events swung in his favour. Michele had called him predictable; the time had come to prove him wrong.

He was running out of men, but more significantly, time. Sure, he could round up many other soldiers who would be ready and able to pull the trigger without a moment's hesitation, but he was astute to realise that if his most trusted and ruthless assassins had been disarmed and taken out with such ease, then there was little hope for a number of "wannabe" assassins, who would have a bullet in their brains before they knew what was happening. There was no more time to lose; he could offer no more excuses to his father, Il Capo, who had more or less presented him with a final opportunity to bring him the Sicilian before his loyalty as his boss and love as his father finally ran out.

And then it came to him.

Benito picked up his cell phone and made two calls: the first to Tommy Byrne; and the second, to Tony Biágio.

Michele and Beth mingled in with the crowds in the Hester Street Fair in the Lower East Side of the New York City borough of Manhattan. From their viewpoint, they could see the black Mustang and were able to keep a watchful eye in the event that someone would turn up soon enough to retrieve the vehicle. Who that someone would be remained to be seen, but Michele was secure in the knowledge that whoever it was would arrive sooner rather than later. Once loyal members of the mob, the bodies of the Mancini brothers were now a liability to their former crew, and if discovered by a member of the public or law enforcement, then they had the ability—even in death—to bring the family down.

Their reputation as merciless killers meant nothing now. Earlier that day they had been ordered to carry out a hit on a mother and her two young children by their underboss, Benito Calabrese. Now, the underboss was met with a scenario he could not have previously envisaged. To get both men out of the picture with more urgency than he had displayed to put them in it. Any feeling of regret was only that their failure to accomplish their orders had compromised their boss, not to mention having handed the Sicilian the upper hand.

In the likelihood that one of the Calabrese crew or associates would arrive soon, Michele and Beth would need to act quickly. Beth followed Michele as he crossed the street and made his way toward a metallic blue Chevrolet Silverado that looked as if it had just been driven out of the showroom.

'Michele,' she said as she watched him step onto the sidewalk and make his way to the driver's side door. 'What are you doing?'

She looked around nervously, but by the time she turned back, Michele was already in the vehicle and had opened the passenger side door.

Beth looked around her again before making her way to the vehicle and climbing inside.

'Could you not have found something bigger?' she asked.

'Like what?'

'I was being sarcastic. How did you know it wasn't alarmed?'

'I didn't.' In an instant, Michele had pulled out the ignition and started the engine.

'You've done this before, right?' Beth asked.

'Many times.'

'What if the owner comes back?'

'With a bit of luck we should be gone by then,' he said calmly.

Beth sighed and turned her attention to the black Mustang parked up only a short distance away.

'I can't believe we did that, let alone, get away with it,' she said.

Maintaining his focus across the street, Michele said, 'Think of it this way, Beth. What are the chances of the police following a man who has a child in the back of his car?'

Beth shook her head. 'I don't follow?'

'A man walks into a bank, makes an armed robbery, and then casually leaves the scene and gets into his car with a child in the back seat, and then drives away.'

'Who would be crazy enough to do such a thing?'

Michele turned to face her.

'What a stupid question,' she said.

Michele laughed. 'No, Beth. I'm merely giving you an example of what lengths people will go to in order to get what they want. Someone with the courage to commit the impossible will more than likely get away with the crime.'

'You're crazy,' she said matter-of-factly.

'Well, that makes two of us.'

And just before Beth was about to say 'do you think anyone will show', a white Toyota Corolla pulled over in front of the Mustang, and a huge man of around six foot six inches of bulk climbed out of the passenger side. He slammed the door closed and then the car drove away as slowly and covertly as it had arrived. The man took a quick look around him, and then opened the door to the Ford Mustang and then climbed inside.

'Time to go,' Michele said.

Michele kept a short yet unsuspecting distance away from his target as it moved on to its destination. The black Mustang was four cars ahead of them and maintaining a respectable speed so as not to attract any unwanted attention from law enforcement.

'Did you see the size of that guy?' Beth said.

'I did.'

'Doesn't it bother you?'

'Should it?'

'I wonder,' Beth said, shaking her head, 'does anything at all frighten you?'

'Going to sleep at night,' Michele said.

Beth turned to look at him, she didn't ask why—she knew the answer.

The driver of the Ford Mustang then made his way along Canal Street, turned left, heading down Hudson Street, and then on to Bond Street.

'Do you think he knows he's being followed?' Beth asked.

'Of course,' Michele said, 'which is why we must make our next move with caution. Right now, the odds are even.'

When the black Mustang turned on to Hubert Street, it indicated right and then slowly pulled over to the side of the road. Michele pulled over at a safe distance away from their target and on the opposite side of the road, so they could observe any movement up ahead. Seconds later, the roller doors of a motor mechanics' garage, called **MIKE AND THE MECHANICS** (after the famous rock band), started to rise from the ground. The Mustang pulled into the middle of the road and then once the shutters were open, swung the car into the building, where the shutters were lowered to the ground once again.

'What now?' Beth asked.

'We wait,' Michele said.

With nothing but the sound of the engine purring away gently, Michele and Beth held their focus on the building where the vehicle had entered, watching intently for any movement without breaking the silence.

Suddenly, the roller doors began to rise again, but before reaching full height, the black Mustang drove out of the garage and on to Hubert Street, this time being driven by a different driver, accompanied by a passenger, and from what Michele could make out, devoid of any back-seat travellers.

Michele watched closely as the roller doors were lowered to the ground once again.

'What do you suppose happened to the bodies?' Beth asked, her voice dragging him away from his thoughts of what was going on inside the building.

'Either in the trunk of the car or being disposed of as we speak,' he responded.

'I had to ask.'

'This is where I make my move,' Michele said. He turned to face her. 'I need you to stay here, Beth.'

'What?'

'It's too dangerous for you to come with me. Here,' he said and handed Beth a .22 caliber handgun.

'I've never held a gun in my life,' she said as she sat studying the loaded weapon in her hand.

'You'll know what to do if you have to,' Michele said. 'And if it comes to it, don't hesitate to use it.' Michele handed her his bag from the back seat and then got out of the vehicle and tucked the .38 revolver into the front of his trousers. 'Keep the engine running and hold on to my bag in case you have to make a run for it.'

'Michele, they'll be waiting for you. There could be an army of them in there.'

'I know,' he said calmly. Too calmly for Beth's liking. 'But the way I see things, I don't have much choice. Besides, I have an appointment with Benito Calabrese and I don't want to disappoint him.'

Beth climbed over to the driver seat and took her place at the wheel. She looked at Michele with an expression that said *is this the last time I'm going to see you?*

'You promised me dinner,' was all she could say.

Michele said nothing, instead, he gave Beth a reassuring smile and then made his way across the road, and toward the building.

Despite the insanity of the situation, Beth still held on to her belief that she would see her companion again. Somehow, she could not imagine it any other way.

Chapter Thirty

With no visible ingress at the front of the garage, Michele walked down the side of the building until he came to a side entrance, which was, predictably, unlocked and evidence that whoever was inside was waiting for him.

Beth was right, this was crazy. He knew that already.

But he had a score to settle, and as far as he was concerned, that made him far more dangerous than any danger that was waiting for him inside.

Michele withdrew the .38 from his trousers and opened the door slowly ready to step inside. With his finger firmly on the trigger, he was ready to open fire if he had to. This was a calculated risk, but so had every move he had made since arriving on foreign soil.

He had made it this far.

There was no turning back now.

Michele scanned his surroundings through the faintest of light, searching for anything untoward. The building was dark and dank inside. Two cars stood aloft on their ramps and half a dozen cars on the ground. He made out what looked like a small office in the corner of the room, merged with stairs which led up to another level of the building. But it was the silence that was unnerving. A vision of being stood alone in a lifeless back alley at night, when suddenly the eyes of many wild cats would open one by one, ready to pounce on their prey.

Michele stepped forward and felt the blow to the right side of his jaw, which caused him to drop the gun to the floor. As he tried to regain his balance, the huge figure of Tommy Byrne stepped out from the darkness and kicked the .38 caliber weapon across the concrete floor and into the shadows.

Michele staggered slightly and then composed himself as he observed the ominous sight of Tommy Byrne rolling up his sleeves in preparation for the fight. At six foot six inches and weighing over twenty stone, he was a menacing figure and a force to be reckoned with.

The blow to his jaw had shaken his brain and had made his legs wobble.

'That's nothing to what you have comin',' the Irishman had warned him.

Michele had fought and beat bigger men than Tommy Byrne, but this was no ordinary man. He was as tough as they come. And if you didn't have enough bullets to take him out, then you were a dead man.

'Just you and me,' the Irishman taunted.

Michele took off his jacket and threw it to one side.

'Let's do it,' he said.

The Irishman had a grin on his face and an expression of surety. The man was a mountain of muscle and an intimidating spectacle, so much so, he had become used to having his opponents beaten before the fight had even started. Tommy gazed fixedly at his opponent who was at least a hundred pounds lighter than himself.

He was physically weak in comparison, at least that's what he thought. Which made him feel all the more confident knowing that he could allow his opponent to come at him with a barrage of shots that would merely render his victim exhausted before the fight had even begun.

'Let's see what you're like without a gun,' the Irishman goaded him. He was ready for the fight, and one that he had already convinced himself was not only a foregone conclusion but one that would be over as quickly as it started.

Michele prepared himself for the arduous task that lay ahead and wondered if he had ever come across a man of such stature in all his life, at least one whose physical makeup looked more animal-like than human. Never before had he been put off by a man's size or reputation, but in his own mind he knew that one wrong move and it could be his last. The Irishman was right, he hadn't fought a battle without a gun for some time. And despite his physical capabilities, this was the one occasion when he would have preferred—given the choice—to have pulled the trigger. He had murdered the pimp on 46th Street without even raising his heartbeat, but this was an entirely different spectacle.

'You killed my friends,' Tommy said.

'I did,' Michele responded unapologetically.

'Not this time around I'm afraid.'

'Let's see,' Michele said.

The Irishman smiled, but Michele sensed the first sign of apprehension. And while it was merely a hint of uncertainty about his adversary, Michele knew that he would have to be at his fighting best if he was to overcome the might of his gargantuan opponent.

The big man raised his hands and took the first step forward. Michele stepped to the right, and then to the left, displaying his agility against the slower movements of his heavier rival. The Irishman who had had his fair share of street fights, maintained his orthodox stance as a boxer, with his hands held up just below his chin, and his elbows tucked in to protect his torso. As he moved in closer toward Michele, he threw a left hook that was more of a wild swing than one of any technical prowess, and Michele leaned back on his right side as he watched the menacing sight of the Irishman's huge fist fly past him.

Tommy let out a smile and then closed in again, throwing another left hook, he followed with a right hook, but Michele had ducked and then danced out of the way. The big man grunted and then opened his hands and signalled the Sicilian to come forward for the fight.

Michele bluffed his step forward, and when Tommy led with a ranging right-hand punch, Michele ducked and then launched a right hand of his own to the Irishman's stomach, followed by a short left hook to his chin, which caused the big man to stagger back momentarily. Michele watched as he shook his head and then smiled, beckoning Michele to come forward for the next round. It would take many punches—and more significantly, in the right places—to wear this man down; however, Tommy believed that he only needed the one punch to put the Sicilian on his back, and from that point, he would make sure he didn't get back on his feet.

'Is that the best you have?' he taunted.

But no sooner had the words left his mouth and Michele had disappeared from his range of vision and hit him underneath the chin with a right uppercut, followed by a left hook to the temple, which sent the Irishman staggering almost six feet back. He shook his head again, however, this time Michele was landing a succession of punches to his body and head, and when he hit him with the palm of his hand in an upward strike at his nose, the big man's nose broke immediately, causing his eyes to water.

Now with the upper hand, Michele wasn't going to let him off the hook. The big man was not only fighting an impregnable opponent, he was struggling to breathe from the effects of a broken nose and a partial loss of sight. But with Michele in close, he had to endure further bombardment and wait for the opportunity to strike, and as he regained his second wind, he managed to grab

Michele around the torso with both arms, and then lift him from the ground. Instead of wasting his energy, Michele brought his head back and then launched forward and his brow landed firmly on the Irishman's nose. Despite the pain, Tommy hung on to the Sicilian and then threw his head forward in a frenzied attack, which caught Michele on the bridge of his nose, causing an agonising shrill to cascade throughout his entire body.

The Irishman hung on. Throwing his huge head forward again, he hit Michele in the same spot, and this time his brain hurt so much, he could see a double-blurred image of the man standing in front of him. When the Irishman landed a third successive head-butt in the same position, he released Michele and watched as his helpless body fell to the ground.

Tommy's shoulders expanded out wide as he walked away from Michele, circling him in a slow methodical walk, he now had time to regain his composure before finishing off the job he had started. He had underestimated the smaller man and had almost paid the price for his arrogance. But he had bided his time, and without having to land a succession of blows to the body—unlike those that had been inflicted on him—he had waited for his opportunity and had almost rendered the Sicilian unconscious.

Michele tried to pick himself up but fell back, almost rolling on the ground. He could see the menacing sight of the Irishman as he circled around him, and wondered if he would be afforded enough time in which to regain his strength and be able to get back to his feet. He heard laughter and some words were mumbled that he couldn't fully understand. And as Michele made another futile attempt to pick himself up from the ground, he sensed the Irishman moving toward him.

Tommy took a deep breath and then looked down at his beaten opponent. 'So,' he said, 'how the mighty Sicilian has fallen. Do you want to know something?' He didn't wait for an answer. 'I've struggled with bigger fry-ups.' He laughed.

'I bet you have,' Michele spluttered.

Michele looked up at him and then the next thing he saw was the Irishman's boot come at his face. When Michele fell back once again, he felt a kick to his ribs, then another, and then another, until he rolled over onto his side and started coughing up blood.

This is it, he thought. *So this is what the taste of death feels like.*

The moment that he realised that he was going to die. His body was numb from the neck down, and his brain had been shaken so badly that his vision was blurred and he couldn't focus. And that was when he thought of Beth. His newfound companion. The woman who had remained by his side.

He wouldn't get the chance to thank her, to tell her how proud he was of her. But there was more to his feelings than mere gratitude, but he was in denial, torn between love and loyalty for his dead wife, and a sense of affection for Beth. Now in the midst of death, he was thinking of a woman he had known only for a very short time and concerned about what would become of her after he had gasped his final breath.

Michele watched through distorted vision as the Irishman made his move toward him in yet another attack on his ailing body. Perhaps this would be the final assault. There was only so much he could take. And any attempt to get up from the ground in order to defend himself would prove futile. Michele held his arms out in a last-ditch attempt to prevent the oversized boot of the Irishman from making contact with his body.

The sound of a single gunshot echoed inside the walls of the building. And as Michele tried to make sense of it all, he turned his head and watched as the Irishman fell to his knees in front of him. As Tommy Byrne fought to catch his breath, two more gunshots were fired in succession, which brought his huge frame to the ground with a thud.

Standing behind him with arms outstretched and a gun in closed hands, was Beth.

'Michele,' she said.

As he made an arduous attempt to get up, Beth dropped the gun and went to aid him. She was crying, and despite the pain and near-death experience that Michele had endured, he managed to break half a smile.

'Hey, Beth,' he whispered.

'I'm here,' she said.

'I thought I told you to stay where you were.'

Beth laughed amongst the sniffles and tears.

'Is that all you can say?'

'Thank you,' he said.

Beth laughed as she wept.

'Can you stand up?' she asked.

'I'll try,' he said. 'But I might need your help.'

'So what else is new,' she said.

Now it was Michele's turn to laugh, but in the process, he coughed up more blood and held on to his aching ribs, each one felt as if they were broken.

With Beth's help, he slowly made his way to his feet.

'Good,' she said softly as if she was talking to a small child. 'Do you think you can make it out of here?'

Michele nodded and now—for the first time since they had met—it was Beth's turn to take the lead. Dazed and struggling to put one foot in front of the other, Michele failed to acknowledge the other body stepping out from the shadows, and before he was able to call out to Beth, she was in the grip of Benito Calabrese, with the barrel of his gun pressed firmly against her head.

Chapter Thirty-One

This was the moment the underboss had been waiting for. Standing only a short distance away from the Sicilian, Benito Calabrese held his left arm around Beth's shoulder, and his gun pressed against her right temple. Michele was unarmed and helpless to intervene; his vision was impaired and his chest felt like it had been crushed by the brute force of the Irishman, Tommy Byrne, who had kicked and stamped on his body with a succession of vicious blows.

Benito looked at Michele with an expression of amusement, happy to remain silent for a moment longer in order to observe this once feared entity, a man who was now beaten and broken. Michele La Barbara, already a legend by those who revered and feared him back in his homeland of Sicily, had beaten the odds and had outwitted and eliminated several members of the most feared Mafia family in New York City.

'Looks like this is the end of the road,' Benito said. 'For both of you.'

With his vision still compromised and his body ailing, Michele shuffled his feet in a pitiful attempt to keep himself from falling. If he was going to die at the hands of Benito Calabrese, he was sure in his own mind that he would not die on his knees.

And that would go for Beth too.

She held no fear, and even with a gun pressed against her head, she refused to show any weakness. Moments ago Beth had pulled the trigger for the first time in her life, and by doing so, she had saved Michele from certain death. However, her intervention had now put her in harm's way to a man who thrived on murder.

Benito had waited patiently in the shadows, waiting to strike at the most opportune moment. He had watched with interest as Beth entered the building, refraining from intervening, his perfidious trait had allowed her to gun down one of his own trusted associates. His fiendish exploit had presented him with not one prize, but two.

'Let her go,' Michele slurred.

Benito smiled and shook his head.

'I don't think so. After all, you're in this together—you and the whore—which means that you will die together. In each other's arms if you wish. Despite what some people may think, I do have some feelings,' he said sarcastically.

'Well,' Michele said, 'take me to your father so we can get this over with.'

'My father,' Benito muttered. He was smiling and shaking his head. 'All in good time.'

Benito pushed Beth forcefully toward Michele, who almost skidded across the floor before falling into his arms. She held on to him, feeling a sense of safety she could not explain, even in the face of death.

'You murdered my brother—my father's son.'

'Tell me something I don't know,' Michele said dryly.

That made Benito laugh.

'Funny you should mention it,' Benito said. 'I was just about to get to that. Besides, I wouldn't want you to die without getting to know the truth.'

Benito lowered the gun to his side but remained at a comfortable distance that would enable him to open fire if either of them decided to make a move.

'The assassination of your wife Mary,' Benito said. 'It was all a set-up.'

The pain Michele felt in his heart far outweighed any physical discomfort he was going through. The mention of her name from a senseless, lowlife hood and the meaningless need to take her from him had left him with a hole in his life. But he remained composed on the outside, ready to hear the truth, no matter how painful such words would prove to be.

'My brother Amadeo had nothing to do with the murder of your wife. In fact, he had no knowledge of your existence. It all started over two years ago when I discovered that your brother Luigi was doing business with associates of mine from Napoli.'

'What are you talking about?' Michele said.

'Your brother was dabbling in my business and making quite a profitable business of his own if the truth is known. It was at that time that my associates put me in touch with your Uncle Gianluca. Oh, he wasn't forthcoming at first, but it didn't take long to persuade him to listen.'

'What business?' Michele asked.

Benito smiled. 'Narcotics, what else,' he said smugly. 'From what I was informed, he was snorting and injecting himself with more stash than he was selling. That was bad for business in more ways than one.'

'Go on,' Michele said.

'So, I needed him out of the way.'

'So why not hire a hitman?'

Benito nodded. 'Funny you should ask. While I was having problems with my business dealings, I was suffering from a more direct problem back here in New York.'

'Your brother Amadeo,' Michele said.

Benito waved his gun in front of him. 'You catch on fast. Amadeo was very much the daddy's boy, and I knew it would only be a matter of time before he would succeed in the running of the family business. So, I devised a plan to get rid of my brother and your brother without bringing any attention to myself.

With Amadeo out of the way, it was simply left to my father to go about his revenge the way that any angry Capo would retaliate. With me at his side of course.' Benito laughed. 'The assassination of your wife was just the beginning… once Gianluca had informed you of who was behind the murder, then it was simply a matter of time. And I've got to say you didn't disappoint me.

'Gianluca wasn't aware that Luigi was being set up over the murder of your wife. No. that would have been too risky to let your uncle in on it. He was simply told what to say and what not to say, if you get my meaning.'

'You met up with Luigi?' Michele asked.

'Not directly. I had Luca Rossi make the trip to Sicily on my behalf.' Benito made the sign of the cross and then said, 'My apologies, my friend. I should never have doubted your loyalty. You took that to the grave with you.

'At the same time, Luca instructed your brother to keep out of our business activities, he also presented him with another glowing opportunity. To take over the Giordano Family.'

'You're crazy,' Michele said.

'Well, it seems that I knew your brother better than you did,' which caused Benito to smile some more. 'From what I understood, he was always a bit of a loose cannon, but with a daily supply of drugs inside him, he became more volatile, and believe it or not, ambitious. So, take out Mary and then let the Calabrese family do the rest. It was really that simple.

'After your wife was murdered we let the dust settle for a while, at least long enough for us to ensure that my brother was in Sicily getting ready for the biggest day of his life. He was an easy target for you, the distraught husband who was out for revenge. For me, Amadeo was a thorn in my side. *God's love*, is what his name stands for, and in my father's eyes, he was his true love, and his affection for my brother had stood out over the years.

'At a young age, Amadeo had managed to create more wealth for the family than anyone else had managed to achieve. Many of his business activities were legal, some not so legal, but he was a valuable asset to the family, and not just because he was my father's son. He was a caporegime, and even though I was underboss, there was always the possibility that he could succeed my father once he passed away.

'So, your uncle made you aware that he had discovered Mary's assassin, and that he was about to be married in Sicily. Perfect. My distraught father was now out for revenge for his son's killer, which then allowed us to take care of your brothers when the time was right. Except Luigi had his eyes on creating his own regime. He was just biding his time, waiting for the moment when he would seize the reins and then take control of the family.

'Any questions?' Benito said.

'You thought that Luca had coughed up which is why you couldn't take the risk of taking me to your father,' Michele said.

'You catch on fast. Killing you might gain my father's wrath, but with you out of the picture, I'm sure in time he'll forgive me. I'll simply inform him that I had no choice.

'Now, as they say,' he said raising his gun. 'Any last requests?'

***

Beth had been sitting behind the wheel of the Chevrolet Silverado, gazing fixedly at the building that Michele had entered. She had insisted that she went with him but to no avail. And having obeyed Michele's commands to sit and wait, she was now all the more nervous than she had been since they had left the hotel early that same morning.

Minutes had seemed like hours as she maintained her position.

Beth paused for an instant and then opened the door, before closing it again. She sat back in her seat and slammed both hands against the steering wheel.

'What's keeping you,' she said to herself, knowing full well that whatever the hell was going on inside the building would be far worse than she had allowed herself to imagine. Beth had been sat in a trance-like state, wondering how long she could sit and wait before making a move of her own when she heard a tap on the driver's side window that broke her from her deep reverie.

Beth turned to see Tony Biágio smiling back at her. The baby-faced assassin waved his gun at her, and then opened the door. 'I'll take that,' he said. Beth handed him the weapon without any resistance and then followed his lead as he waved his gun for her to step out of the car.

Whatever had been going through Beth's mind as she stepped out onto the street would never have prepared her for what was to come next.

Tony Biágio leaned in the car and picked up Michele's bag and then pointed his gun at Beth and told her to move. Beth observed that customary smile of a man, which usually came before a beating or something much worse. She feared that what was to come would be much worse than what she had ever experienced before, and wondered if she would meet the same fate as her friend Kimberley. Beth glanced at the prominent scar that ran down the left side of Tony's face and wondered what he had done to deserve it. More so, what had happened to the poor soul who had dared to inflict harm on him?

'Move,' he said again and nudged her with the barrel of his gun.

Beth crossed the road and proceeded to walk toward a black Cadillac XTS that was parked up adjacent to where she had been sitting. She approached the vehicle with caution, however, mindful that whatever was waiting for her inside would ensure that she would never see daylight again.

Tony Biágio opened the passenger door and then told Beth to get in. She did as she was told and after he closed the door, she watched as he made his way round to the driver's side of the vehicle.

'Hello, Beth,' came the voice from behind her. 'So good of you to join us.'

Beth remained still as Tony got into the car, waiting for that moment when she would feel the barrel of the gun pressed against the back of her head. The signal that the game was finally over.

'You were waiting for someone?'

'Yes,' Beth said cautiously.

'Michele La Barbara?'

Beth nodded.

The man leaned forward toward her, and Beth felt a chill come over her which she supposed had come from the *other side*.

'My name is Alberto Calabrese. Does that name mean anything to you?'

Beth nodded. 'Yes,' she said in almost a whisper.

'Good,' he said. 'Today is your lucky day, Beth. I'm about to cut you a deal.'

Beth caught the eyes of the old man gazing at her through the rear-view mirror, and for a moment, had felt the devil looking back at her. *Cut you a deal*, meant only one thing.

Betray Michele.

No way!

'So this is what I would like you to do, Beth. I want you to follow Michele into the building and remain at his side.'

'What?' she said.

'That's right. Lorenzo,' he said as he sat back.

The consigliere took his captain's place and leaned forward toward Beth holding a wire. He unbuttoned Beth's blouse and then taped the wire above her bra on her left breast. Beth refrained from any resistance to his touch. It wasn't the first time that a man had unbuttoned her blouse without her permission, however, the family advisor had made no attempt to take advantage of her, nor had he any intention of doing so. Checking it was firmly in place, he buttoned up her blouse just enough to conceal the wire.

'There,' he said as he sat back in his seat. 'We're all set.'

'What's all this about?' Beth asked.

'It's really simple, Beth. We want you to go inside the building and wait.'

'Wait for what?' she asked.

'Until we tell you differently.'

The old man leaned forward again. 'What role you play now will determine how the rest of your life unfolds. Unfortunately, I can't promise you that the same goes for the man you are out to protect, however, I'm willing to wait a little longer before I cast judgement.

'It's in your hands, Beth,' he said. He patted her shoulder and then sat back in his seat. 'Tony.'

Tony Biágio got out of the car and made his way round to the passenger side door and opened it. 'Get out,' he said to Beth, who looked up at him with wondering eyes.

When Beth stepped out onto the sidewalk, Tony handed her the bag, along with the .22 caliber handgun. Beth looked at the gun in her hand and met Tony's eyes and the smile that followed. He was pointing his gun only inches away from her stomach, and ready to take her out if he so much figured that she had some crazy thought of retaliation.

She didn't.

And for some reason that she could not explain at the time, she decided that the best, perhaps the only course of action, was to follow through with the instructions she had been given. Whatever the hell that plan was supposed to be. But one that she hoped would not only save her own life but the life of the man she had fallen in love with.

Alberto lowered the rear passenger side window and looked up at Beth.

'Stick to the plan, Beth.'

Beth met his eyes and then turned her attention toward the building that Michele had walked into but had so far failed to walk out from.

She was oblivious to the life that was slowly fading away from her.

The man from Sicily needed her help now more than ever.

Chapter Thirty-Two

Beth had barely time to consider when or if at all the cavalry were going to show up when the sound of the roller door rising slowly from the ground distracted Benito from carrying out his merciless act. As the daylight poured into the building, the black Cadillac eased its way inside, and after coming to a halt, Tony Biágio stepped out and made his way around the vehicle and opened the rear passenger door. He then made his way over to the entrance of the building and pressed the button that would send the roller doors back to ground level. As the light faded yet again, two men climbed out from the vehicle and then stepped forward.

'What the…' Benito said.

'Drop the gun, Benito.' Tony Biágio—his friend—was pointing his gun at him.

Benito glanced at the three men, and then turned his attention back to Tony, now pointing his gun at him.

'You set me up?' Benito said.

'You set yourself up, Benito,' Tony returned.

'Father,' Benito said. 'It seems that you have arrived here just on time.'

Alberto raised his hand and then stepped forward, making his way slowly toward Michele, the two men gazing fixedly at one another through the dim light. Alberto Calabrese had waited for this moment for so long—to stand face to face with the man who had murdered his son. Both men held their gaze without uttering a word and then the Capo turned his attention to Beth, who looked back at him with more courage and trust than she had done so only a short time ago. Alberto raised his hands and opened her blouse enough only to release the wire that had been taped to her upper left breast.

Michele's eyes moved from Beth to Alberto, and then the three of them turned to face Benito.

Alberto Calabrese had wanted the man who had murdered his son for so long it seemed; he had hardly thought of anything else. He had been instrumental in luring the Sicilian away from his homeland to make a journey of over four and half thousand miles. *Or so he was led to believe*. He had heard every word, every confession, from his cold-hearted son, whose goal all along had been to take his position as the overall boss of the Calabrese family. The first step to take out the one threat to his future position of Il Capo, his own brother, Amadeo.

'Father?' he said in a surprised, unsettled tone. 'What's going on? How did you—'

'Save it, Benito. We have just heard your confession,' Lorenzo piped up. 'We've been suspicious of your activities for some time, so much so, we decided to check things out for ourselves.'

He could sense both hatred and bewilderment from those eyes that gazed back at him.

'The wire,' Lorenzo said and then smiled. 'Call it a favour from someone in law enforcement who owes me a favour.' Lorenzo winked, but Benito had failed to see it.

'Tony,' Benito said, now pointing his gun at him. 'You turned me in?'

Tony Biágio remained silent. He had had no choice and his decision to betray his boss and closest friend was something that he would have to live with.

Alberto raised his hand to signal he'd heard enough.

'If I had not have heard the words from your own lips I would never have believed it,' Alberto said. 'How could you order the death of your own brother?'

But it wasn't a question that demanded an answer—but it was a significant moment for Alberto Calabrese, who had on this night lost another son.

The ageing boss pulled a gun from his coat pocket and pointed it at Benito. His son.

'You would kill your own son, your own flesh and blood?' Benito said.

'You're not my son,' he said, and without further warning or hesitation, Alberto Calabrese pulled the trigger, and as the bullet entered the centre of his son's forehead, he watched as his facial expression released itself of all anger and hatred before his body fell to the ground.

Alberto Calabrese stepped forward and looked down at his son's body, his eyes open and glaring back at him in wonderment. 'God forgive me,' he said quietly. The first time he had ever asked for forgiveness. Slowly, he knelt down and closed his son's eyelids, wishing for a single moment that it had been him who was lying there.

Finally, the ageing Don stood up straight and turned to face Michele La Barbara, the man who he had wanted in front of him for so long. Maintaining eye contact, he stepped away from his son's dead body and made his way toward the Sicilian until he was standing before him.

'When I discovered you were the man who murdered my son, I wanted you dead. No,' he closed his eyes and shook his head, 'more than that… I wanted you to feel the pain that I have had to endure each day and night since my boy was killed.

'But now, I understand that you too have been grieving over the death of your wife and unborn child. We are but two victims who have been brought together by the same tragedy that has befallen us.'

Michele nodded.

'I'm sorry for your loss too,' Michele said, and the boss of the Calabrese family, who could see the truth or lies in a man's eyes, looked at Michele and understood that he was gazing into the eyes of an honourable man. 'Now, I must return home and bury the dead, just as I vowed to do so.'

Alberto looked at Michele and then sighed. 'I've lost count of the times that I've actually pulled the trigger or the many lives that I have taken over the years. But never would I have ever imagined that I would point a gun at my own son. We've known for some time that Benito was out of control. His quest for power was becoming a concern to us, but never did it enter my mind that he was behind the murder of Amadeo. His wicked acts of betrayal have finally brought the family down.'

Michele and Beth looked at one another and then Michele turned to face Don Calabrese, who had now extended his hand in friendship. Having waited patiently for the moment when he would have Michele La Barbara in front of him—kneeling before him—now, he felt only remorse for a once-formidable enemy.

Michele took Alberto's hand firmly, and as the two men gazed at each other, they shook hands, the animosity toward one another was now over.

For Michele, it was now time to go home.

Michele had taken Beth from a life that she would never return to. A world that now had no meaning to her, other than the revulsion of being subject to sex and slavery. But she could never go back. Not after the journey, she had experienced with Michele. And nor would she want to. But where would she go from here? She had no family, her friend—her best friend was dead, so the only family she had come to know were those who maintained their grip of fear on her, and who had stalked her in the hope for her return.

She had no one. Except for the one man she had sworn her allegiance to. A stranger, who had become her closest and dearest companion for the short time that they had been together. A loyal man, who was in love with only one woman—his dead wife. There could be no other woman in Michele's life, that much she was certain of. And it wasn't until this moment in her life that she now understood what love meant.

The word *love* had never had any meaning—not for family, friends, or lovers. But fate had determined that she would meet the one man who would turn her life inside out, for all the right reasons. She would be tested—that was how the universe worked. Nothing comes easy, not even love, but she had come to realise that they had crossed paths that night for a reason. However, one question remained?

How did Michele feel about her?

She could only wonder.

While Michele was still an unknown entity with law enforcement in New York City, he was still cautious about making it to the airport without being apprehended by airport security or the police. The fight with the Irishman had left him worse for wear, and while he wanted to get on the next flight home, right now, he just wanted to rest and sleep.

He had been one kick away from fighting for his life.

He had arrived with only his personal belongings in a bag, and that was how he would return home, except for the ammunition and cell phones he had obtained during his mission. They would be handed over to Alberto Calabrese, and the bodies, disposed of without so much of a trace. The days ahead would unravel more clues as to mob-related murders, but there would be nothing to link the Il Capo to any of the crimes, even a witness statement from Beatrice Rossi would fall on deaf ears if the matter resurfaced.

Having agreed that Michele would stay overnight in a hotel and get some rest, consigliere Lorenzo Esposito, acknowledged that he would take care of the flight details, tickets, and a personal lift to the airport, and would guarantee his anonymity over the Sicilian's remaining hours in the city.

The light had almost faded as the men prepared themselves to leave the building, the old man offering to drive the couple to a hotel where they would go undetected.

Michele glanced at Beth, her forlorn figure left only to wonder how her world would transpire after her companion left the city, never to return.

'What about Beth,' he said.

'What about her?' Lorenzo said curiously.

'Can you arrange for her to come with me?'

The consigliere looked at his boss and then nodded. 'Sure,' he said, 'I can get her a phoney passport and a flight back to Italy with you… if that's what you want?'

Michele turned his attention back to Beth, whose facial features were now obscured in the dimming light.

'Would you like to come with me, Beth? It will be a new start—for both of us.'

Beth held back the tears as she faced Michele. 'Yes,' she said. 'If you'll have me.'

A smile surfaced across Michele's beaten face. 'Sure,' he said. 'Why not.'

'What will become of you now?' Alberto asked.

Michele took a deep sigh. 'A new life perhaps, a new beginning. And you?'

The Capo looked at his consigliere, who he could see was just as curious as to his response. 'Retirement. It's been a long time coming. I started this family many years ago… I guess the time has come for me to close the door and to leave this life behind.

'What do you think, consigliere?'

Lorenzo looked at both men and smiled. 'Retirement sounds good,' he said approvingly.

251

Chapter Thirty-Three

Life had taken a most bizarre and unexpected turn for Beth, who had gone from a common whore on the streets of New York City, onward to a new life on different shores. From the time that Michele had requested for her to accompany him back to his homeland of Sicily, he had neither expressed why he had made such a gesture nor stated how he felt about her.

Did he have feelings for her, she wondered? Or was this just companionship? Having heard the harrowing story of how his wife Mary and unborn child had been murdered at the hands of his own brother, Beth wondered how he would now cope, both mentally and emotionally.

Michele had spoken little since they had stayed overnight at the hotel, and had remained reticent about the vile chain of events that had seen his entire life rocked from its very foundation. It had been hard enough to accept that Mary was gone from his life but to discover the true identity of her assassin, had only added to his burden. Luigi, his younger brother, who he had raised to become one of the most feared mobsters of La Cosa Nostra. His thirst for power was ego-driven; the madness that followed had been through an endless supply of drugs, all part of the grand design to which would inevitably lead to ruin.

And now Michele had to return home to bury his brother, just as he had vowed to do so. And as for the life—the only life he had ever known—it was over.

The flight home enabled Michele to digest what had happened since the morning of that fateful phone call, and despite the deception and acts of violence that had torn his family apart, he no longer felt alone. Beth had changed all that. Their meeting was destined somewhat, and his decision to request her to come back with him to Sicily, was not out of pity or feeling that he had a duty of responsibility. On the contrary, Beth had drawn him close to her in ways he could never have imagined.

Beth had lived most of her young adult life as a prostitute, whereas Michele La Barbara, was the boss of the most powerful Mafia family in Sicily. But no more; as far as Michele was concerned, the life he had lived for so long as he could remember was now in the past. There were of course matters of importance that required his immediate attention when he made his return to the island, and then afterwards, it was the beginning of the rest of his life.

As Beth sat gazing out of the passenger window at the thick blanket of clouds below, she felt the warmth and safety of Michele's hand as he placed it on top of her own. She turned to look at him and smiled, reassured to some extent at least, that her journey to foreign shores would bring them even closer together.

After all, Beth hadn't come along for the ride… throughout her young life, she had succumbed to one door opening and then another one slamming shut in her face. In essence, there had been few surprises. She had accepted Michele's offer to accompany him because she wanted to—not because she needed to.

As she looked down at his huge bulk of a hand, she felt only warmth and a gentleness that somehow she had always known existed. Then, as if compelled to do so, she was drawn to his eyes—those eyes of his that either penetrated a person's soul or portrayed something more endearing. Now, as she searched his mind for answers, she felt sadness, warmth, and love.

Palermo, Sicily

Having arrived back in Palermo, Michele and Beth made the short journey to La Kalsa, and to the home of Rosa Rossi. After a warm embrace (and a dressing down from the old lady because of his facial bruising and inability to withstand a firm hug from one as elderly and frail as she), Michele introduced Beth to Rosa and Lupo, who kept close by the old lady, as if making a statement that she was his new owner and he was here to stay.

Rosa made Beth feel welcome, and it was here she would stay until Michele had sorted out unfinished business. Her safety was paramount. And with the old lady living in almost obscurity from the world of organised crime, and now with her trusted guard dog at her side, this was for Beth, the safest haven on the island.

'You'll be safe here. Beth.'

'And what about you?' she said.

'I'll be back soon enough. I promise,' he said.

With the old lady allowing the couple to have a moment of privacy, Beth took the opportunity to speak up about the one thing that was at the forefront of her mind.

'There's something I need to say to you before you go…'

'It can wait,' Michele said abruptly, cutting her off just in time. 'I have to go, and then when I return'—he allowed himself the merest suggestion of a smile—'we'll talk.'

As the couple embraced, Michele caught sight of Rosa, who was looking at them from the kitchen, smiling, and full of new hope.

Roberto Del Panucci was sitting at his desk when Michele entered his office. Having been instructed to allow his brother, Luigi, to remain on the premises until his return, he had carried out his list of demands to the letter.

Upon Michele's departure, the undertaker had been aware that the beaten, disfigured corpse of the man once called "The Fiend", would deteriorate in little time if not attended to. And despite the skills that he had adopted since he had opened his practice, there was only so much he could do to the body that would permit him to resemble the brother that Michele once knew.

'Don Michele,' he said.

Michele nodded. 'Roberto Del Panucci, I have come to see my brother. Is he ready?'

'Sì,' Panucci said already standing. He made his way from the desk and locked the front door to his office to ensure that they would not be disturbed. 'Please, come this way,' in which he led Michele to the next room where his brother had been laid to rest.

Panucci opened the door and allowed Michele to enter first, and as he slowly made his way toward the open coffin, he looked down at his brother, who was now dressed in a black suit, white shirt and black tie, and wearing black leather shoes. His face, almost doll-like in a feature he almost looked revived, was smooth now compared to the contorted expression that had gasped its last breath.

'You have done well, Roberto. Grazie.'

Panucci nodded.

'Please,' Michele said, 'leave us for a moment.'

'Certo,' Panucci said and then left the room for the brothers to share their final moment together.

Michele looked down at the open coffin, gazing at a brother he once knew from another lifetime. The man he had become had been groomed by self-ego, obsession for power, and an addiction to drugs.

Somehow, despite the disloyal trait of Benito Calabrese, he never questioned whether he was telling the truth about Luigi's involvement in his wife's murder.

He knew that to be the truth.

Somehow, he had always suspected that her killer was someone close to him.

'Why?' he said as he looked down at his brother. 'You had it all… what more could you have possibly wanted? Your thirst for power over your love and honour for your family has cost you your life, and those of many others.

'I made a promise to you that I would see to your burial, and despite the crimes that you are guilty of against my wife and the family, I will keep true to my word.

'Perhaps we will meet again in another lifetime—perhaps not. Now, it's time for you to rest in peace. I hope you find it.'

Michele followed Roberto Del Panucci to the burial ground, a much larger cemetery in a different location to where his wife, Mary, was buried. The ground had already been prepared, and the groundsmen, ready and waiting to lower the coffin into the ground.

The only matter outstanding was the headstone, which Michele would ensure was ordered to his specification and put in place, not in his honour of his dead brother, but to honour his agreement.

As Michele watched the first shovels of earth fall onto the coffin, he felt neither sadness nor hatred, only an acceptance that he had fulfilled his end of the bargain.

This was the place where he would say a final farewell to a family he once loved. Any thoughts of betrayal or hatred thereafter would simply be ignored. He would move on to a different life where organised crime did not exist, a world that would allow him no memories of a nefarious past.

Uncle Gianluca had raised him and introduced him to the life of a mobster. The same man who had once been a father figure to him had finally betrayed him while ordering the death of Luigi and leaving Giovanni and his wife in the hands of the Calabrese family in New York City. As a family—a unit—at one time they had been untouchable. Now, after murder on both sides of the globe, the life of

La Cosa Nostra was now over. At least until a new wave of mobsters decided that it was their time to make their mark on the world.

As he looked down at his brother's coffin for the final time, Michele whispered the words, 'Ciao, Luigi. Possa la tua anima riposare in pace.'

(Bye, Luigi. May your soul rest in peace.)

Michele drove from one cemetery to another, first, calling into the market where he picked up a single red rose.

Once again, he found himself kneeling beside his wife's headstone, holding the rose in his hand, he was lost for words. The last time he had visited her grave, had been to tell her he was going away on a journey, and despite that having been only days before, it had felt like a lifetime.

With only an hour or so to go until the evening sun would disappear below the horizon, the air was cool, and somehow, more comforting. Since his first visit to the cemetery, it had somehow become the one place where he had discovered sanctuary, a calmness away from the harsh reality that existed outside the walls of this hallowed ground. A place he had once feared to tread, had since become a garden of comfort.

He had agreed that he would bring Rosa to pay her respects, but on this day, his visit was of a personal and private note. Michele steadied himself, ready to speak to his wife for what might be the final time, he searched for the words that would express his true feelings.

'Thank you,' he said, 'for being there for me, Mary. But most of all'—his eyes were glazed and a tear formed and then rolled down the left side of his beaten face—'thank you for being in my life.

'I've something to tell you, Mary. Although,' he smiled, 'I guess you already know what I am about to say. I've met someone. A young woman called Beth. I think you would like her. Yes,' he said with affirmation, 'you would like her.'

Michele placed the rose carefully at the base of the headstone, and then took a deep breath before he unlocked the chain from his neck and opened the locket. Looking at Mary in all her beauty, he then closed the locket and then placed it inside the engraved vase that stood as a symbol of his love for her. Next, he took off his wedding ring, placing it in the vase, he finally put the lid back on, signifying an end to the grief that had accompanied him since her untimely death.

'I have to go,' he said tearfully. 'I will never forget you.'

Michele kissed his fingertips and then placed them on top of her gravestone.

'Ti amerò sempre,' he said.
(*I will always love you.*)

Afterword

New York City had witnessed a series of murders over a forty-eight-hour period that led law enforcement agencies to conclude that such bloodshed was mob-related and therefore the result of organised crime. Investigations had begun after the gruesome discovery of the notorious city pimp, Marv Brown, who was discovered in a back alley off 46th Street, with his neck completely broken by way of a savage attack. Because there had been no witnesses to the assault, investigations into the murder would be limited in terms of a successful outcome.

The victim had been involved in a number of criminal activities and had a wide network of illicit dealings that ranged from prostitution, drug dealing and alleged connections with the mob. With a greater number of enemies than allies, and no eyewitnesses to confirm any leads to whom may have been responsible for the attack, then there was little for the NYPD to go on at this time, other than to leave the case open on the off chance that someone would come forward with some credible information.

The following day, just after 12.30pm, the body of a young woman was pulled out of the Hudson River. The naked body of the woman was later identified as Kimberly Jones, a former prostitute, who had been discovered with her wrists bonded with tie wraps and tied behind her back. Forensic reports clarified that her death had been due to strangulation and that her body had been dumped into the river soon afterwards. The homicide of a pimp and then the discovery of a young prostitute a short time after had led law enforcement to consider that there was a plausible link between the murders.

Later that day, at approximately 7.25pm, it was reported that a car had exploded on Queens, which led to the discovery of two bodies burnt beyond recognition. It was discovered that the owner of the vehicle, Franco De Blasi, had been in the driver's seat when the vehicle had exploded, however, remains of another body had been found scattered around the surrounding area.

Initially, the body could not be identified, but it was reported that there had been a disturbance in an apartment block opposite to where the burnt wreckage of the car was found, and further reports that Franco De Blasi had been seen entering that same apartment block on a number of occasions. Following further investigations, it was confirmed that two men had shared apartment number 33c, one of the men being Franco De Blasi, the other, his lover, Vincenzo Conti.

With the NYPD on high alert, the FBI led by Special Agent Dick Campbell, took their lead in the investigations, their focus of attention now firmly on the mob and organised crime. While there was little information regarding Franco De Blasi, there had been reports or at least suspicions of his links to the Mafia, and more notably, the Calabrese family, albeit nothing that would firmly substantiate that claim. Up until his death, Franco De Blasi had been a covert operator, obeying the code of silence, he had left no trail of his criminal affairs other than mere speculation.

But it was the following day when a cab driver had reported an incident on 125 E 50th Street, who alleged that he had pulled over for a young woman outside of the Benjamin Hotel, who had got into the passenger side, however, followed seconds after by a man who got into the rear, and carrying a gun which he pointed at the woman. He then went on to say that a third person got into the back of the cab, at which point he decided to get out of the vehicle and make a run for it. Along with his cab number, his vague description of the two men and young woman led to every available police officer scouring the city in a desperate search to find them.

With Dick Campbell notified of the incident, he gathered his team together in the hope that the information he had received would lead to a breakthrough. But any hope of apprehending the suspects was dashed when the call came through that a vehicle had been reported on fire on Riverside Park. By the time law enforcement and fire services had arrived on the scene, the vehicle was all but a burnt-out wreckage, but as the incident on Queens less than twenty-four hours previous, there was yet another body that was burnt beyond recognition.

As for the other two suspects, there was neither any sign of them nor any evidence to suggest where they had gone to. And to exacerbate the situation further, it would be at least another twenty-four hours before forensic pathologists would be able to put a name to the body.

By the time Special Agent Dick Campbell and his team arrived at the Rossi home in West Village, they made a forced entry on the property only to discover they had entered another crime scene. With forensics covering every inch of the property, and retrieving any samples of blood, brain tissue or pieces of skull from the living room, it would be some time later before they were able to come up with further information or any possible IDs. In the meantime, an immediate APB was conducted for Beatrice Rossi and her two children, who, it appeared, had either been abducted or had fled the scene in a hurry. With law enforcement from every state informed of the vehicle registration number, it was hoped that the Rossi family would be found sooner rather than later, and more significantly, that they were found alive and well.

Having finally located Beatrice Rossi and her children at her parents' home in Boston, she was taken to a local police station where she was questioned over the scene of events that had led to her home becoming a crime scene. While she remained reticent as to her husband's involvement in any form of organised crime, she testified to the sequence of events that had occurred that day, providing a full statement as to the two strangers who had called at her home, and more significantly, the reason they had called. Fearing for the safety of her children, Mrs Rossi explained that she had followed their instructions to the letter, and despite having knowledge of her husband's demise, she remained grateful that their intervention had saved her and her children from certain death.

As far as Beatrice Rossi was concerned, there was no going back to the place she had once called her home, and even to the extent that she had no desire to make a return to pick up any possessions. The only matter that remained of any importance in New York, was the cremation of her husband's body, which she personally vowed to see to, regardless of the risks involved, however, unaccompanied by her two children.

Two days later in New York City, and under the protection of two police officers, Beatrice Rossi attended a brief service that then led to the cremation of her husband's body. The life she had become accustomed to with the man she had loved since high school, was all but a distant memory. After the service she immediately left for Boston, where, with the full support of her parents, she would begin a new life with her two children, never to return to the place that she had once called her home.

As for police and FBI investigations, it seemed that those responsible for the crime spree that had hit the city over a period of fewer than seventy-two hours, had been ahead of law enforcement every step of the way. The two strangers who had hijacked a cab outside of the Benjamin Hotel and then arrived at the Rossi home only hours later were never seen or heard of again.

It appeared that the NYPD and the FBI had finally hit a dead end in their investigations. And despite Franco De Blasi and Luca Rossi having alleged links to La Cosa Nostra, there was little evidence to support that they worked for the Calabrese family, and therefore, nothing to justify making an arrest of any kind.

Having been witness to the confession made by his former friend and underboss, Tony Biágio was able to deal with the part that he had played in becoming a trusted companion, to an informer. His final order from Il Capo had been to dispose of his son's dead body by whatever means necessary, but to ensure that he would never be seen again. With an area of over 538 acres, Forest Park in Queens would be an ideal location and Benito Calabrese's final resting place.

Tony had left the scene with his underboss in the boot of the car, gone home to grab a shovel, and then headed out alone to undertake his final orders. After fulfilling his obligation to his boss, he returned home, showered and packed up his clothes and most personal possessions, and then left the city, never to be seen or heard from again.

Benito Calabrese's wife, Marie, had received a visit at her home from Alberto and Lorenzo that same evening, where they informed her of her husband's death. Hysterical at first, she finally calmed, knowing the life that her husband had chosen, would one day result in his demise. News that she would neither be able to see nor bury her husband was a grave matter that only added to her burden, but again, one that she had to accept knowing that if she complied with law enforcement in any way, the luxurious life, family and a legacy of businesses that she had been afforded, would come crashing down in one fatal swoop.

As for consigliere, Lorenzo Esposito, he welcomed the decision made by his boss to leave the life behind them, and so embarked on a new venture by way of creating his own law firm. After spending many years as a major player in organised crime, the former advisor to the Calabrese family had now become completely legitimate. Fate had been kind to him, for had Benito Calabrese have taken over from his father as he had planned to do so after his murderous campaign, then Lorenzo would have been a dead man soon after.

As it was, his boss had changed his destiny, and the fortune of others by taking the life of his own son. With his past life behind him, Lorenzo Esposito became wildly known as one of the best defence lawyers in the city. While his profession had taken on a more legitimate meaning, he had, in essence, continued on a similar path, however, one that had enabled him to be from the outside looking in.

Each morning as he entered his office, and on an evening when he returned home to his wife, he was reminded of the second chance he had been presented with. A former right-hand man to the most powerful Mafia boss in New York, the former consigliere had been able to leave the life of La Cosa Nostra behind him and return to the normality of modern-day society.

After the murder of his sons, Amadeo and Benito, Alberto Calabrese, head of the notorious New York City crime family, made the decision to walk away from the organisation that he had created so many years before. During his long term as Il Capo, he had become a dominant figure in the city, and as far as law enforcement had been concerned, untouchable. He was smart, and his ability to stay out of the limelight and abide by the strict rules of omertà had ensured that his reign as head of the family remained intact for so long.

But having gone through a year of heartbreak after the death of his youngest son, Amadeo, he now had blood on his own hands. From now, he would continue to live out each day praying for forgiveness, while at night, made to relive the moment when he had shot and killed his eldest son and underboss of the Calabrese family.

It would only be a matter of time before their paths would cross again.